A CORPSE IN THE GARDEN, A CLUE
IN THE RAILWAY STATION,
A RED HERRING IN THE SANATORIUM . . . AND
ALWAYS A BRAINTEASING SOLUTION

MORE MURDER MOST COZY

"The Second Mrs. Porter" by Melba Marlett
When a beautiful woman awakes in a remote
private hospital without her memory, she is
beset by the suspicion that she is taking the
place of a murdered heiress.

"The Paintbox Houses" by Ruth Rendell
An eighty-four-year-old amateur sleuth sits
knitting by her window and spies an act of il-
licit love . . . followed by what surely must be
murder.

"White Wings" by Elizabeth Goudge
Two spinster sisters fallen on hard times set up
an antique shop in a seaside town only to be
confronted by a crusty old seaman who needs
a place to stay . . . and perhaps someone to
con.

"The Mahogany Wardrobe" by John H. Dirckx
A boardinghouse for young ladies has a concealed locker, a secret entrance, and a knotty
puzzle of a murder for Inspector Franklin of
the Homicide Bureau to unravel.

MORE MURDER MOST COZY

More Mysteries
in the Classic
Tradition
From *Ellery Queen's
Mystery Magazine*
and *Alfred Hitchcock's
Mystery Magazine*

Edited by Cynthia Manson

A SIGNET BOOK

SIGNET
Published by the Penguin Group
Penguin Books USA Inc., 375 Hudson Street, New York, New York 10014, U.S.A.
Penguin Books Ltd, 27 Wrights Lane, London W8 5TZ, England
Penguin Books Australia Ltd, Ringwood, Victoria, Australia
Penguin Books Canada Ltd, 10 Alcorn Avenue, Toronto, Ontario, Canada M4V 3B2
Penguin Books (N.Z.) Ltd, 182–190 Wairau Road, Auckland 10, New Zealand

Penguin Books Ltd, Registered Offices: Harmondsworth, Middlesex, England

First published by Signet, an imprint of New American Library,
a division of Penguin Books USA Inc.

First Printing, July, 1993
10 9 8 7 6 5 4 3 2 1

Grateful acknowledgment is made to the following for permission to reprint their
copyrighted material:

"The Man on the Roof" by Christianna Brand, copyright © 1984 by Davis Publications,
Inc., reprinted by permission of the Mysterious Literary Agency; "The Boxdale Inheritance" by P. D. James (originally titled "Great Aunt Allie's Flypaper"), copyright ©
1979 by P. D. James, reprinted by permission of the Elaine Greene Literary Agency;
"The Paintbox Houses" by Ruth Rendell, copyright © 1980 by Ruth Rendell, reprinted by permission of George Borchardt, Inc.; all stories previously appeared in
Ellery Queen's Mystery Magazine, published by Bantam Doubleday Dell Direct, Inc.

"Sanctuary" by Agatha Christie (from Double Sin and Other Stories) copyright ©
1954 by Agatha Christie, © renewed 1982 by Agatha Christie Limited, reprinted
by permission of the Putnam Publishing Group and Harold Ober Associates, Inc.;
"The Mahogany Wardrobe" by John H. Dirckx, copyright © 1985 by Davis Publications, Inc., reprinted by permission of the author; "White Wings" by Elizabeth Goudge,
copyright © 1938, 1941 by Elizabeth Goudge, reprinted by permission of Harold Ober
Associates, Inc.; "The Second Mrs. Porter" by Melba Marlett, copyright © 1986 by
Davis Publications, Inc., reprinted by permission of the author; "The Plum Point
Ladies" by Henry T. Parry, copyright © 1976 by Davis Publications, Inc., reprinted
by permission of the author; all stories previously appeared in Alfred Hitchcock's
Mystery Magazine, published by Bantam Doubleday Dell Direct, Inc.

PUBLISHER'S NOTE
These stories are works of fiction. Names, characters, places, and incidents either
are the product of the authors' imaginations or are used fictitiously, and any resemblance
to actual persons, living or dead, events, or locales is entirely coincidental.

Contents

Foreword

Here is the companion edition to the first volume in a series titled *Murder Most Cozy*. There is a limitless wealth of mystery stories that fit the "cozy" category both in narrative style and tone. Gems of this genre, from *Alfred Hitchcock's Mystery Magazine* and *Ellery Queen's Mystery Magazine*, are nestled in this collection. This will come as no surprise to readers when they see that world-renowned Agatha Christie, P. D. James, Christianna Brand, and Ruth Rendell are among the authors included here.

Our heroines are for the most part amateur female sleuths who, through their inquisitive natures, uncover the wrongdoing of others. On the surface, our gentle heroines move in circles in which acquaintances appear most amiable. Yet our savvy protagonists quickly unmask the evil that lurks in the most unlikely places.

Should the gentlemen among our prospective readers hesitate here, however, let us hasten to observe that their compatriots strongly abound in rich and important roles. There are Ms. Goudge's seafaring man, Ms. Brand's Inspector Cockrill, and Ms. James's Adam Dalgliesh.

The settings range from vicarage to boardinghouse, from a carefree picnic to an ominous convalescent home, from the sparkling seacoast to the darkness of hidden spaces. The plot twists are clever, the storytelling sure. In short, here is a collection we hope you will settle down cozily to enjoy.

—*Cynthia Manson*

The Boxdale Inheritance

by P. D. James

"You see, my dear Adam," explained the Canon gently, as he walked with Chief Superintendent Dalgliesh under the Vicarage elms, "useful as the legacy would be to us, I wouldn't feel happy in accepting it if Great Aunt Allie came by her money in the first place by wrongful means."

What the Canon meant was that he and his wife wouldn't be happy to inherit Great Aunt Allie's fifty thousand pounds, if sixty-seven years earlier she had poisoned her elderly husband with arsenic in order to get it.

As Great Aunt Allie had been accused and acquitted of just that charge in a 1902 trial which, for her Hampshire neighbors, had rivaled the Coronation as a public spectacle, the Canon's scruples were not altogether irrelevant. Admittedly, thought Dalgliesh, most people faced with the prospect of fifty thousand pounds would be happy to subscribe to the commonly held convention that, once an English Court has pronounced its verdict, the final truth of the matter has been established once and for all. There may possibly be a higher judicature in the next world but hardly in this. And so Hubert Boxdale would normally be happy to believe. But, faced with the prospect of an

9

unexpected fortune, his scrupulous conscience was troubled. The gentle but obstinate voice went on:

"Apart from the moral principle of accepting tainted money, it wouldn't bring us happiness. I often think of that poor woman, driven restlessly round Europe in her search for peace, of that lonely life and unhappy death."

Dalgliesh recalled that Great Aunt Allie had moved in a predictable pattern with her retinue of servants, current lover, and general hangers-on from one luxury Riviera hotel to the next, with stays in Paris or Rome as the mood suited her. He was not sure that this orderly program of comfort and entertainment could be described as being restlessly driven round Europe or that the old lady had been primarily in search of peace. She had died, he recalled, by falling overboard from a millionaire's yacht during a rather wild party given by him to celebrate her eighty-eighth birthday. It was perhaps not an edifying death by the Canon's standards but Dalgliesh doubted whether she had, in fact, been unhappy at the time. Great Aunt Allie (it was impossible to think of her by any other name), if she had been capable of coherent thought, would probably have pronounced it a very good way to go. But this was hardly a point of view he could put forward comfortably to his present companion.

Canon Hubert Boxdale was Superintendent Adam Dalgliesh's godfather. Dalgliesh's father had been his Oxford contemporary and lifelong friend. He had been an admirable godfather: affectionate, uncensorious, genuinely concerned. In Dalgliesh's childhood, he had always been mindful of birthdays and imaginative about a small boy's preoccupations and desires.

Dalgliesh was very fond of him and privately thought him one of the few really good men he had known. It was only surprising that the Canon had managed to live to seventy-one in a carnivorous world in which gentleness, humility, and unworldliness are hardly conducive to survival, let alone success. But his goodness had in some sense protected him. Faced with such manifest innocence, even those who exploited him, and they were not a few, extended some of the protection and compassion they might show to the slightly subnormal.

"Poor old darling," his daily woman would say, pocketing pay for six hours when she had worked five and helping herself to a couple of eggs from his refrigerator. "He's really not fit to be let out alone." It had surprised the then young and slightly priggish Detective Constable Dalgliesh to realize that the Canon knew perfectly well about the hours and the eggs, but thought that Mrs. Copthorne, with five children and an indolent husband, needed both more than he did. He also knew that if he started paying for five hours she would promptly work only four and extract another two eggs, and that this small and only dishonesty was somehow necessary to her self-esteem. He was good. But he was not a fool.

He and his wife were, of course, poor. But they were not unhappy—indeed it was a word impossible to associate with the Canon. The death of his two sons in the 1939 war had saddened but not destroyed him. But he had anxieties. His wife was suffering from disseminated sclerosis and was finding it increasingly hard to manage. There were comforts and appliances which she would need. He was now, belatedly, about to retire and his pension would be small. A legacy of fifty thousand pounds would enable them both to live in comfort for the rest of their lives and would also, Dalgliesh had no doubt, give them the pleasure of doing more for their various lame dogs. Really, he thought, the Canon was an almost embarrassingly deserving candidate for a modest fortune. Why couldn't the dear, silly old noodle take the cash and stop worrying?

He said cunningly: "Great Aunt Allie was found not guilty, you know, by an English jury. And it all happened nearly seventy years ago. Couldn't you bring yourself to accept their verdict?"

But the Canon's scrupulous mind was totally impervious to such sly innuendos. Dalgliesh told himself that he should have remembered what, as a small boy, he had discovered about Uncle Hubert's conscience— that it operated as a warning bell and that, unlike most people, Uncle Hubert never pretended that it hadn't sounded or that he hadn't heard it or that, having heard it, something must be wrong with the mechanism.

"Oh, I did, while she was alive. We never met, you know. I didn't wish to force myself on her. After all, she was a wealthy woman. My grandfather made a new will on his marriage and left her all he possessed. Our ways of life were very different. But I usually wrote briefly at Christmas and she sent a card in reply. I wanted to keep some contact in case, one day, she might want someone to turn to, and would remember that I am a priest."

And why should she want that, thought Dalgliesh. To clear her conscience? Was that what the dear old boy had in mind? So he must have had some doubts from the beginning. But of course he had; Dalgliesh knew something of the story, and the general feeling of the family and friends was that Great Aunt Allie had been extremely lucky to escape the gallows.

His own father's view, expressed with reticence, reluctance, and compassion, had not in essentials differed from that given by a local reporter at the time.

"How on earth did she expect to get away with it? Damned lucky to escape topping if you ask me."

"The news of the legacy came as a complete surprise?" asked Dalgliesh.

"Indeed, yes. I only saw her once at that first and only Christmas, six weeks after her marriage, when my grandfather died. We always talk of her as Great Aunt Allie, but in fact, as you know, she married my grandfather. But it seemed impossible to think of her as a step-grandmother.

"There was the usual family gathering at Colebrook Croft at the time I was there with my parents and my twin sisters. I was barely four and the twins were just eight months old. I can remember nothing of my grandfather or of his wife. After the murder—if one has to use that dreadful word—my mother returned home with us children, leaving my father to cope with the police, the solicitors, and the newsmen. It was a terrible time for him. I don't think I was even told that my grandfather was dead until about a year later. My old nurse, Nellie, who had been given Christmas as a holiday to visit her own family, told me that, soon after my return home.

"I asked her if Grandfather was now young and beautiful for always. She, poor woman, took it as a sign of infant prognostication and piety. Poor Nellie was sadly superstitious and sentimental, I'm afraid. But I knew nothing of Grandfather's death at the time and certainly can recall nothing of that Christmas visit or of my new step-grandmother. Mercifully, I was little more than a baby when the murder was done."

"She was a music-hall artist, wasn't she?" asked Dalgliesh.

"Yes, and a very talented one. My grandfather met her when she was working with a partner in a hall in Cannes. He had gone to the South of France with his man-servant for his health. I understood that she extracted a gold watch from his chain and, when he claimed it, told him that he was English, had recently suffered from a stomach ailment, had two sons and a daughter, and was about to have a wonderful surprise. It was all correct except that his only daughter had died in childbirth, leaving him with a granddaughter—Marguerite Goddard.''

"That was all easily guessable from Boxdale's voice and appearance," said Dalgliesh. "I can only suppose the surprise was the marriage?"

"It was certainly a surprise, and a most unpleasant one for the family. It is easy to deplore the snobbishness and the conventions of another age and, indeed, there was much in Edwardian England to deplore, but it wasn't a propitious marriage. I think of the difference in background, education, and way of life, the lack of common interests. And there was the disparity of age. Grandfather had married a girl just three months younger than his own granddaughter. I cannot wonder that the family were concerned, that they felt that the union could not, in the end, contribute to the contentment or happiness of either party."

And that was putting it charitably, thought Dalgliesh. The marriage certainly hadn't contributed to their happiness. From the point of view of the family, it had been a disaster. He recalled hearing of an incident when the local vicar and his wife, a couple who had actually dined at Colebrook Croft on the night of the murder, first called on the bride. Apparently old Augustus Boxdale had introduced her, saying: "Meet the prettiest little variety artiste in the business. Took a gold watch and notecase off me without any trouble. Would have had the elastic out of my pants if I hadn't watched out. Anyway, she stole my heart, didn't you, sweetheart?"

All this was accompanied by a hearty slap on the rump and a squeal of delight from the lady, who had promptly demonstrated her skill for extracting the

Reverend Arthur Venable's bunch of keys from his left ear.

Dalgliesh thought it tactful not to remind the Canon of this story.

"What do you wish me to do, sir?" he inquired.

"It's asking a great deal, I know, when you're so busy. But if I had your assurance that you believed in Aunt Allie's innocence, I should feel happy about accepting the bequest. I wondered if it would be possible for you to see the records of the trial. Perhaps it would give you a clue. You're so clever at this sort of thing."

He spoke without flattery but with an innocent wonder at the strange vocations of men. Dalgliesh was, indeed, very clever at this sort of thing. A dozen or so men at present occupying security wings in HM prisons could testify to Chief Superintendent Dalgliesh's cleverness, as indeed could a handful of others walking free, whose defending counsel had been in their own way as clever as Chief Superintendent Dalgliesh.

But to reexamine a case over sixty years old seemed to require clairvoyance rather than cleverness. The trial judge and both learned counsels had been dead for over fifty years. Two world wars had taken their toll. Four reigns had passed. It was highly probable that, of those who had slept under the roof of Colebrook Croft on that fateful Boxing Day night of 1901, only the Canon still survived.

But the old man was troubled and had sought his help and Dalgliesh, with a day or two's leave due to him, had the time to give it.

"I'll do what I can," he promised.

The transcript of a trial which had taken place sixty-seven years ago took time and trouble to obtain even for a Chief Superintendent of the Metropolitan Police.

It provided little comfort for the Canon. Mr. Justice Bellows had summed up with that avuncular simplicity with which he was wont to address juries, regarding them as a panel of well-intentioned but cretinous children. And the facts could have been comprehended by any child. Part of the summing up set them out with lucidity:

"And so, gentlemen of the jury, we come to the night of December twenty-sixth. Mr. Augustus Boxdale, who had perhaps indulged a little unwisely on Christmas Day, had retired to bed in his dressing room after luncheon, suffering from a recurrence of the slight indigestive trouble which had afflicted him for most of his life. You will have heard that he had taken luncheon with the members of his family and ate nothing which they, too, did not eat. You may feel you can acquit luncheon of anything worse than over-richness.

"Dinner was served at eight P.M. promptly, as was the custom at Colebrook Croft. There were present at that meal Mrs. Augustus Boxdale, the deceased's bride; his elder son, Captain Maurice Boxdale, with his wife, his younger son, the Reverend Henry Boxdale, with his wife; his granddaughter, Miss Marguerite Goddard; and two neighbors, The Reverend and Mrs. Arthur Venables.

"You have heard how the accused took only the first course at dinner, which was ragout of beef, and then, at about eight-twenty, left the dining room to sit with her husband. Shortly after nine o'clock, she rang for the parlor maid, Mary Huddy, and ordered a basin of gruel to be brought up to Mr. Boxdale. You have heard that the deceased was fond of gruel, and indeed as prepared by Mrs. Muncie, the cook, it sounds a most nourishing dish for an elderly gentleman of weak digestion.

"You have heard Mrs. Muncie describe how she

prepared the gruel according to Mrs. Beaton's admirable recipe and in the presence of Mary Huddy, in case, as she said, 'The master should take a fancy to it when I'm not at hand and you have to make it.'

"After the gruel had been prepared, Mrs. Muncie tasted it with a spoon and Mary Huddy carried it upstairs to the main bedroom, together with a jug of water to thin the gruel if it were too strong. As she reached the door, Mrs. Boxdale came out, her hands full of stockings and underclothes. She has told you that she was on her way to the bathroom to wash them through. She asked the girl to put the basin of gruel on the washstand by the window and Mary Huddy did so in her presence. Miss Huddy has told us that at the time she noticed the bowl of fly papers soaking in water and she knew that this solution was one used by Mrs. Boxdale as a cosmetic wash. Indeed, all the women who spent that evening in the house, with the exception of Mrs. Venables, have told you that they knew it was Mrs. Boxdale's practice to prepare this solution of fly papers.

"Mary Huddy and the accused left the bedroom together and you have heard the evidence of Mrs. Muncie that Miss Huddy returned to the kitchen after an absence of only a few minutes. Shortly after nine o'clock, the ladies left the dining room and entered the drawing room to take coffee.

"At nine-fifteen P.M., Miss Goddard excused herself to the company and said that she would go to see if her grandfather needed anything. The time is established precisely, because the clock struck the quarter hour as she left and Mrs. Venables commented on the sweetness of its chime. You have also heard Mrs. Venables' evidence and the evidence of Mrs. Maurice Boxdale and Mrs. Henry Boxdale that some of the ladies left the drawing room during the evening, and Mrs. Venables has testified that the three gentlemen remained together until Miss Goddard appeared about three-quarters of an hour after to inform them that her grandfather had become very ill and to request that the doctor be sent for immediately.

"Miss Goddard has told you that when she entered her grandfather's room he was just finishing his gruel and was grumbling about its taste. She got the impression that this was merely a protest at being deprived of his dinner rather than that he genuinely considered that there was something wrong with the gruel. At any rate, he finished most of it and appeared to enjoy it despite his grumbles.

"You have heard Miss Goddard describe how, after her grandfather had had as much as he wanted of the gruel, she took the bowl next door and left it on the washstand. She then returned to her grandfather's bedroom and Mr. Boxdale, his wife, and his granddaughter played three-handed whist for about three-quarters of an hour.

"At ten o'clock Mr. Augustus Boxdale complained of feeling very ill. He suffered from griping pains in the stomach, from sickness and from looseness of the bowels. As soon as the symptoms began, Miss Goddard went downstairs to let her uncles know that her grandfather was worse and to ask that Doctor Eversley should be sent for urgently. Doctor Eversley has given you his evidence. He arrived at Colebrook Croft at ten-thirty P.M. when he found his patient very distressed and weak. He treated the symptoms and gave what relief he could, but Mr. Augustus Boxdale died shortly before midnight.

"Gentlemen of the jury, you have heard Marguerite Goddard describe how, as her grandfather's paroxysms increased in intensity, she remembered the gruel and wondered whether it could have disagreed with him in some way. She mentioned this possibility to her elder uncle, Captain Maurice Boxdale. Captain

Boxdale has told you how he handed the bowl with its residue of gruel to Doctor Eversley with the request that the doctor should lock it in a cupboard in the library, seal the lock, and keep the key. You have heard how the contents of the bowl were later analyzed and with what results."

An extraordinary precaution for the gallant captain to have taken, thought Dalgliesh, and a most perspicacious young woman. Was it by chance or by design that the bowl hadn't been taken down to be washed up as soon as the old man had finished with it? Why was it, he wondered, that Marguerite Goddard hadn't rung for the parlor maid and requested her to remove it? Miss Goddard appeared the only other suspect. He wished he knew more about her.

But, except for those main protagonists, the characters in the drama did not emerge very clearly from the trial report. Why, indeed, should they? The British accusatorial system of trial is designed to answer one question: is the accused guilty beyond reasonable doubt of the crime charged? Exploration of the nuances of personality, speculation, and gossip have no place in the witness box.

The two Boxdale brothers came out as very dull fellows indeed. They and their estimable, respectable sloping-bosomed wives had sat at dinner in full view of each other from eight until after nine o'clock (a substantial meal, that dinner) and had said so in the witness box, more or less in identical words. The ladies' bosoms might have been heaving with far from estimable emotions of dislike, envy, embarrassment, or resentment of the interloper. If so, they didn't tell the court.

But the two brothers and their wives were clearly innocent, even if a detective at that time could have conceived of the guilt of a gentlefolk so well respected, so eminently respectable. Even their impeccable alibis had a nice touch of social and sexual distinction. The Reverend Arthur Venables had vouched for the gentlemen, and his good wife for the ladies.

Besides, what motive had they? They could no longer gain financially by the old man's death. If anything, it was in their interests to keep him alive in the hope that disillusion with his marriage or return to sanity might occur to cause him to change his will. So far, Dalgliesh had learned nothing that could cause him to give the Canon the assurance for which he hoped.

It was then that he remembered Aubrey Glatt. Glatt was a wealthy amateur criminologist who had made a study of all the notable Victorian and Edwardian poison cases. He was not interested in anything earlier or later, being as obsessively wedded to his period as any serious historian—which indeed he had some claim to call himself. He lived in a Georgian house in Winchester—his affection for the Victorian and Edwardian age did not extend to its architecture— and was only three miles from Colebrook Croft.

A visit to the London library disclosed that he hadn't written a book on the case but it was improbable that he had totally neglected a crime close at hand and so in period. Dalgliesh had occasionally helped him with the technical details of police procedure. Glatt, in response to a telephone call, was happy to return the favor with the offer of afternoon tea and information.

Tea was served in his elegant drawing room by a parlor maid wearing a frilly cap with streamers. Dalgliesh wondered what wage Glatt paid her to persuade her to wear it. She looked as if she could have played a role in any of his favorite Victorian dreams and Dalgliesh had an uncomfortable thought that arsenic might be dispensed with the cucumber sandwiches.

Glatt nibbled away and was expansive.

"It's interesting that you should have taken this sudden and, if I may say so, somewhat inexplicable interest in the Boxdale murder. I got out my notebook on the case only yesterday. Colebrook Croft is being demolished to make way for a new housing estate and I thought I would visit it for the last time. The family, of course, haven't lived there since the 1914–18 war. Architecturally, it's completely undistinguished, but one grieves to see it go. We might drive over after tea if you're agreeable.

"I never wrote my book on the case, you know. I planned a work entitled *The Colebrook Croft Mystery* or *Who Killed Augustus Boxdale?* But the answer was all too obvious."

"No real mystery?" suggested Dalgliesh.

"Who else could it have been but Allegra Boxdale? She was born Allegra Porter, you know. Do you think her mother could have been thinking of Byron? I imagine not. There's a picture of her on page two of the notebook, by the way, taken by a photographer in Cannes on her wedding day. I call it Beauty and the Beast."

The old photograph had scarcely faded and Great Aunt Allie half smiled at Dalgliesh across nearly seventy years.

Her broad face, with its wide mouth and rather snub nose, was framed by two wings of dark hair swept high and topped, in the fashion of the day, by an immense flowered hat. The features were too coarse for real beauty, but the eyes were magnificent, deep-set and well spaced—and the chin round and determined. Beside this vital young Amazon, poor Augustus Boxdale, clutching his bride as if for support, was but a very frail and undersized beast. Their pose was unfortunate. She almost looked as if she were about to fling him over her shoulder.

Glatt shrugged. "The face of a murderess? I've known less likely ones. Her Counsel suggested, of course, that the old man had poisoned his own gruel during the short time she left it on the washstand to cool while she visited the bathroom. But why should he? All the evidence suggests that he was in a state of post-nuptial euphoria, poor senile old booby. Our Augustus was in no hurry to leave this world, particularly by such an agonizing means. Besides, I doubt whether he even knew the gruel was there. He was in bed next door in his dressing room, remember."

Dalgliesh asked: "What about Marguerite Goddard? There's no evidence about the exact time when she entered the bedroom."

"I thought you'd get onto that. She could have arrived while her step-grandmother was in the bathroom, poisoned the gruel, hidden herself either in the main bedroom or elsewhere until it had been taken into Augustus, then joined her grandfather and his bride as if she had just come upstairs. It's possible, I admit. But it *is* unlikely. She was less inconvenienced than any of the family by her grandfather's second marriage. Her mother was Augustus Boxdale's eldest child who married, very young, a wealthy patent-medicine manufacturer. She died in childbirth and the husband only survived her by a year. Marguerite Goddard was an heiress. She was also most advantageously engaged to Captain the Honorable John Brize-Lacey. Marguerite Goddard—young, beautiful, in possession of the Goddard fortune, not to mention the Goddard emeralds and the eldest son of a Lord—was hardly a serious suspect. In my view, Defense Counsel—that was Roland Gort Lloyd, remember—was wise to leave her strictly alone."

"A memorable defense, I believe."

"Magnificent. There's no doubt Allegra Boxdale

owed her life to Gort Lloyd. I know that concluding speech by heart—

" 'Gentlemen of the Jury, I beseech you in the sacred name of Justice to consider what you are at. It is your responsibility, and yours alone, to decide the fate of this young woman. She stands before you now, young, vibrant, glowing with health, the years stretching before her with their promise and their hopes. It is in your power to cut off all this as you might top a nettle with one swish of your cane. To condemn her to the slow torture of those last waiting weeks, to that last dreadful walk, to heap calumny on her name, to desecrate those few happy weeks of marriage with the man who loved her so greatly, and to cast her into the final darkness of an ignominious grave.'

"Pause for dramatic effect. Then the crescendo in that magnificent voice. 'And on what evidence, gentlemen? I ask you.' Another pause. Then the thunder. 'On what evidence?' "

"A powerful defense," said Dalgliesh. "But I wonder how it would go down with a modern judge and jury."

"Well, it went down very effectively with that 1902 jury. Of course, the abolition of capital punishment has rather cramped the more histrionic style. I'm not sure that the reference to topping nettles was in the best of taste, but the jury got the message. They decided that on the whole they preferred not to have the responsibility of sending the accused to the gallows. They were out six hours reaching their verdict and it was greeted with some applause.

"If any of those worthy citizens had been asked to wager five pounds of their own good money on her innocence, I suspect that it would have been a different matter. Allegra Boxdale had helped him, of course. The Criminal Evidence Act, passed three years earlier, enabled him to put her in the witness box. She wasn't an actress of a kind for nothing. Somehow she managed to persuade the jury that she had genuinely loved the old man."

"Perhaps she had," suggested Dalgliesh. "I don't suppose there had been much kindness in her life. And he was kind."

"No doubt, no doubt. But love?" Glatt was impatient. "My dear Dalgliesh! He was a singularly ugly old man of sixty-nine. She was an attractive girl of twenty-one!"

Dalgliesh doubted whether love, that iconoclastic passion, was susceptible to this kind of simple arithmetic but he didn't argue.

Glatt went on: "The prosecution couldn't suggest any other romantic attachment. The police got in touch with her previous partner, of course. He was discovered to be a bald, undersized little man, sharp as a weasel, with a buxom wife and five children. He had moved down the coast after the partnership broke up and was now working with a new girl. He said regretfully that she was coming along nicely, thank you gentlemen, but would never be a patch on Allie, and that, if Allie got her neck out of the noose and ever wanted a job, she knew where to come. It was obvious, even to the most suspicious policeman, that his interest was professional. As he said: 'What was a grain or two of arsenic between friends?'

"The Boxdales had no luck after the trial. Captain Maurice Boxdale was killed in 1916, leaving no children, and the Reverend Edward lost his wife and their twin daughters in the 1918 influenza epidemic. He survived until 1932. The boy Hubert may still be alive, but I doubt it. That family always were a sickly lot.

"My greatest achievement, incidentally, was in tracing Marguerite Goddard. I hadn't realized she was still alive. She never married Brize-Lacey, or indeed anyone else. He distinguished himself in the 1914–18 war, came successfully through, and eventually married an eminently suitable young woman, the sister of a brother officer. He inherited the title in 1925 and died in 1953.

"But Marguerite Goddard may be alive now for all I know. She may even be living in the same modest Bournemouth hotel where I found her. Not that my efforts in tracing her were rewarded. She absolutely refused to see me. That's the note that she sent out to me, by the way. Just there."

It was meticulously pasted into the notebook in its chronological order and carefully annotated. Aubrey Glatt was a natural researcher; Dalgliesh couldn't help wondering whether this passion for accuracy might not have been more rewarding spent other than in the careful documentation of murder.

The note was written in an elegant upright hand, the strokes black and very thin but clear and unwavering.

Miss Goddard presents her compliments to Mr. Aubrey Glatt. She did not murder her grandfather and has neither the time nor the inclination to gratify his curiosity by discussing the person who did.

Aubrey Glatt said, "After that extremely disobliging note, I felt there was really no point in going on with the book."

Glatt's passion for Edwardian England obviously extended to a wider field than its murders and they drove to Colebrook Croft high above the green Hampshire lanes in an elegant 1910 Daimler. Aubrey wore a thin tweed coat and deerstalker hat and looked, Dalgliesh thought, rather like a Sherlock Holmes, with himself as attendant Watson.

"We are only just in time, my dear Dalgliesh," he said when they arrived. "The engines of destruction are assembled. That ball on a chain looks like the eyeball of God ready to strike. Let us make our number with the attendant artisans. You will have no wish to trespass, will you?"

The work of demolition had not yet begun, but the inside of the house had been stripped and plundered, the great rooms echoed to their footsteps like gaunt and deserted barracks after the final retreat. They moved from room to room, Glatt mourning the forgotten glories of an age he had been born too late to enjoy, Dalgliesh with his mind on the somewhat more immediate and practical concerns.

The design of the house was simple and formalized. The first floor, on which were most of the main bedrooms, had a long corridor running the whole length of the facade. The master bedroom was at the southern end with two large windows giving a distant view of Winchester Cathedral tower. A communicating door led to a small dressing room.

The main corridor had a row of four identical large windows. The brass curtain rods and wooden rings had been removed (they were collectors' items now), but the ornate carved pelmets were still in place. Here must have hung pairs of heavy curtains giving cover to anyone who wished to slip out of view. And Dalgliesh noted with interest that one of the windows was exactly opposite the door of the main bedroom. By the time they had left Colebrook Croft and Glatt had dropped him at Winchester Station, Dalgliesh was beginning to formulate a theory.

His next move was to trace Marguerite Goddard, if she were still alive. It took him nearly a week of weary searching—a frustrating trail along the South Coast from hotel to hotel. Almost everywhere his inquiries were met with defensive hostility. It was the usual story of a very old lady who had become more demanding, arrogant, and eccentric as her health and fortune waned—an unwelcome embarrassment to manager and fellow guests alike. The hotels were all modest, a few almost sordid. What, he wondered, had become of the legendary Goddard fortune?

From the last landlady, he learned that Miss Goddard had become ill, really sick indeed, and had been removed six months previously to the local district general hospital. And it was there that he found her.

The ward sister was surprisingly young, a petite dark-haired girl with a tired face and challenging eyes. "Miss Goddard is very ill. We've put her in one of the side wards. Are you a relative? If so, you're the first one who has bothered to call and you're lucky to be in time. When she is delirious she seems to expect a Captain Brize-Lacey to call. You're not he, are you?"

"Captain Brize-Lacey will not be calling. No, I'm not a relative. She doesn't even know me. But I would like to visit her if she's well enough and is willing to see me. Could you please give her this note?"

He couldn't force himself on a defenseless and dying woman. She still had the right to say no. He was afraid she would refuse him. And if she did, he might never learn the truth. He wrote four words on the back page of his diary, signed them, tore out the page, folded it, and handed it to the sister.

She was back very shortly.

"She'll see you. She's weak, of course, and very old, but she's perfectly lucid now. Only please don't tire her."

"I'll try not to stay too long."

The girl laughed: "Don't worry. She'll throw you out soon enough if she gets bored. The chaplain and the Red Cross librarian have a terrible time with her. Third floor on the left. There's a stool to sit on by the bed. We will ring the bell at the end of visiting time."

She bustled off, leaving him to find his own way.

The corridor was very quiet. At the far end, he could glimpse through the open door of the main ward the regimented rows of beds, each with its pale-blue coverlet, the bright glow of flowers on some of the tables, and the laden visitors making their way in pairs to each bedside. There was a faint buzz of welcome, a hum of conversation. But no one was visiting the side wards. Here, in the silence of the aseptic corridor, Dalgliesh could smell death.

The woman propped high against the pillows in the third room on the left no longer looked human. She lay rigidly, her long arms disposed like sticks on the coverlet. This was a skeleton clothed with a thin membrane of flesh, beneath whose yellow transparency the tendons and veins were as plainly visible as an anatomist's model. She was nearly bald and the high-domed skull under its spare down of hair was as brittle and vulnerable as a child's. Only the eyes still held life, burning in their deep sockets with an animal vitality. But when she spoke, her voice was distinctive and unwavering, evoking as her appearance never could the memory of imperious youth.

She took up his note and read aloud four words:

" 'It was the child.' You are right, of course. The four-year-old Hubert Boxdale killed his grandfather. You signed this note Adam Dalgliesh. There was no Dalgliesh connected with the case."

"I'm a detective of the Metropolitan Police. But I'm not here in any official capacity. I've known about this case for a number of years from a dear friend. I have a natural curiosity to learn the truth. And I have formed a theory."

"And now, like that poseur, Aubrey Glatt, you want to write a book?"

"*No.* I shall tell no one. You have my promise."

Her voice was ironic.

"Thank you. I am a dying woman, Mr. Dalgliesh. I tell you that not to invite your sympathy, which it would be an impertinence for you to offer and which

I neither want nor require, but to explain why it no longer matters to me what you say or do. But I, too, have a natural curiosity. Your note, cleverly, was intended to provoke it. I should like to know how you discovered the truth."

Dalgliesh drew the visitors' stool from under the bed and sat down beside her. She did not look at him. The skeleton hands still holding his note did not move.

"Everyone in Colebrook Croft who could have killed Augustus Boxdale was accounted for except the one person nobody considered—the small boy. He was an intelligent, articulate child. He was almost certainly left to his own devices. His nurse did not accompany the family to Colebrook Croft and the servants who were there over Christmas had extra work and also the care of the delicate twin girls.

"The boy probably spent much time with his grandfather and the new bride. She, too, was lonely and disregarded. He could have trotted around with her as she went about her various activities. He could have watched her making her arsenical face wash and, when he asked, as a child will, what it was for, could have been told 'to make me young and beautiful.'

"He loved his grandfather, but he must have known that the old man was neither young nor beautiful. Suppose he woke up on that Boxing Day night, overfed and excited after the Christmas festivities? Suppose he went to Allegra Boxdale's room in search of comfort and companionship and saw there the basin of gruel and the arsenical mixture together on the washstand? Suppose he decided that here was something he could do for his grandfather?"

The voice from the bed said quietly: "And suppose someone stood unnoticed in the doorway and watched him?"

"So you were behind the window curtains on the

landing looking through the open door?" Dalgliesh said.

"Of course. He knelt on the chair, two chubby hands clasping the bowl of poison, pouring it with infinite care into his grandfather's gruel. I watched while he replaced the linen cloth over the basin, got down from the chair, replaced it with careful art against the wall, and trotted out into the corridor and back to the nursery. About three seconds later, Allegra came out of the bathroom and I watched while she carried the gruel into my grandfather. A second later I went into the main bedroom. The bowl of poison had been a little heavy for Hubert's small hands to manage and I saw that a small pool had been spilt on the polished top of the washstand. I mopped it up with my handkerchief. Then I poured some of the water from the jug into the poison bowl to bring up the level. It only took a couple of seconds and I was ready to join Allegra and my grandfather in the bedroom and sit with him while he ate his gruel."

"I watched him die without pity and without remorse. I think I hated them both equally. The grandfather who had adored, petted, and indulged me all through my childhood and deteriorated into this disgusting old lecher, unable to keep his hands off this woman even when I was in the room. He had rejected me and his family, jeopardized my engagement, made our name a laughing stock in the County, and all for a woman that my grandmother wouldn't have employed as a kitchen maid. I wanted them both dead. And they were both going to die. But it would be by other hands than mine. I could deceive myself that it wasn't my doing."

Dalgliesh asked: "When did she find out?"

"She knew that evening. When my grandfather's agony began, she went outside for the jug of water. She wanted a cool cloth for his head. It was then that she noticed that the level of water in the jug had fallen and that a small pool of liquid on the washstand had been mopped up. I should have realized that she would have seen that pool. She had been trained to register every detail. She thought at the time that Mary Huddy had spilt some of the water when she set down the tray and the gruel. But who could have mopped it up? And why?"

"And when did she face you with the truth?"

"Not until after the trial. Allegra had magnificent courage. She knew what she stood to gain. She gambled with her life for a fortune."

And then Dalgliesh understood what had happened to the Goddard inheritance. "So she made you pay?"

"Of course. Every penny. The Goddard fortune, the Goddard emeralds. She lived in luxury for sixty-seven years on my money. She ate and dressed on my money. When she moved with her lovers from hotel to hotel, it was on my money. She paid them with my money. And if she has left anything, which I doubt, it is my money. My grandfather left very little. He had been senile and had let money run through his fingers like sand."

"And your engagement?"

"It was broken, you could say, by mutual consent. A marriage, Mr. Dalgliesh, is like any legal contract. It is most successful when both parties are convinced they have a bargain. Captain Brize-Lacey was sufficiently discouraged by the scandal of a murder in the family. He was a proud and highly conventional man. But that alone might have been accepted with the Goddard fortune and the Goddard emeralds to deodorize the bad smell. But the marriage couldn't have succeeded if he had discovered that he had married socially beneath him, into a family with a major scandal and no compensating fortune."

Dalgliesh said: "Once you had begun to pay, you

had no choice but to go on. I see that. But why did you pay? She could hardly have told her story. It would have meant involving the child."

"Oh, no! That wasn't her plan at all. She never meant to involve the child. She was a sentimental woman and she was fond of Hubert. No, she intended to accuse me of murder outright. Then, if I decided to tell the truth, how would it help me? After all, I wiped up the spilled liquid, I topped up the bowl. She had nothing to lose, remember—neither life nor reputation. They couldn't try her twice. That's why she waited until after the trial. It made her secure forever.

"But what of me? In the circles in which I moved at that time, reputation was everything. She needed only to breathe the story in the ears of a few servants and I was finished. The truth can be remarkably tenacious. But it wasn't only reputation. I paid in the shadow of the gallows."

Dalgliesh asked, "But could she ever prove it?"

Suddenly she looked at him and gave an eerie screech of laughter. It tore at her throat until he thought the taut tendons would snap violently.

"Of course she could! You fool! Don't you understand? She took my handkerchief, the one I used to mop up the arsenic mixture. That was her profession, remember! Sometime during that evening, perhaps when we were all crowding around the bed, two soft plump fingers insinuated themselves between the satin of my evening dress and my flesh and extracted that stained and damning piece of linen."

She stretched out feebly toward the bedside locker. Dalgliesh saw what she wanted and pulled open the drawer. There on the top was a small square of very fine linen with a border of hand-stitched lace. He took it up. In the corner was her monogram delicately embroidered. And half of the handkerchief was still stiff and stained with brown.

She said: "She left instructions with her solicitors that this was to be returned to me after her death. She always knew where I was. But now she's dead. And I shall soon follow. You may have the handkerchief, Mr. Dalgliesh. It can be of no further use to either of us now."

Dalgliesh put it in his pocket without speaking. As soon as possible he would see that it was burnt. But there was something else he had to say. "Is there anything you would wish me to do? Is there anyone you want told, or to tell? Would you care to see a priest?"

Again there was that uncanny screech of laughter, but softer now.

"There's nothing I can say to a priest. I only regret what I did because it wasn't successful. That is hardly the proper frame of mind for a good confession. But I bear her no ill will. One should be a good loser. But I've paid, Mr. Dalgliesh. For sixty-seven years I've paid. And in this world, Mr. Dalgliesh, the rich only pay once."

She lay back as if suddenly exhausted. There was a silence for a moment. Then she said with sudden vigor: "I believe your visit has done me good. I would be obliged if you'd return each afternoon for the next three days. I shan't trouble you after that."

Dalgliesh extended his leave with some difficulty and stayed at a local inn. He saw her each afternoon. They never spoke again of the murder. And when he came punctually at two P.M. on the fourth day, it was to be told that Miss Goddard had died peacefully in the night with apparently no trouble to anyone. She was, as she had said, a good loser.

A week later, Dalgliesh reported to the Canon.

"I was able to see a man who has made a detailed study of the case. I have read the transcript of the trial and visited Colebrook Croft. And I have seen one other person closely connected with the case but who is now dead. I know you will want me to respect confidence and to say no more than I need."

The Canon murmured his quiet assurance.

Dalgliesh went on quickly: "As a result, I can give you my word that the verdict was a just verdict and that not one penny of your grandfather's fortune is coming to you through anyone's wrong doing."

He turned his face away and gazed out of the window. There was a long silence. The old man was probably giving thanks in his own way. Then Dalgliesh was aware of his godfather speaking. Something was being said about gratitude, about the time he had given up to the investigation.

"Please don't misunderstand me, Adam. But when the formalities have been completed, I should like to donate something to a charity named by you, one close to your heart."

Dalgliesh smiled. His contributions to charity were impersonal—a quarterly obligation discharged by banker's order. The Canon obviously regarded charities as so many old clothes: all friends but some fitted better and were consequently more affectionately regarded than others.

But inspiration came.

"It's good of you to think of it, sir. I rather liked what I learned about Great Aunt Allie. It would be pleasant to give something in her name. Isn't there a society for the assistance of retired and indigent variety artists, conjurers, and so on?"

The Canon, predictably, knew that there was and could name it.

Dalgliesh said: "Then I think, Canon, that Great Aunt Allie would have agreed that a donation in her name would be entirely appropriate."

The Man on The Roof

by Christianna Brand

Sergeant Crum, who, with the assistance of only a fledgling constable, runs the tiny police station in the village of Hawksmere, rang up Chief Inspector Cockrill in Heronsford. "It's the Duke, sir. Phoned to the station and says he's going to shoot hisself."

"The Duke? What Duke? Your Duke, up at the castle?"

Sergeant Crum took a leisurely moment to reflect that in his own small neck of the woods they were hardly so rich in the gilded aristocracy as to necessitate discrimination. Inspector Cockrill, however, had not waited for an answer.

"What have you done about it?"

"Tried to get my constable, sir. Gets his dinner in the village, he does, being his home is there—the Sardine Tin, they call it these days, since the old people—"

"Yes, well, never mind your constable's domestic arrangements—"

"—and they told me he'd suddenly rushed off," continued Crum placidly. "Said he'd heard a shot or something of that. *They* hadn't heard nothing, but the old people are getting a bit—"

"Well, get after him fast, for goodness sake! I'll be there in half an hour at latest."

The sergeant pursued his unhurried way and at the North Gate leaned out of his car to question the lodgekeeper—and, learning that His Grace had gone down a two–three hours ago towards South Lodge, cursed himself mildly for not having thought of that and started on the long haul round the castle walls to what had once been the opposite entrance. South Lodge, of course! Fisher couldn't have heard a shot fired up at the castle.

The constable met him at the little wooden gate of the graveled path that led up to the lodge, clinging as though for support to his bicycle. Over his large, rather handsome young face was spread a strange pall of grey. He said, "He's dead, Sarge."

"Dead? He's done it?"

"Seems like it. He's lying on the floor in the parlor. Lot of blood around."

"You're sure? You didn't make certain?"

"Door's locked, sir. I looked in at the window, but it's too small to get through. And anyway—"

"I was held up. Started for the castle first. You came here direct?"

"Yessir. I heard the shot, I guessed what it might be. I knew he'd be here—I saw him this morning, turning in at the gate. So I got on me bike and came over."

The lodge was in fact a lodge no longer. In the not too distant past, its magnificent wrought-iron gates had been removed and the gap bricked up except for a small postern door. And the high wall ringing the castle and its grounds, rebuilt in a curve that now left the little house standing outside on its own, in an expanse something under an acre of dull, flat land, was at present covered in a blanket of Christmas snow about two inches deep. A hedge completed a sort of high ring around the building, with a break in it to admit of a small wooden gate leading up to the tiny porch over the front door.

The redundant lodgekeeper had been allowed to remain in residence until the accession of the present Duke about three years ago, when he had been evicted with his poor old wife, so that His Grace, whose single bleak passion was the collection and destruction of butterflies, might convert the place into a sort of playroom for himself and his hobby. Considering that there must, up at the castle, be at least seventy rooms which might equally have served his purpose, the dispossessed might be forgiven for suggesting resentfully—but not to the Duke—that a nook might have been created for him there.

Now, in the light snow, two narrow lines, clearly the marks of the constable's bicycle tires, led up and away from the front door—the return journey having apparently been decidedly wobbly. There was no other mark in the snow.

"No sign of his footsteps."

"No. It hadn't started snowing when I saw him going in through the gate." For whatever reason, the constable had lost more color. "That was a couple of hours ago."

"Oh, well." Sergeant Crum abandoned a secret hope that by delaying his errand until the Inspector should come, he might shift onto other shoulders the onus of the whole alarming affair, for sudden death is not a commonplace in quiet little Hawksmere, nestling under the calm shadow of the castle up the hill. He started off through the light flurry of swirling snow, some vague instinct suggesting that it might be well to avoid the tracks of the bicycle tires. You could see where the constable had propped his machine against the wall of the house and gone up the two or three steps. Snow was shuffled as his footprints came down and appeared to move round to the right.

"I ran round to the side window," said Fisher, following his glance. He indicated a small window to their left. "You can't see in so well from there."

"Yes, well, you'd know, wouldn't you?" said Sergeant Crum.

The door was secured by a Yale lock, the sort that clicks shut of itself, to be opened, when the door is closed, only by its own particular key. "Mm," said the sergeant. He tramped in the constable's footsteps leading round the house, and returned with his rugged countryman's visage the same curious shade of grey. "Certainly *looks* very dead," he said uncomfortably and lifted up his heart in a wordless prayer.

The prayer was answered. There came the throbbing of a car in the snowbound stillness and Chief Inspector Cockrill stood at the little gate. For once his shabby mackintosh was not trailing over one shoulder but was worn with his arms in the sleeves, and pushed back upon his noble head with its spray of fine grey hair was the inevitable ill-fitting hat. Inspector Cockrill is known to pick up any hat that happens to be at hand, to the considerable inconvenience of the true owner. Anything that does not actually deafen and blind him is perfectly acceptable to the Terror of Kent.

He remained for a long time intently surveying the scene: the little house in its flat white circle of snow, ringed in by the wall and the hedge so as to be almost invisible to anyone not looking in over the gate. Nice setting for a locked-room mystery, he thought: which God forbid! Fortunately, it appeared to have been a good, straight-forward suicide, heralded in advance by the gentleman himself. And from what he had heard, there would be few to mourn the passing of the sixth Duke of Hawksmere—very few indeed.

A pretty little building, almost fairylike in its present aspect, its highly ornamental pseudo-Gothic façade aglitter with its dusting of snow. An octagonal room, flat-roofed, with a small side window where the lodgekeeper might sit watching for the first signs of approaching vehicles all ready to leap out and open the gates. Into this room, the door opened directly. There was an opposite door leading to the back of the house—two or three small rooms and the household offices: Only the front had been designed to be seen. The rest was cut off and hidden away behind it, considerably less decorative in appearance. The room was furnished only with a desk and a trestle table, upon which were distributed the tools of the Duke's preoccupation, a typewriter, and sheaves of paperwork. There was no other furniture in the house.

Inspector Cockrill stood quietly, taking it all in. The door leading to the other rooms was locked and bolted on this side. There could be nobody else in the house unless they had entered by a back door or window: and in fact there was nobody there. The body lay across the front door, so that, upon entering, one saw nothing but the head and shoulders (turned away from the door) and an outflung hand and arm. The shot had gone through the right temple and out through the other side of the head, somewhat higher up; a bullet was lodged much where one would have expected it to be, high up on the post of the opposite door. An open thermos jug stood on the desk with a puddle of cooling coffee left inside, and there was a piece of foil that had evidently been wrapped round a packet of sandwiches. The time was still early afternoon.

It was almost an hour before, having set in motion the wheels of investigative law, Mr. Cockrill decided: "Well, I'd better go up to the castle and see them there." But before he went, he summoned the constable to stand before him—very pale, hands hanging faintly twitching at his sides. "So, boy. Fish your name is, is it?"

"Fisher, sir," said the constable, hardly daring to contradict.

Inspector Cockrill conceded the point. "Well, now, once again—you heard this shot?"

"Having me dinner I was, sir, at home with me gran and grandad and Mum and Dad and all. And I heard this shot and I thought, the old bastard has done it at last. I mean," said the constable in a terrible hurry, "His-Grace-has-done-himself-in-at-last, sir!"

"You knew of this habit of the Duke's of constantly threatening suicide?"

"Being as he often rang up the station—which he did today, sir."

"Mm. Who else heard the shot?"

"Well, no one, Mr. Cockrill, sir. Gran and Grandad, they're a bit deaf and me mum and dad was arguing and the kids all quarreling, kicking up a row as usual. Besides—"

"Besides?"

"They'd've only said good riddance, and to leave things be."

"Oh?" said Cockie coldly. "Why would they have said that?"

"Well, account of—I mean, nobody liked the old— I mean, nobody liked the Duke, sir, did they?"

"You, however, stifled your feelings and dashed off to his assistance?"

"Only me duty, sir," said Constable Fisher.

"How did you know he'd be here?"

"Well, I saw him arriving," the constable explained. "And he always did spend most of the day here, brought down his sangwidges and coffee and that."

"And seems to have consumed them. Does that strike you as rather odd?"

"What, like 'the prisoner ate a hearty breakfast'?"

The Inspector bent upon him an appreciative eye. "Exactly. Who eats up his lunch before he sets about killing himself?"

"If a gentleman had—well, like moods, sir. And it was a while ago: the coffee's gone quite cold."

"Yes, well . . . Now once again, Constable. You were at this door within six or seven minutes of your hearing the shot? The door was locked. You went round to the window and looked through. The window round at the side of the room, not to this one next to the door, which is nearest."

"You can't see the whole room from the little window, sir. Even from the other one, I couldn't see much. But I could see a good bit of him. I—well, I got a bit rattled, sir, seeing him lying there like that, sort of dead like."

"Very dead like," said Cockie sardonically. "You didn't think of going in and trying to resuscitate him?"

"But he was dead, sir. His head—" He puffed out his cheeks and put a hand over his mouth.

"You'll get used to it," said the Inspector, more kindly. "It shakes one, the first time. So you got on your bike and rode back to the gate? A bit wobbly, those tire marks, the returning ones."

"Yes, well, I was a bit—I didn't know what to do, sir, till the sergeant came."

"In other words, you lost your head."

To Sergeant Crum he said, grumbling: "A wretched young rookie! The Duke of Hawksmere, no less, announces his forthcoming suicide and who's on the spot? This great, green baby of a rookie constable, not yet dry behind the ears." He glanced up at the castle frowning down, formidable, upon them from the hilltop. "God knows what on earth the Duchess is going to say . . ."

What the Duchess in fact said was, comfortably, "Oh, well, he was always threatening suicide, *wasn't* he? His farewell notes simply litter the place. If the police had always had someone important at the ready, no other work would have got done at all."

But that poor boy, she added, must have been scared stiff, all on his own, having to cope. "And you say it's not really quite so simple?"

Not simple at all. But for the moment he dodged it. He said, gratefully: "Your Grace takes it very calmly."

They sat in her private room with its charming pieces of period furniture, made cozy by large, comfortable armchairs. The Duchess had always seemed to him, in many ways, like a comfortable armchair herself: warm and well cushioned and to all the world holding out welcoming arms. "Well, yes—I can't pretend to be heartbroken, he was only a fairly remote cousin, you know, and such a misery, poor man!" Her son, the young Duke, had died in an accident up at his University three years ago and his cousin succeeded to the title.

"I stayed on here at the castle with him, though I longed to retire to the Dower House and be on my own. But he was a mean man, he cared nothing for the estate and the people—he was doing a lot of harm all over the place. Now his brother will succeed him and he's a very different kettle of fish. He loves it, and Rupert, his boy, and darling little Becca, they really do care about it, too. And what a change for them! Poor as church mice they all were till Cousin Hamnet inherited. Everyone thinks that if you belong to a great old family like ours, you must naturally be rich, but of course, apart from the title, that needn't be so at all. And they certainly weren't." It was on account of this, she believed, that Hamnet had never got married; though now, as a matter of fact, there were murmurs about his doing so.

"So Hamnet was pretty happy to succeed?"

"Well—not happy as we've seen. He was not a happy man. A depressive, I suppose the psychiatrists would say, and he certainly got no joy out of being

Duke of Hawksmere. But there *is* a joy, you know, in being at the center of it all and caring about the land—running it properly, looking after the people, one's own people. It sounds condescending, referring to them as 'our people,' but they do become like one's own, so many have been for generations with the family. One gets very protective towards them, and I'm thankful to say that Will, the new Duke, and darling Rupert and Becca have the feeling very strongly. I must confess," said the Duchess, "that I've loved it all. Even the bazaar-opening I've secretly rather enjoyed."

"Nobody opens a bazaar like Your Grace," said Cockie handsomely.

"Well, a new Grace will be opening them now, and they're all so happy to be here—now forever. The children were here a lot in their school hols, inseparable friends with the family down at South Lodge. Poor Dave, a bad attack of calf-love, it was rather touching, all great hands and feet and blushing like a peony every time she came near him."

Inspector Cockrill, unfamiliar with any South Lodge family and ignorant of whoever Dave might be, preferred to probe a little further into the family of the new Duke. "They're all staying here at the moment, I understand?"

"Yes, for Christmas. I'm so happy having them here."

"A handsome pair, I believe. Tall, are they? Take after their father?"

"Oh, my dear, no—*ants*! I mean, compared with my own beautiful son, they seem so dark and little."

"Pretty lightweight, are they?"

"Both of them." She looked at him warily. "Why should you ask? You've got something up your sleeve, you old devil! You've been holding out on me."

"No, no," said the Inspector, "I just wanted to get

the facts from you, unprejudiced. And so I have. And in return I'll offer Your Grace a fact, which I wouldn't do for most people, so please keep it absolutely to yourself." But he could hardly bring himself to speak it aloud. "Have you ever heard, Duchess, of a locked-room mystery?"

"You mean like detective stories? Doors bolted, windows barred, wastes of untrodden—" She broke off, incredulous. "You don't mean it? The lodge down there in the middle of all that snow?"

"The constable rode up to the front door on his bike. He walked a little way round to a side window and back. He rode back down to the gate. He and his sergeant then walked up to the house. *I* walked up to the house. Apart from those footsteps coming and going and the two lines coming and going of the bicycle tires there isn't a break in the whiteness all round about that place. Ringed round by the wall and the hedge, the lodge sitting like a cherry in the middle of an iced cake. Not a single sign."

"Oh, well," said the Duchess, "what's really so odd about that? Naturally, he'd have let the door close when he went into the lodge—the Duke, I mean. And in this weather he'd keep the windows shut. He went down before the snow began. Had this gun with him—presumably in case he came on suicidal at any time, which he was always doing; and he did come on suicidal. He rang up the police station as usual, sat down and composed yet another note, and this time, for a change, poor old Ham, he really did shoot himself. I mean, you say he was just lying there?"

"Almost right across the doorway," said Cockie. "Right hand flung out, fingers curled as though the gun had just fallen from them. The first thing you saw as you pushed open the door—his hand with his fingers half curled. Death instantaneous, shot at very close range, and no question of one of these medical freaks when a man moves about a bit, even walks a little distance after death. He died at once and lay where he had fallen."

"And in fact the constable even heard the shot. So where's the mystery?" said the Duchess reasonably. "Where's your locked room?"

"The locked room is the lodge," said Cockie, "locked in, as it were, in all that untrodden snow. A man dead in the lodge, very recently dead, death instantaneous, from a gunshot wound at very close range. And the mystery is very easy to state and not at all easy to answer. The mystery is, where is the gun—?"

"Where—?"

"—because it isn't lying there close to his right hand where it ought to be, and it isn't anywhere else in the lodge, and it isn't anywhere outside in all the snow." The cigarette held in his cupped hand sent its pale smoke spiraling up between his fingers, and he flung the butt suddenly, with an almost violent movement, into the heart of the flickering fire. "So damn the blasted thing," he said. "Where the hell *is* it?" And apologized immediately, "I beg Your Ladyship's pardon!"

"Oh, no, don't apologize," said the Duchess. "I do see. It's dreadful for you." Well, and dreadful for all of them, she added with growing recognition of what it must mean.

For if the Duke of Hawksmere hadn't shot himself at last, who had done it for him?

And how did that person get away?

And what did he do with the gun?

They sat for a long time in silence, thinking it over. The Chief Inspector said at last, reluctantly: "There seems to be only the one possible solution."

"Mm," said the Duchess. She looked at him rather unhappily. "Are you thinking what I'm thinking?"

"Just a question of what on earth could have been the motive," said the Inspector, shrugging.

"Motive? Oh!" She looked quite horrified. "You're not thinking what I'm thinking after all, Cockie." And what he *was* thinking was absolutely, absolutely, said the Duchess earnestly, "abso*lute*ly *wrong*."

The handful of men at the disposal of the police had been supplemented by carefully selected village helpers, and at South Lodge there was much pushing and thrusting and beating about hedges and ditches in search of the missing weapon. Result: exactly nil. By now, in the magical way that such things happen, the local press at least had got wind of the affair and their reporters had come swarming over in a fever of excitement from the neighboring small towns: doubtless Fleet Street would soon be upon them. Already they were creating a dangerous nuisance, slouching about in the inevitable filthy old mackintoshes, humped under the weight of swinging cameras, trampling all over the sacred ground.

"Couldn't do much about it," said the Inspector's own sergeant, Charlie Thomas, from Heronsford. "What with the search and all, there aren't enough men to keep them back. It's like a blob of mercury, you think you've got them all under your thumb and suddenly they're scattering into little blobs all over the place again. But, anyway, with fresh snow falling we couldn't do much more in the way of investigation, Chief. All the tracks are disappearing and we'd sorted out every last detail of what might have been a clue."

The Inspector stood for a long, long time looking outside at the ring of wall and hedge surrounding the flat expanse of white, tramped round through the churned-up snow to the window through which Constable Fisher had peered, trembling, for his first sight of the Duke's dead body. (Later the constable had been hoisted up by way of the same window frame to look over the many-spired parapet for any sign of the revolver. "No, Sarge," he had reported, "nothing up here!" From no other vantage point could it have been thrown there.)

And no gun anywhere else in the house. Not in the room where the Duke had died nor in the empty rooms out at the back. The connecting door had been locked and bolted from this side, all the windows and the back door had been similarly fastened—boarded up in most cases. It was as though someone, having made all safe from within, had come out into the octagonal room and locked the intervening door behind him. Nor was there any sign of anyone having been in the back of the house for many long months. Inspector Cockrill gave vent to a satisfied sigh. He liked things to be exact.

It was late evening when, having left in charge trusted henchmen of his own, he collected his sergeant and drove with him back to Heronsford. The night was dark but star-lit, all aglitter where the headlights picked out the leafless twigs of the hedges, frost-laden. He sat in the passenger seat, the cigarette smoke curling up through his nicotined fingers. "Well, then, Charlie—what do you make of it?"

"Not a lot," said the sergeant, eyes on the unrolling white ribbon of the road.

"Sealed room. No marks in the snow that aren't accounted for."

"Time of death?" prompted the sergeant.

"The doc says very recent. Works out at about the time young Fish says he heard the shot."

"Fisher," said Charlie.

"I don't know why I keep thinking it's Fish. Well—so?"

"Well, so there are questions to be asked," said the sergeant. "No acrobatic leaps possible, or trapeze acts or any of that stuff: the distances between the lodge and anything else are much too great. So number one would be, could anyone have been hiding in the lodge? Answer—we searched it thoroughly, even the roof outside, and positively there was not. Well, we were looking for the gun, but if a man had been there we'd hardly have missed him.

"Question two—and this one I know you're a bit fond of: why were the returning bicycle marks so wobbly? Answer—the wretched lad was scared out of his wits, having been first on the scene and found the Duke dead—his hands were probably shaking like jellies on the handlebars. Even Crum observed that he was pale and distressed. Question three, then: did he really hear the sound of the shot?—no one else did. Answer—sure enough, we have only his word for it. Question four then is: was it really the Duke who telephoned the station? And the answer to that is that Sergeant Crum, who took the message, is so thick he would never think to question it.

"Number five: why did Crum then bat off up to the castle when the constable was supposed to have heard the shot from his home, which he couldn't possibly have done if it had been fired up at the castle? That gets the same answer—the man is as thick as two planks. Question six: did the Duke really write the suicide note which was propped up on the desk? Answer—yes, probably, but it could have been written under coercion. Finally—and this is the sixty-million-dollar one—how did the murderer get away, taking the gun with him? Answer—"

"Or answers . . ."

"Pretty obvious, Mr. Cockrill, don't you think? Only one way, really. Different versions of the same, depending upon who the murderer *was*."

"Except in the case of the one I think of as number four."

"Four?" said the sergeant, almost as though they were playing a word game. "I've only got three."

Inspector Cockrill ran over them, ascribing to each a motive or motives. "I've only just now decided to add in this fourth one. In that case, the motive could be anything: His Late Grace was a deeply unlovable man." They sat silent a little while, musing over it all, while the little car crept across the light carpet of snow—in this narrow, little-used byroad hardly disturbed at all. The sergeant said at last: "It's odd that with the first three the motive in each case seems to be vicarious—if by that I mean, on behalf of other people."

"Well, I'd hardly say that: other people would benefit, certainly. In the first, it would certainly seem so vicarious, as you call it, as to be very hard to believe." He added rather gloomily that they mustn't forget that the Duchess appeared to have a candidate of her own and one without even a motive. "And that makes five."

The sergeant was hardly impressed. "Oh, well, sir— the Duchess!"

The Inspector had sat all this time nursing the enormous hat on his bony knees. Now, as they reached his gate, he scrambled out, clapping it back onto his head. "Yes, well— 'the Duchess' you say, my lad. But the Dowager Duchess of Hawksmere, let me tell you, is an exceedingly shrewd old bird. And I'm a bit scared of her. There's nothing she'd stop at to protect 'our people,' let alone her own family." He slammed-to the door of the car and stood hunting through the pockets of the disreputable old mac in search of his keys. "Oh, thank goodness, here are the damn things. I'm in need of a hot drink and bed. Good night, Charlie. Go off home now and sleep well. Tomorrow is another day."

Another day. For all but the late Duke of Hawksmere,

lying so quiet and stiff in his metal cold-box, split like a herring to reveal his body's secrets: with nothing to disclose, however, but the recent consumption of a sandwich meal, and a gunshot wound in the head . . .

The new day was less than gladdened for Inspector Cockrill by the arrival of the Chief Constable of the county. A choleric, ex-military man, he huffed and puffed a good deal, unable to face the grotesquerie of a locked-room mystery right there in their midst, and for comfort settled on the solid facts relating to the missing weapon. Well, yes, said Inspector Cockrill, a common enough type of weapon left over from the last war—impossible to say how many ex-officers might, for one reason or another, have failed to hand back their revolvers at the conclusion of hostilities. The passage through bone, explained the experts, would make it difficult to ascribe the bullet to any one particular gun.

"Was the late Duke known to have possessed such a revolver?"

"If you recall, Sir George, you yourself undertook to question him on the subject."

"Yes, well, so I did call on him and ask him. But delicately, you know, stepping very delicately. He hardly seemed to know what I was talking about. But he certainly didn't deny that he had such a weapon."

Very helpful, reflected Cockie.

"Well, you can't march in with a sniffer-dog and search a place like the castle," said the Chief Constable huffily. Besides, he added, these people who were always threatening suicide never really did it.

"Nosir," said Cockie in the authentic accents of Police Constable Fisher at his most wooden. He explained the probable difficulties in ascribing the bullet to the late Duke's, or indeed to any revolver.

"Which, anyway, you've lost," the Chief Constable reminded him sourly.

"Oh, yessir, so we have," said the Inspector, more in the Sergeant Crum line this time. Sort of thing that could happen to anyone, the voice suggested.

At first light, the search for the missing gun had begun again—village people, tremendously eager and helpful, said Cockie. Although, he added limpidly, none of them had liked the Duke, most of them having understandable grudges against him. To tenants so long accustomed to the cherishing rule of the Dukes of Hawksmere, with the family arms around "our people," he had seemed a mean, to them a dangerous man.

The Chief Constable was as appalled as the Inspector could have wished. "Good God, man, they'll all be on the side of the killer! You don't know *who* may have found the thing and be harboring it somewhere. They must be taken off at once—search them, search their homes, search every house in the village!"

He stumped off angrily to wreak further havoc from the comfortable ambiance of the Heronsford police station and Chief Inspector Cockrill was able to give out, with a lightened heart, that these arbitrary orders came not from himself—as if he would—but from the Chief Constable in his un-wisdom. He must, however, have considerably overrated his superior's enthusiasm—Sir George would never have contemplated an intrusion into the castle itself.

The search there was more easily concluded than might have been expected—by anyone but the Inspector himself. "Under some papers in a drawer of the late Duke's desk," he explained to the Dowager Duchess. "Surprise, surprise!" he added sardonically.

"*Not* a surprise." said the Duchess. "After all, it may not be the one that was used. I hear the bullet may not prove to be traceable. Perhaps he didn't have this one with him. He presumably didn't always lug one around with him."

"So how did he propose to shoot himself down at the lodge? He rang up the station and said he was about to do so."

"Well, someone rang up the station. Would Sergeant Crum necessarily have questioned the voice? And there'd be suicide notes all over the place. Whoever it was could just have used one of those."

"Your Grace ought to be in my job," said the Chief Inspector respectfully.

"Do you know, Cockie," said the Duchess on a note of not very sincere apology, "in this particular case, I really believe I should."

Mr. Cockrill felt in duty bound to report to his Chief Constable, though by no means to unravel matters clearly for him. "Her Grace put the gun there herself, of course, as I knew she would."

"The *Duchess*?"

"The Dowager. It was in a package sent up with her letters this morning. Well, of course, her post has been prodigious. Posted last night here in Hawksmere. Everyone's been in and out of the village, in and out of Heronsford, up and down to London like yoyos, lawyers and so forth: a Duke doesn't die like ordinary men, let alone get himself murdered. The post alone may tell us something," suggested Cockie. "Don't you think?"

It patently told the Chief Constable nothing whatsoever. He huffed and puffed and went off at a tangent. "Why should the Duchess do such a thing?"

"Protecting her family?"

"For heaven's sake—her family! You're not suspecting the new Duke of Hawksmere in a business like this?"

"He had everything to gain. But, well, no—"

"Well, then, young Rupert. You wouldn't—"

"His father has succeeded the sixth Duke. He is

now heir to the title. And he loves the place and the people on the estate deeply. The family own half the county. He was horrified by the way the late Duke was treating them. And he was threatening to marry and get an heir for himself. We have to consider young Rupert."

"Good heavens, Cockrill, I shall never live this down!"

"Or there's the girl," continued Cockie remorselessly. "She felt the same about it all. And of course her parents now become Duke and Duchess instead of being just hard-up nobodies."

Sir George looked as though spontaneous combustion were just around the corner. The daughter of the Duke! Or the heir to the dukedom! But comfort was at hand. He demanded triumphantly, "Just explain to me how either of them could have got away from the building? The tire marks, the footmarks, are all accounted for, and there are no others. So how could either of those young people have got away from the place?"

Oh, well, as to that, said Cockie, tremendously off-hand, one could think of three or four explanations in each case; surely Sir George must have worked them out for himself? And he suddenly caught sight of Charlie Thomas and must rush off and join his sergeant, if Sir George would excuse him . . .

To Charlie, he said: "I can't resist pulling the old buffer's leg."

"You'll get yourself into trouble one of these days, Boss," said the sergeant, laughing. But what on earth, he wondered, was going to happen next?

"What will happen next," said Cockie prophetically, "is that a letter will arrive, suggesting a new and totally unexpected suspect and a new and totally unexpected method of getting away from the lodge—snow surroundings, bike marks, footprints, and all."

*   *   *

And duly the letter arrived and was handed over to them by the Duchess herself. "In this morning's post. Addressed to me. The postmark? But, Cockie dear, you've no notion what the mails have been like—with the Duke's death, you know, all the business letters and the sympathetics, poor loves, so tricky for them to know just what to say! I mean, 'So sorry to hear that your cousin has been murdered. Whatever will you do about the funeral? Yours affectionately, Aunt Maude.' The children are reading through them in fits of giggles, they are so naughty! But as to the postmarks, I'm afraid we just slit all the envelopes open and threw them away. It's not like the Americans who put their addresses on the back—I never get used to it. But out they've gone, and with this sort of cheap writing paper there wouldn't be a matching envelope, we'd never trace which belonged to which."

Nor had the typewriter proved traceable to anyone in or around Hawksmere. Probably done in a pretense of testing a demonstration model somewhere up in London, Cockie thought. A very old trick. Style, predictably illiterate.

"Dear Dutchess," ran the letter, "I am well away now and soon will be abroad so to save truoble for others I confes to the murder of tghe duke of Hawksmear he was a relaiton of yuors but he was a dead rotter and he deseved to die. I went doun befor the sno began he let me in I told him he mite as well comit suiside but he siad he would not now as he was hopeing to het marrid he did not seam to have a gun but I had bruoght one along with me in case. I cuold not make him write a suiside note but there was one rihgt there on the desk just lying about.

"By now it was snoing and I pushed the gun in his back and mad him ring up the police station and say he was going to shoot hisself then I put tghe gun near his head and shot him. When I opend the door it was very quite I haerd a bycicle bell and I went back and closed the door when I hared the person go away I cam out and I saw footsteps in the snow going round the house and I followed them and there was a window. I climbed up by the window on to the roof and when the jurnalists cam crowding round I showed myself and a policeman came and hauled me down so I said I only wanted to get a shot of the snow with the footmarks, as if I was a jurnalist and they quit beleived me. I better say I saw a policeman was being hoisted up to see if tghe gun was on the roof, so I lay up against the parapet where he would be leaning over to look and unles he bent right over he wuld not see me and he did not he only calld out no gun here. That is all. There was a lot of peeple hated tghe duke long before he was a duke and I was one of them. Yuo need not look any feurther."

"Well, well, well," said Cockie, handing over this effusion to his sergeant. "What did I tell you?" He went on down to the lodge and summoned the constable. "Well, now, Fish—"

"Fisher, sir," said the constable a trifle desperately.

"All right, never mind that. You were the man sent up to see if the gun had been thrown onto the flat roof of this room. Why did you choose to climb up via the side window?"

"It couldn't have been thrown from any other point, sir. There's a porch over the front steps and there weren't any other marks in the snow."

"The gun could have slithered back and come to rest just under the parapet. You didn't think to hook yourself right over the edge and look downwards and inwards?"

"The gun wouldn't have done that, Mr. Cockrill, sir." He made a chucking movement with his hand. "It would slither away, sir, not backwards. But any-

way, with the snow it would probably just stay where
it fell. So it would be about in the middle of the roof.
And it wasn't."

"So if a man were hiding close up under the parapet
where you looked over—?"

"I could well have missed seeing him," Fisher admitted. "I wasn't looking there." And come to think
of it, he suggested, a man *had* tried to climb up on
the roof—two or three in fact—but each time been
hauled back before he got there. "Them journalists,
sir. If anyone got far enough, he would have seen if
a gun had been thrown up there."

In fact, several of the culprits had been traced but
none admitted having got up as far as the roof, and
the consensus had been that this was true. Still, it
might be well for Cockrill to scan the newspapers for
press photographs of the snowy ground, taken from a
high angle . . .

He came back to Constable Fisher. "The late Duke
had a good many enemies? You yourself hardly loved
him, I daresay?"

The constable's air of ease gave way to pallor and
tensed-up fingers. "I never hardly set eyes on him,
sir. Him being the Duke and all."

"Till the day before yesterday?"

"And by then he was dead, sir."

"Yes, so he was. It must have been a shock, peering
in at that close-shut window? Now, tell me again—
why that particular window?"

"You can't see right into the room from the nearer
one, sir. Not into the whole of the room."

"No you can't, can you? But how did you know
that?"

"Well, sir, being as my gran and grandad used to
live here—"

"They *lived* here?" said Cockrill, and glanced with
a sort of gleam towards his sergeant. "They *lived*

here? And were chucked out by the Duke, I suppose? And had to squash in with the rest of your big family, all in one little cottage—the old folks cranky and carping, I daresay, as old people are when they see too much of the young—your parents resentful and answering back, all those noisy brothers and sisters worse than ever, and everyone miserable. In other words—the Sardine Tin!"

"Except I think it must be more peaceful, sir, in a sardine tin."

No wonder, reflected the Inspector, that I kept thinking of him as Fish. "Never mind your constable's domestic arrangements," he had said, choking off Sergeant Crum's ill-timed explanations, and all that time . . . "All right for the moment, then, Fisher." But to Charlie he said: "Well, Sarge—the simplest explanation, after all? It was only that being more or less strangers to these parts we had no idea that such a motive existed. But now—"

A shot that nobody else had heard. Down to the lodge on one's bicycle and up to the front door. The Duke, placidly consuming sandwiches, is easily persuaded to admit the uniformed figure of the local rozzer. Some excuse—the police require the handing over of the revolver which His Grace is understood to have illegally in his possession. Gun in hand, force the telephone call to the police station. With any luck, Sergeant Crum will go batting off up to the castle, thus giving one more time. Force the production of the suicide note and then—one shot and it's done.

It's done: but all of a sudden, it's horrible. Back away to the open front door, gun in hand, having forgotten in one's panic to throw it down beside the outflung hand. Stand there, shaking, trying to wipe off one's fingerprints and—horror!—the door is blown shut by the whirl of the wind that is sending the snow-flakes aflurry and one is locked out on the step with the gun in one's hand! Round to the window in hopes it may open sufficiently to throw the gun into the room. But it is tightly closed—and at any moment Sergeant Crum may arrive!

Down to the gate, then, awobble with nervousness, on one's bike and when the hue and cry goes forth, join eagerly in. For who will think of looking in the pocket of the heroic discoverer of the crime, for the weapon which brought it about?

Nervous? Yes, of course he would be nervous. But so what? A man is dead whom all the world detested, Gran and Grandad can come back to the cozy little home, Mum and Dad will be free and happy again, and the pack of younger brothers and sisters will be safe from the ceaseless censure of the older generation and settle down happily once more. Her Grace can move out to the dear little Dower House, the new Duke is a kind and generous man, Rupert, friend of one's childhood, will be heir to the dukedom, and long-loved Becca will be rich and happy and always down here at Hawksmere to be adored from afar. And how grateful, could they have known, would everyone for miles around have been to the begetter of all this happiness . . .

But first the gun. One cannot carry it around in a uniform pocket, and where to hide it in the narrow confines of the village to which one is now restricted? Post it off to the castle, then, with a message to the Duchess, "Please put this back where it belongs, for all our sakes." Her Grace must recognize that the thing has been done by someone here on the ducal estates, by one of "our people." Her Grace won't make trouble for anyone who will throw themselves upon her mercy, and Her Grace knows very well how to protect herself . . .

Charlie Thomas had been mulling it over, muttering

at intervals into the recital, "Mm, mm." Now he said: "And the letter?"

"Ah," said Cockie, for the first time losing confidence a little. "The letter."

"Very interesting, that letter. Not in fact the work of an illiterate. The mistakes are deliberate. A writer who spells 'brought' as 'bruoght' knows what letters there are in that difficult word. A true illiterate would write 'brort' or something. And this isn't an accomplished typist. It's easy to hit a *g* when you intended an *h* and he keeps putting *tghe*. But Fisher types very well and I don't think he's bright enough to have thought all this up. So that would bring us to—"

"The new heir," said Cockie none too happily. "Young Rupert."

"It's one thing for a lad to want to help his grandparents to get back their old home," said Charlie. "But Rupert's dad becomes a Duke, they're all in the money, and, what's probably the most important point, 'our people' will be safe from the tyrant, who was threatening to marry and spawn a breed of mini-tyrants forever."

"So how do you suggest he got away, leaving no trace in the snow? You don't suggest that Rupert was the man on the roof?"

"There never was any man on the roof, sir, *was* there? Just some damn journalist, trying to be cleverer than the rest; and *he* was hauled down and whoever he may have been, he wasn't Rupert. But we've both thought of ways in which someone other than Fisher could have got away from the lodge . . ."

There was the sound of hooves chiff-chuffing across the grass and a light voice exhorted: "Now, darlings, be good horses and just stay there!" and, with a thump at the door, the two young people came into the room.

"Look here, Inspector, you're *not* accusing poor

Dave of murdering Cousin Ham?" demanded Lady Rebecca on a note of scorn.

An ant she might be, but a very pretty ant, the cloud of dark, soft hair crowned by a shabby little riding bowler. The brother was as dark and scarcely taller, very slender, and no less shabbily fitted out. Poor as church mice, the Duchess had said, and clearly their late cousin had not been generous with handouts, despite his sudden acquisition of title and great wealth. Inspector Cockrill said mildly: "Are you referring to Police Constable Fisher?"

"Yes—we've just met him in the lane, and he's petrified."

"If he did kill the Duke, that would be fairly natural."

"He no more killed the Duke than I did!" Rupert said.

"In fact, my boy, we were just discussing that very possibility. That you *did.*"

"*Me?* What a lot of rubbish! Why on earth should I want to kill rotten old Cousin Hamnet?"

"Just because he *was* rotten old Cousin Hamnet."

The brother and sister were leaning back negligently against the edge of the table, feet crossed in their well worn riding boots. "Good lord," said Rebecca, "you're not going to suggest that he was the man on the roof, beloved of our Aunt Daisy—the Duchess Daisy," she elaborated. "And if you are, how did he get away from the lodge without leaving great humping footprints in the snow?"

"Well," said the Inspector easily, "we had an idea that he might have used a bicycle."

"Oh, that's great!" said Rupert. "I haven't even got a bicycle."

"But your dear friend Dave—he had a bicycle."

It rocked them a little, but the boy said nonchalantly enough, "Don't tell me—let me guess. I borrowed Dave's bicycle."

"At gun-point," suggested Becca, mocking, her pretty little nose in the air.

"Or by cajolement. He would be very much on your side."

"You seem to have a simple faith in the trustworthiness of your force," said Rupert.

"Well, but—to such a good friend. And it does all seem to fit."

"It doesn't fit at all," said Rebecca. "We were together the whole afternoon, out riding." She saw as she spoke the weakness of this double alibi and added, "My Aunt Daisy saw us from the window. She'll tell you so."

"I'm sure she will," said the Inspector drily.

Rebecca slid down from her perch on the table edge. "So we'll be going home now because I can assure you that Dave didn't do it and neither did Rupert, so just *don't* be silly about it."

"No, indeed, since you put up so convincing a case. On the other hand," suggested Cockie, "you leave yourself undefended."

"*Me?*" said Becca as her brother had said before her.

"You had exactly the same possible motives as your brother. One or the other of you came down here before the snow fell—"

"Why one or the other—why not both of us?"

"Because only one person could have ridden away on that bicycle, with or without Constable Fisher." The sergeant opened his mouth to speak, but Mr. Cockrill quelled him. "You came down here before the snow fell, one or the other of you. You started a long argument with your cousin about the running of the estate—about his possible marriage, perhaps. But it was all no good. You lost your temper, the gun was lying around as usual, ready for use if the fancy took him—and you picked it up. By that time the snow had fallen, but while you stood panicking on the doorstep, there appeared the gallant Saint Dave to the rescue on his trusty bicycle. No need in your case, Lady Rebecca, for any gun-pointing or even cajolement: up you scramble and, wobbling a bit with the extra weight and general insecurity, you duly arrive at the gate. Off you scarper and the friend of your childhood is left, rather scared, but glowing with the knowledge that he has saved—well, I'll still say one or other of those he loves."

"Not bad," said Rupert with a determined air of superiority, but looking, all the same, a little pale. "But surely there must be other candidates, not just Becca and me?"

"There aren't, you know. Your father is too big and heavy to have shared a bike with Fisher, who's a big chap too—I've tried an experiment and the bicycle broke down—and what's more, he has an alibi rather more convincing than that of a brother and sister out riding, watched by Her Grace, your cousin Daisy. Someone from round about? Well, the police aren't entirely idiots, you know, whatever you may believe to the contrary, and we've made very thorough investigations—you can count them all out."

"So you seriously think you have a case against us—against one of us?"

"Or Constable Fisher," said Cockie placidly.

Rupert slid down and stood beside his sister. "Well, we'll be going now, if you'll excuse us. You can bring the handcuffs up to the castle any time. Come on," he said to his sister. "We'll go and lay this mouse at the feet of our ever present help in times of trouble and see what *she* has to say to Mr. Cockrill about it."

The Inspector waited until the shuffle of hooves had trotted off into silence. Then he stretched himself.

"Well, Charlie, at least we've got that off our chests." And perhaps another time, he added laughing, his sergeant would refrain from breaking out into expostulation when his superior officer dropped a clanger.

"It was you saying that only one person could have ridden away on the bike—with or without Fisher. Of course, anyone who had ridden the bike up to the lodge could just have ridden it back again—and any bike, for that matter, it needn't be Fisher's. The tire marks were snowed over before we really got at them."

"Well, it doesn't matter either way. The tracks were made by the constable: he'd seen into the room, he described it to Sergeant Crum. The tire marks were made by him, riding his own bike—quite possibly giving a lift back to the gate to someone of a fairly small physique. And we've eliminated everyone except that precious pair." He heaved himself up and shrugged on his dreadful old mac, thrust that hat onto his head, and gave it a thump which brought it down over his eyes. "Damn the thing, it never used to be as big as this," he said, irritably shoving it up to his forehead. "I'll get on up to the castle now and, in my turn, place my poor mouse at the feet of Her Ladyship. Who, however, is their cousin and not their aunt."

"Does it matter?" said Charlie, surprised.

"Not a bit," said the Inspector and folded himself, mac and hat and all, into his little police car. "See you, Sarge!"

"In one piece, I hope," said Charlie rather doubtfully.

The Duchess of Hawksmere met him in the vast hall, where she stood surrounded by his trio of suspects. "Oh, Cockie—how nice to see you! Now you, my loves," she said to the young ones—apparently without affectation on either side, including among her loves the village constable—"go off and get some coffee and buns or something and don't make any more fuss." One freckled hand on the bannisters, she began to haul herself up the stairs. "Sorry to be so slow, Inspector, but my arthritis is giving me hell today." At the door of her sitting room, she ushered him in. "Find a chair for yourself, but first pour me a drop of vodka, like an angel, and help yourself to whatever you like. And no nonsense about being on duty and all that—we're both going to need it, I promise you."

The Chief Inspector thought that upon his side, at any rate, this would certainly prove only too true. He cast the mac and hat upon a chair and sat down with her before the agreeably flickering fire. "Well, Duchess?"

"Well, Cockie! I thought you'd come up after the kids, with all their dramas, and here you are, and we can settle down and have a real good yat."

Only the Duchess of Hawksmere, reflected the Inspector, would refer to a serious discussion of a murder in the family as a good old yat. "I have to walk circumspectly, my lady."

"Oh, not with me. I mean nobody ever does: it's because I'm so dreadfully uncircumspect myself. So I thought," she suggested with her own particular brand of authority and humility, "would it be possible for you to outline for me the cases you have against all these young people? Because I really do think I can help you, you know."

He thought it over. It was all highly unconventional, but he, no more than Her Grace, had never been, would never be, a slave to that sort of thing. Moreover, he was curious about her own so-far-undisclosed candidate. "If it honestly will go no further?"

"Cross my heart and wish to die," said the Duchess, making a sign upon her well upholstered bosom.

"Well, then . . ." Somewhat gingerly and with many ifs and ands, he outlined one by one his suspicions of the young heir, Rupert, and his sister, the Lady Rebecca. "And then as to Fish—"

"Fisher," said the Duchess. "I do think it's so hurtful to get people's names wrong. I do it all the time myself, but I'm old so it doesn't count. Besides, I call everyone darling, such an actressy habit, I simply hate it: but at least they don't realize that half the time it's because I can't think who on earth they are!"

"Duchess, you are trying to charm me," said Cockie severely.

"Am I? Well, perhaps I am—I never know I'm doing it. But we need a little gaiety in all this awfulness, don't we? So, well then, that brings us to the man on the roof—the letter."

Chief Inspector Cockrill expatiated at length upon the letter. Don't let's be silly about that, was the unexpressed burden of his reflections. Aloud he said: "We know that that was just a diversion."

"But a very potent diversion, Chief Inspector, wouldn't you say? I mean—hardly to be denied outright, at least with any certainty. No possible proof for or against, is there?" She fixed him with a quizzical look which told him that he might as well be a bazaar that Her Grace was about to open. He knew he was at her mercy—and would love every minute of it. "But first, Cockie dear—another drink?"

"Not another drop, Duchess, thank you."

"Oh, but you must, or I can't. And you know that I can't get weaving till I'm in vodka up to the ankles. I get so tired," said the Duchess, looking as wan as every evidence of robust health would allow, "and when I'm tired, my mind simply won't work—I'm helpless."

It seemed to Inspector Cockrill highly desirable from his own point of view that Her Grace should remain without reviving vodka, but she had him in thrall. He reluctantly poured out two small rations

("Oh, Cockie, for goodness sake!") and more gener-ously topped them up. "So now, my dear, what are we to do? Because you know perfectly well that my two young ones couldn't possibly have killed the man, and neither could poor, dear Dave. So we come back to the letter. And who wrote the letter."

"You wrote the letter yourself, Duchess, and posted it on one of your necessary expeditions up to London. Or didn't post it at all—just 'found it' among your letters."

"Well, what a thing to suggest! But really very perspicacious of you, Cockie. Yes, of course. I thought it might come in nicely for covering every eventuality: because if you could just settle for that—only keeping it to yourself, of course—and never be able to find a trace of the murderer, well, who could say a word against you?"

"My Chief Constable, for one, could say a word against me and would, most vociferously."

"Oh, that pompous old fool! Nobody will listen to a word he says; you just leave him to me. All you need do is cast about like mad, dragging in Scotland Yard and Interpol and all that lot, trying to trace the letter, trying to ferret out all Hamnet's old enemies, which after all would take you back twenty or thirty years—and finally give up and say the case is closed or whatever the expression is."

"No case is ever closed," said Cockie severely.

"Well, keep it a bit open, but just never solve it. Because what the letter says is true. Millions of people simply hated poor old Ham, long before he was ever a Duke. He was a misery to himself, always saying he wanted to die, never having the courage to get around to doing it. And now the lovely man on the roof has done it for him and everyone will simply love him for it and never want him to be caught at all."

"Except me," said the Chief Inspector somberly.

"Well, I do call that rather lacking in appreciation of my efforts to help you!"

"You don't suppose that *I'd* be content with some cooked-up nonsense, no one ever knowing the truth?"

"Well, but someone does know the truth, don't they, Cockie? I mean, I've told you all along, haven't I? *I* do."

"Your Grace has never had the ꞓodness to divulge it to *me*."

"Oh, Cockie, how cross and sarcastic! Well, I ˙˙ divulge it now. But only," said the Duchess, downing the last of her second vodka tonic, "if you promise, promise, promise never to do anything about it."

"Are you asking me to let a criminal go free?"

"No, I'm not. I don't think there is any criminal—except the man on the roof. I think Hamnet did at last really go ahead and commit suicide. Ate his lunch, thought things over—he was always a bit dyspeptic after meals—and reached for the gun. And then—" She put out her pudgy hand with its carefully tended, varnished nails and touched his own nicotined fingers. "Trust me. You'll be grateful to me, honestly you will. I'm not practicing any deceit upon you—and it will solve everything."

You are old, he thought, and stout and arthritic and nowadays no beauty, but damn you—"All right," he said grudgingly. "So?"

"So—that boy, Cockie. You kept on saying it yourself—to be first on the scene of the bloody death of the Earl of Hawksmere, no less—a baby, a great, raw green rookie of a baby policeman, not yet dry behind the ears. In a total panic—wouldn't he be? What he said was the truth, my dear—he heard the shot, leapt on his bike, and pedaled like a lunatic down to the lodge and up through the snow to the front door. And the door was open. Hamnet always left an escape route—rang up in advance so that if ever he did take the plunge, someone could get there in time to haul him back to life. The door was open—how would anyone have heard the shot if it had been fired from behind sealed-up windows and doors? He looked inside and the first thing he saw was the Duke's head, dreadfully wounded, and the revolver lying there, fallen from the dead hand. So—what would any of us do? He panicked and, in an automatic impulse bent down and picked up the gun."

"Oh, my God!" said the Inspector.

"Yes, it was a bit Oh-my-God, wasn't it, since the number-one lesson a policeman is taught is never ever to touch anything at the scene of the crime. He would have thrown it down at once, I daresay, but another lesson came into his mind as he began to calm down—watch out for fingerprints! He got out his hankie or whatever and started wiping his own off the gun and—horror of horrors— there comes a flurry of wind and the door blows shut!"

"Leaving him locked out, with the gun still in his hands. Nips round to the side window to see if he can throw it back in, but the window's tight shut. So he shoves the thing into his pocket and, very nervous, wobbles back to the gate, and when Sergeant Crum arrives—not the most observant of men—goes into his act. The door was closed, he could only see the body by looking in through the window . . ."

"Yes. Well, there you are, Cockie—and there *he* was, poor wretched boy, and just think of his state of mind. Marching about all evening searching for the weapon when all the time it was in his uniform pocket. And now, for days, he'll be kept on duty in the village—and where in little Hawksmere can such a thing remain hidden for any length of time, with everyone searching for it? So what does he do? He posts it off to me. Of course, he can't be sure I've guessed the truth, but people have got into a sort of habit of thinking I'll cope. And that's all, really, except for the lovely, convenient man on the roof, made up for you by me."

He sat almost paralyzed in the deep armchair, looking at her smiling face. "Constable Fisher lost his head and just picked up the gun. Is this what you really believe?"

"It's the simple truth, my dear. And simple is the word."

"He's admitted it?"

"I haven't asked him. It was so obvious."

Not to the assembled forces of the law, it hadn't been. "But to prefer to be suspected of murder—?"

"He could always tell the truth in the end."

"Why not have told it from the beginning?"

"My *dear*," said the Duchess, "you'd have had his guts for garters."

He leapt to his feet. "One thing's for certain—I'll have them now."

"Yes, well—the only thing is, if this story gets out you'll look a bit of a fool, old love, won't you?"

Chief Inspector Cockrill, the Terror of Kent—a bit of a fool, right here on his own patch. "Hey, now, Duchess, if you *don't* mind—"

"Oh, but I do mind," she said. "I don't like to think of you looking foolish." And she pleaded, "Let the boy go! He's been through a bad time, you can be pretty sure of that; he won't do it again. There's nothing against Rupert and Becca, there's been no crime! This is what actually happened and that's the end of it. But the man on the roof—there he is, all worked out so nicely for you and it all hangs together perfectly, now doesn't it? Someone out of the past caught up with the wicked Duke and you never had a hope in hell of catching up with the someone from the past. Gradually the whole affair will fade and Chief Inspector Cockrill, for a miracle, has failed to Get his Man;

but for the rest, everyone is happy." And one couldn't help thinking, said the Duchess, confiding to the fireplace, that it is less humiliating to fail to solve a very difficult case than to have failed to solve such a very simple one as a young officer losing his head.

"No one must ever know," said the Inspector; and it was capitulation.

"Good heavens, no. I'll talk to Dave Fisher and tell him what I've guessed and that to save his skin I've played a naughty game all round, and just to pipe down and never get it into his head to confess because he'd get me into trouble. I could even suggest that you rather suspect that this might have happened, but you have to investigate every possibility."

"Except the right one," said Chief Inspector Cockrill rather stiffly. He collected his droopy mackintosh from the back of the chair, clapped the hat on his head, and hastily removed it, in the presence of Her Ladyship. "And honestly—not one word of this to anyone?"

"Oh, not a word," vowed the Duchess, even now casting about in her mind for someone one could safely confide in. For really it had been rather a bit of fun. "But I *told* you."

"You told me—?"

"That in this case, I really should have been in your job," said the Duchess. She too rose. "I say, Inspector—what about one more little one? I really think we could do with it. Do join me!"

Inspector Cockrill paused a moment and then cast down his hat and coat again. "Do you know, Duchess—I think I will," he said.

The Second
Mrs. Porter

by Melba Marlett

She opened her eyes and didn't know where she was.
The word "orientation" swam into her mind. "That's
it," she thought. "I am very, very comfortable, but
I am not oriented." The shortcoming did not seem
important to her. She was wrapped in a beautiful
peace, a consciousness of well-being that was intox-
icating. The light blue robe that invested her shoulders, the delicately striped afghan that covered her
knees were airy miracles; the narrow hands that lay
in her lap were smooth and pink-tipped. She flexed
them, enjoying the smooth response of the muscles.
"What wonderful hands," she thought, surprised,
pleased. They were as strange to her as everything
else.

Drowsily she studied the handsome room. It seemed
to be a kind of bed-sitting room, furnished in muted
blues and greens, with everything precisely placed.
Her eyes traversed it slowly, lingering on the pretty
bed against the far wall, on the enchanting little bou-
doir chair, on the bowl of ruffled white flowers—were
they sweet peas?—was there a flower called that?—
on the low table, on the mirror whose reflection dou-
bled the size of the room and showed her a woman
in a light blue robe, lying on a chaise longue by a

71

wide window. She knew at once that she was looking
at herself, but she had no feelings of recognition, nor
any great interest in the matter. She turned her head,
without raising it, toward the window. Through the
thin white curtain she looked at a wide green lawn,
enlivened with petunia beds, marked with tall accents
of cypress and oak. The sunshine had a late-afternoon
slant to it. Odd to have bars on a window that gave
on such a handsome view.

When she woke again, it was evening, and she was
in bed. Across the room, in lamplight now, she saw
the chaise longue, the afghan neatly folded at its foot.
A woman dressed in white was stacking dishes on a
tray, her back to the bed.

Her mind supplied the word she should use. "Nurse,"
she said.

The woman turned around so sharply that the dishes
clattered. Then her face smoothed and she approached
the bed. "Well, Mrs. Porter," she said. "I'm glad
you're so much better this evening. Is there anything
I can get for you?"

She had a feeling that she should be very careful.
The dishes gave her an inspiration. "I'm hungry," she
said.

"I'm not surprised. You had very little supper.
What would you like?"

Of course, she had not had supper at all. She would
have remembered eating supper. Careful, careful.
"Some ice cream? Perhaps some tea?" She hadn't the
faintest notion of what either thing was. They were
only words that had come into her head.

The nurse smiled and picked up the tray. "I'll bring
them right away." The door swished shut behind her.

She wanted nothing more than to stay right where
she was and enjoy the room in solitude, but she had
a presentiment of trickery that made her slide from
the bed and circle the room, looking for—well, any-

thing that would give her an advantage in the guessing game. They were trying to make her believe she was in a hospital, though this room, with its bars at the windows, was not like her concept of hospital. (Funny how she knew some things without knowing how she knew them. It was the important things she *didn't* know that she must discover.) They wanted her to think she was sick, though there could not be another person on earth who had such a feeling of health. They said she was Mrs. Porter, but she didn't recognize the name.

As if on command she opened a dresser drawer and it was full of letters. They were addressed to Mrs. Robert W. Porter, Women's Memorial Hospital, and each one had been neatly slit open, its contents not so neatly put back. (She nearly laughed. I suppose they'll try to tell me I've read every one, she thought.) Quickly she slid several of them out of their envelopes, just far enough to see the opening lines. "Dear Ellen," they began. And "Darling Ellen" and "My poor Ellen." The dates ranged wildly through different months of different years. She put them back precisely and closed the drawer. If this was part of the scheme to convince her that she was Mrs. Porter, what a lot of trouble they had gone to, with those variegated scripts and writing papers. I suppose there is a Mrs. Porter somewhere, she thought, climbing back into bed.

The minute she saw the tray, she recognized both ice cream and tea (how could she have forgotten?) and began to consume them, daintily, to make them last longer. Their deliciousness absorbed her completely, as if they were the first food she had ever eaten.

When she looked up, a tall man in a gray suit was standing beside the nurse.

"I'm your doctor," he said. "Dr. Lindsay. Remember me?"

"Yes," she said, falsely. "How are you?"

"The point is, how are *you*? Mrs. O'Hara called me and I came right down. What about your vision? Can you see me quite clearly?"

If you only knew, she thought, how *very* clearly I can see you, with the excitement in your eyes and voice and the significant little looks you and Mrs. O'Hara are exchanging. "Certainly," she said.

"No blurring? No double vision?" He took a small silver tube from his pocket. "I'm going to shine this little light in your eyes. It'll take only a few minutes. It won't hurt you."

The light shining into one eye did not preclude the vision of the other. Through it, she studied the texture of his skin and guessed his age to be forty. Younger than herself; the woman she had seen in the mirror must be at least forty-five. "You have reddish whiskers, Dr. Lindsay," she said.

He snapped off the light and stepped back. "Haven't shaved since this morning. Do you know your name?"

"My name is Ellen Porter," she said. "I'm in Women's Memorial Hospital. I think I have been here for a long time." It was the right thing to have said. She heard the intake of his breath.

"And Mrs. O'Hara, here. Do you know her?"

Something hinged on this answer. The electricity in the room tingled along her nerves. "I'm sorry," she said. "I don't know Mrs. O'Hara."

"Of course you don't," he said, triumphantly. "She's brand new. Just came on this evening." He turned to the nurse. "Well, Mrs. O'Hara, you're a miracle worker. Now if you two girls will just settle down for tonight, I'll see Mrs. Porter the first thing in the morning. The nurses have been telling me that they find that chaise comfortable for napping, and I don't believe Mrs. Porter will be requiring much attention."

It was time to take a giant step. "I won't be requiring anything at all tonight," Ellen said. "Is there any other place where Mrs. O'Hara could sleep?" She made appealing gestures against their consternation. "It seems to be that I've been with people forever. It would be so—normal, to have my room to myself."

The word "normal" turned the tide. Yes, Mrs. O'Hara could be elsewhere, close at hand, for frequent checks. The night light in the bathroom could be left on. And yes, certainly, she could have more ice cream for breakfast. The request pleased them inordinately. They went away smiling.

Most of that night she spent in the bathroom, reading the letters from the drawer, one by one under the night light, with the bathroom door closed. Periodically she returned to her bed, to act the perfectly sleeping patient. If Mrs. O'Hara did surprise her, it would be in a normal situation, and she would at once flush the letter away. But Mrs. O'Hara came at only the right intervals.

By the time her table clock said three, she was back in bed, thinking hard about Ellen Porter. The woman was incomprehensible to her, to anyone with common sense. Mrs. Porter, it seemed, was a woman of great wealth who spent her time in litigation and in giving offense. Her husband, Robert, from whom she had been estranged—no mention of divorce, however— had been injured in an automobile accident. Her remaining family consisted of some distant cousins, who appeared to have hopes of becoming her heirs. There were references to the unsatisfactory behavior of a Mr. Arthur Crandall, who was Mrs. Porter's attorney and made of the same kind of stone as she was. Over and over the letters said, "You have so much, we have so little." Sue's education—therapy for Tony—

subsistence for an aging great-aunt. Small requests, really, to make of a woman who had millions. Most expressed a perfunctory hope for her better health, but one, signed Gregory Porter, was belligerent: "You can hide in that hospital till Hell freezes over, but we'll get you into court the minute you leave. You have never fulfilled your father's promises to us, though we signed those papers on the strength of them and in good faith. Robert says that he is willing to settle; but that he can't prevail upon you. Five years, or ten, the going gets tougher, but we can wait. How does it feel to know that so many people wish you were dead?"

Well, Mrs. Porter *was* dead, or would they have dared to give her name to a stranger? (If only I knew my real name, she thought, I suppose it's some medicine they give me.) But Mrs. Porter must also be made to seem alive for some reason, so a conspiracy was being engineered to that end, and somehow she had become involved in it, an empty-headed puppet on God-knew-whose strings. I have to play along, she thought, because I don't know what else to do; but somewhere along the way I'll escape them, if I'm very patient and very clever.

The game was to learn from them while they thought they were learning from her, and she found it easy for two reasons. First, Dr. Lindsay and the staff seemed to want her to set her own pace in "remembering," as they called it; and, second, her senses remained magnificently acute, so that in the faces and voices of the people around her she caught the smallest and most fleeting changes. Watching their souls move behind their eyes gave her the clues to what they wanted her to say.

She learned to be bold on occasion. "Why don't I have visitors?" she asked Dr. Lindsay after a month of their daily interviews. "I should think that Mr. Crandall might have come by now. Or Robert."

Plain as day was the astonishment behind the professional mask. "Do you *want* to see your husband?"

"Of course," she said, promptly. "I realize that we weren't on the best of terms, but still—has he recovered from the accident?"

The jolt of that threw him against the back of his chair, but he kept his voice calm. "Yes, he's recovered. What do you remember about—the accident?"

"Nothing, really. Only that there was one. When did it happen?"

"Five years ago."

"As long as that?" She rubbed her forehead so that she could study him between her fingers. "Was I—in it? Is that what brought me here?"

His face was all confirmation, though he averted his eyes. "Don't worry about it. You're coming along so well. No use to force these things. That's why we're not allowing you visitors until a little later."

She smiled at him. "That makes me feel better. I know I wasn't one of the world's most popular women, but I did think *somebody* ought to come by."

"They'll come as soon as we let them."

"And write as soon as you let them?"

He made a note on the chart before him. "I have no objection to letters. We screen them, you see, so if there's anything too troublesome, we can protect you from it."

"Oh. You read them first?"

"Yes. Every letter that comes in is pre-read by staff. Don't mind the inked-out sections. They're for your own good."

But there had been no inked-out sections at all in the neatly-opened letters she had read that first night and which, without notice or explanation, had disappeared from the dresser drawer by the next time she opened it. Had they decided those letters were a mistake? And how could they let her have visitors when the very first one would see that the woman who was supposed to be Ellen Porter was really no such person?

Serious as her predicament might be, she found she could not worry about it with any consistency. Life was marvelously pleasant, now that she was "fully ambulatory." The private nurses, with their professional nosiness, were removed; and, with the coming of Wally West, she was given the beatific freedom of the hospital grounds.

Wally was a tall, spidery eighteen-year-old with a shimmering mind and the composure of a saint. He was a senior at the high school in Northfield, the little town whose church steeples were visible down in the valley, and he was employed by the hospital, late afternoons, as a Walker.

"More like a Tagger-Alonger," Wally said. "You just walk where you want to, and I tag along. If you want to talk, we talk. If you don't want to, I keep quiet. The thing is, don't worry about talking. I always have plenty to think about."

At first she was content just to walk, miles a day, over the meadows and woodland that belonged to the hospital. Then Wally began to insist that she sit down every now and then.

"Dr. Lindsay says you're losing too much weight," he said. "Let's sit on this bench and watch the squirrels."

"And talk," she said, agreeably.

"Okay. But I better tell you that the doctor gets a written report from me about you, once a week. I have an agreement with him that I can tell my patients that. Don't want to go around feeling like a judas or something."

"That's all right. I have nothing to hide."

"I told 'em that already. I said to Dr. Lindsay, 'Mrs. Porter's getting so well, she doesn't need me.' But he says to keep on anyway."

"And I say so, too." The October air was marvelous, and she raised her face to it. "I don't *feel* ill, you know. I'm not even sure what's supposed to be wrong with me."

"Well, plenty *was*. When I first came to work here, more than a year ago, they told me they'd inherited you from some other hospital. You were just a bundle in a chair—you know, like a vegetable—didn't talk or see or hear. The nurses got you up and dressed you, and walked you, and put you to bed again, and you weren't *with* it. Now, well, you're a miracle. You don't even look like yourself. I'd never recognize you as the same woman."

"Did you see me close up, Wally? Did you come right up and look into my face? Surely I'd remember that."

"No, I just saw you from a distance, being trundled around. You looked like this." He slid down limply on the bench, pushed his hair over his eyes, let his head and jaw go slack. "Strictly nobody home. The sickest person in the whole hospital." He slid upright again. "I wrote a composition about you for my English class. Didn't use your name, of course, that wouldn't have been right. I called it 'The Woman Who Went Away.' Got an A on it, too."

"I'd like to read it. Could I?"

"If Dr. Lindsay says so. I'll ask him."

"Don't." The word was too impulsive and she hastened to lighten it. "It's good policy to let sleeping doctors lie."

"I couldn't let you see it without his permission, Mrs. Porter. Something in it might set you back, it takes a psychiatrist to know."

She reached over and patted his hand. "That's all right, Wally. Don't worry about it."

By September, she knew every path and twig on the hospital's back acreage. Her favorite spot was a little curving abandoned garden, where re-seeded pansies and poppies struggled with a heavy invasion of weeds. "Wonder why they let this go?" she said to Wally. "It must have been very pretty once, and you can see half the country from up here."

"What I like about it is that it has *benches*. What do you say we sit for a few minutes?"

"You sit, and I'll—I'll *weed*."

It was a happy inspiration. Besides the kneeling and pulling that stretched her muscles and warmed her blood, there was the pleasure of seeing a design unfold. Here there had been a big clump of bleeding-heart, and here had been—was it foxglove? And over everything were the weeds, vigorous and furiously stubborn.

Day after day she struggled with them, panting with determination. Some had surface roots and came away easily, but, if she didn't get every scrap of them, they regrew, almost overnight. Others had roots that went down a foot, and all of them reappeared at a moment's notice.

"I'm getting to be an expert on weeds," she said to Wally. "They're fascinating in a curious kind of way. Sometimes I dream about them at night. Sort of a nightmare, where I keep pulling and pulling, and the weeds just stay as thick as ever! I wish I had a book about them. Maybe there's one in the hospital library."

"Well, you're making an impression here," said Wally, grinning. "Only three weeks' work and you've cleared a space at least two feet square. Did you always like to garden?"

"Yes," she said, firmly, wondering if it were true.

"Then maybe you have some gardening books at

home, and Dr. Lindsay could have them brought for you."

"Of course," she said, smoothly. "I wonder why I didn't think of that myself. You know, next Monday I'm going to start right in the middle there, where it's thickest. Maybe, just maybe, it was planted in a clock pattern, and the middle ought to tell me."

The very next day, at their morning session, she broached the subject to Dr. Lindsay. "Are there any books about weeds? I'd like some."

"Wally says you're really going after them. I've been asking around, and nobody seems to know anything about your weeded-over garden. Must have been part of the original planting, forty years ago. It might show up on an old landscaping map, if I could find one." He had noticed her hands, and he was shocked. "My God, Mrs. Porter, the least you can do is wear gloves when you go digging! I can't have people thinking you take care of our grounds single-handed! And, yes, I'll see that you get some gardening books."

"I need some different clothes, too," she said. "Nothing in my closet really fits me anymore. I'm a different shape than I used to be. My waistline's the same, but I'm rounder above and below it."

"We'll get one of the nurses to take you down to the village to shop—and maybe to help you research weeds in the Carnegie library there. How will that suit you?" He leaned across and handed her a typewritten page. "This is from Mr. Crandall, came yesterday. It's not much more than a request to come and see you." His eyes were so intent upon her that she had to look away to keep from laughing. "I'm going to have to let him come, I suppose. He's a member of the trust that's been handling your affairs while you've been with us."

"I know that he's my lawyer," she said, casually. "I didn't know about the trust." She folded the letter and put it back on his desk. "Is Robert a member of the trust, too?"

"I don't think so. Perhaps they ask his advice, I wouldn't know. Considering that the two of you weren't on good enough terms at the time of the accident to be living together, the court decided to— "

"If we weren't living together, how did we come to be in that car together?"

"That's what the police wanted to know. There was quite an investigation, particularly when it looked as if you weren't going to live. But then you began to recover—"

She laughed. "A vegetable in a chair! How encouraged they all must have been!"

"Believe me, Mrs. Porter, it took medical miracles to get you even as far as the vegetable stage." He leaned back in his chair and smiled at her. "Don't bother to pretend that you remember anything from that earlier period. There was neurological damage that had to be repaired. You could not possibly recall anything from that first six months after the accident."

She tried to look prettily indignant. "Pretend? Why should I pretend?"

"I'm not sure. I have the feeling, off and on, that you're playing games with me. Please don't do it."

And I have the feeling that you're playing games with *me,* she thought swiftly, and that the name of today's little game is Get Her to Confide in You. "Dear Dr. Lindsay," she said, appealingly, "it's only that I like to please you. I'm not treacherous, only feminine. Sometimes I think I know what you want me to say, so I *say* it!"

"Whether it's true or not?"

"Well, after I say it, it always *seems* true."

He shook his head. "We'll never get you put back together that way."

"I'm not sure I want to be put back together," she

said, daringly. "I wasn't as nice a person then as I am now."

That surprised him, but he rallied. " 'Healthy' and 'nice' aren't always the same thing, Mrs. Porter, and its 'healthy' we're trying for. The more honest you try to be, the more quickly I can let you leave here."

The leap of hope in her heart surprised her by its strength. "Should I want to leave here?"

"Yes."

"And I'm not healthy enough now?"

"No. There's something—well, I'm not satisfied with your adjustment. You've been through a dreadful ordeal—pain, surgery, a long invalidism, partial re-building of your face, loss of memory—and none of it seems to have touched you at all. This indicates a lack of realization that is, well, worrisome."

For the first time she was convinced that he was a completely honest man, and she nearly told him the whole story. How Ellen Porter must be dead or in hiding, and that she (infuriatingly nameless) had somehow been substituted, and that no one had supposed she would recover enough (from whatever had been done to her) to know the difference, but that somehow she had. And, just as swiftly, she saw that it would be wrong to involve this young doctor by alerting him. As long as they both appeared innocent and unaware, they would be safe, she was sure of it.

She ventured one cautious question. "This is not the first hospital I've been in, is it, and you're not the original doctor to take my case?"

"No. There were three—maybe four, I can look it up—other hospitals, and, as for doctors—" he threw up his hands "—I must be the thousandth. Some day I'll show you your medical file. It's a foot thick. By the time you were turned over to us, everybody thought that you were merely custodial, you see. Then you surprised us by getting better, and I began to cherish the hope of a complete cure. Unfortunately, in a case like yours, it's the patient who has to do most of the work, and all you've demonstrated is a disposition to avoid the effort."

"I won't pretend anymore," she said, smiling at him with genuine affection, but, of course, it was a promise she could not possibly keep.

That interview marked the end of her comfortable isolation. She had known there were other patients in the hospital, hundreds of them she was told, but she had seen nothing of them except at a distance. Her quarters were in a small wing of the building that was restricted, apparently, to her own use. They included her large room and bath, a small kitchen where trays were left for distribution elsewhere on the floor, the offices of Dr. Lindsay and his secretary, and an elegant meeting room labeled Hospital Board that, as far as she had observed, never had a meeting in it. It was a marvel that so busy an institution should have so quiet a corner. Every afternoon and evening, from her window she saw the cars, creeping up the long and distant drive from the main road (which she had never seen) to fill the two large parking lots; and, at ten o'clock at night, there might still be the car lights of a departing late visitor. Yet all day long, up to now, she had spoken to no one but Dr. Lindsay, a floor nurse or two, and Wally. Now she was going to be put through a period of social testing, and she must be doubly on guard.

The shopping trip to the village was easy. The stores were good, her accounts limited only by the number of times she wished to sign her name—which she was careful to do in a schoolbookish hand that had no distinguishing marks, she hadn't the slightest notion of what Ellen Porter's signature should be like—and her mentor, a young nurse's aide named Miss Raymond, pleasant and only mildly watchful. But oh, the exhilaration of being outside again, of becoming, for a few hours, one of the everyday inhabitants of the everyday world! From where they were walking on Main Street, she could see the depot set on the edge of the town and the tracks fanning out from it, and, for a wild minute, she estimated the number of blocks she would have to run to reach it and her possible rate of speed, as matched against Miss Raymond's. She reproved herself immediately for such silliness. If she escaped that way, they would search the world over for her until they found her and brought her back to her luxurious jail. The only good way to leave was with their full connivance and approval, which she must earn by showing them *(who?)* that she was perfectly willing to play the role they had assigned her.

Even this knowledge could not keep her from savoring the day—October's blue and gold, the leaf smoke, the calling of children to each other in school play yards, the good lunch at the little restaurant on the square where the marble Civil War soldier stood holding his rifle, the lovely things they showed her in the stores. She bought presents for the nurses and huge boxes of candy for the clerical help; serviceable skirts and sweaters, but in pretty colors, for herself; a bottle of perfume for Miss Raymond; a bright jacket for Wally; a handsome leather box for Dr. Lindsay's desk; and, on impulse, a round glass paperweight that responded to the light by throwing back a hundred different shades of blue.

Miss Raymond said the paperweight was the prettiest thing she had ever seen. "A person could look at it forever, Mrs. Porter. Is it for your little desk by the window?"

"No, it's not for myself at all. It's for Robert." It came out so easily that it must have been in her mind from the beginning, yet she would take an oath that she had never contemplated giving Robert a gift, nor even considered the prospect of meeting him. "He's—he's my husband."

"Yes, I know, and he ought to be awfully pleased. Well, shall we go find your books?"

Across the street, granite steps led up to a door marked Carnegie Public Library, where, undoubtedly, there were reference books that would tell her all about the very rich Ellen Porter. "Miss Raymond, if you have some shopping of your own to do, I promise to stay in the reading room till you come back. Why don't you—"

"No, indeed, Mrs. Porter. I'm not going to leave you for a moment."

"I only want to see some gardening books. I want to read about weeds."

"Gardening books are all right," said Miss Raymond, "if you show me the titles of what you read, and if I'm sitting right beside you." She had the grace to look apologetic. "Your reading is still controlled, you see. Dr. Lindsay's orders."

"Oh, dear, just when I felt so free! Come along, then, and tell the librarian what I can look at."

The librarian said they had no books on weeds, only some government pamphlets, but any book on gardens was bound to mention weeds, it seemed to her, and Miss Raymond concurred. So gardening books were heaped on the table in front of Mrs. Porter, and she turned the pages resignedly, while her nurse became immediately absorbed in fashion magazines.

But luck was with her. The third book she opened was entitled *Famous Gardens of the World,* and Chapter Ten was headed "Mrs. Robert Porter's Garden at Quercorum in Connecticut"! It was illustrated by a full-page picture, in color, of Mrs. Porter, standing near her prize delphinium, with a great white stone house stretching away behind her. Her heart began to beat suffocatingly, but she controlled her breath and composed her face. Both the pictured woman and the house were completely strange to her.

Greedily she assimilated what information she could. Ellen Porter had married her second cousin, Robert Porter, more than twenty years ago. The marriage was childless but the void had been filled with the diversions of the wealthy—travel, the maintenance of six residences (only the one in Connecticut was identified), yachting, the breeding of race horses, the exchanges of visits with friends. Mrs. Porter looked after her own business affairs. "It was my branch of the family that made the money," she was quoted as saying, "and I feel it my responsibility to look after it. Robert is really not a businessman so it all works out for the best."

She studied the picture for a long time. The real Ellen Porter was at least fifteen years older than herself, with a high-bridged nose, deep frown lines, a tight straight-lipped mouth. The conspirators had been careful about the only two characteristics that plastic surgery could not change; height and eye color. "So I'm tall, and my eyes are blue," she mused, "but where did they find me? When was the substitution made? Whatever my real identity, I must have had friends, relatives. But I suppose they wouldn't recognize me now, anyway." She smoothed her hair, feeling the tiny scars hidden there. "So there can be no danger to anyone, as long as my memory doesn't return, completely—and with all that surgery, I bet they've made sure that it won't."

Then she turned the page and saw the picture labeled "Robert Porter." How long she stared at it, she had no idea. When she raised her eyes, Miss Raymond was still reading her magazines, the librarian was helping some teenagers with the card catalogue, all was as it had been. Except that now she was in love with

Robert Porter, who must be one of the handsomest and most appealing men in existence.

Alive with plans that would bring Robert to her, she was politic with Dr. Lindsay the next morning and spoke casually about Mr. Crandall's eventual visit. "What if I want to make changes in my business affairs, Dr. Lindsay. Am I allowed to? I mean, is my signature legal?"

"It will be, the minute I vouch for it, Mrs. Porter. I'm not ready to do that, yet. Mr. Crandall has your power-of-attorney, however, and I daresay he'll be inclined to act on your suggestions."

She smiled at him. "You don't consider me sane?"

" 'Sane' is a word I rarely use. I just think you're not—ready."

And that afternoon, as if to corroborate him, came the relapse, shockingly, suddenly, out of the blue. One minute she was weeding in the very middle of the Hidden Garden, calling occasional remarks to Wally on his bench; the next, she was staring down at something smooth and hard that her fingers were encountering, under the mat of weeds. It was a metal plate, brass it seemed, and as she tore the weeds away, she saw the writing on it. "To the memory of—" it began. She scraped and pulled, deliberately averting her eyes until she could see it all. "To the memory of Ellen Porter, 1900–1962, this garden, of her own planning, is gratefully dedicated." Streaked with dirt, panting from exertion, she stared at it, openmouthed. So Ellen Porter was dead, and this is where they had buried her.

A black cloud of terror swept down on her, suffocating, paralyzing. She fought it off, got to her feet, ran—somewhere, anywhere. She heard Wally's voice calling to her, but she could not stop. She collapsed, finally, against the wall of the hospital, near the side door that they always used, and felt Wally's grasp on her arms.

"Mrs. Porter, what's happened? Are you all right? Mrs. Porter?"

She saw a nurse and an orderly racing up behind him. "Yes," she managed to gasp, "I'm—all right. Saw—a snake. Always been—scared to death—of snakes."

"Good grief! I think you just set a new world's record for the half-mile." He turned to the newcomers. "She saw a snake."

But the staff was suspicious, alert. They put her to bed for the rest of the day, had the private nurses back again for forty-eight hours, chatted amiably to her—and watched. Dr. Lindsay paid her a special visit. "Seems funny to see you in bed again," he said. "Just a precaution against your having overdone it."

"It was a silly way to act. I feel so apologetic."

"We went up to look for your snake, but we didn't find one." He took her wrist between his fingers. "That seems to be a pretty little garden you've unearthed. We're going to ask the hospital board to let us restore it. It shouldn't have been let go." He put her hand down on the coverlet and patted it. "Must have been a shock to you, coming across your own name like that. It was your Aunt Ellen, you know, who gave us this hospital."

"I'd—forgotten."

"No ingratitude involved on our part, just a shortage of gardeners during the war. It's only a memorial kind of thing. Your aunt is buried in Rome, I believe."

She could not keep her voice from sounding defensive. "It *did* look like a grave, you know."

"And who did you think was buried there?" he asked gently.

Her thoughts ran around like mice in a cage, while

the silence grew and grew. "I—I don't believe I thought at all," she said, finally. "It was—how does Wally say it?—a gut reaction."

"Is that your best analysis? I can't quite believe that, Mrs. Porter."

"Then work on it till you can!" she said, crossly. "Some things aren't easy!" In his shout of surprised laughter her tension eased. "And you can just take that night nurse out of my room tonight, too. I can't sleep with another person in the room—unless it's Robert." The last three words amazed her—she had not meant to say them—but she realized that they were absolutely right. "*When* are you going to let Robert come?" she asked, and burst into tears.

"Mr. Crandall can come week after next," he said, "and Robert a week or so after that." He handed her a handkerchief. "That's rushing things, but if you refuse to be patient and rational—"

"I have been *extremely* patient, Dr. Lindsay."

"And rational?"

She smiled at him, while she wiped her eyes. "Women aren't supposed to be rational. Ask anybody."

He went away laughing, and the dangerous moment was past. Heavens, he was such a young man, hard to mislead, but not difficult to charm!

That night she received the first of the shocking notes.

She had fallen asleep reading, her bed light on. When she awoke, the door to her room was swinging slightly, and she called, "Come back. I'm awake." But no one came, and she guessed that the draft had been caused by the opening of an outside door in some distant corridor. It had happened before, on windy evenings.

Then she turned to put her book on the bedside table, and there lay the note. It was on plain white paper—torn from her own tablet, she thought later—folded once, handwritten in large, jagged, black letters.

Insist on Robert's coming to see you. Be sure to mention the Gregory Porter lawsuit to Arthur Crandall, beforehand. Robert always wanted that settled.   E.

She lay motionless for a long time before she could summon the nerve to re-read it. Not once did she doubt that it was from the real Ellen Porter; the positiveness of the words and the insolence of the ugly handwriting were absolutely convincing. She was glad to put a match to it, to see it fall into black flakes in the ashtray.

It cost her a real effort to turn off the light, though leaving it on would, she knew, eventually bring nurses to ask questions. For hours she lay awake, ears strained for any hint of approach, but there were only the usual hospital night sounds, hushed, as always in this isolated room. In the first dim light of morning, she reached for her pen and wrote a note of her own.

Dear Mrs. Porter:
   I want to cooperate, but I don't understand my situation. Now that you are well enough to get around, I don't see why I am needed any more at all. Is there any place where we could meet and talk? I am very willing to be helpful—it's the only way I know to get out of here—but I could do much better if I knew what was expected of me.

She could not decide on a signature, so she simply folded the note and left it where the other had been.

Ten minutes later, she sat up suddenly, tore the note into tiny shreds, and burned it, too, though her hands were shaking so badly she had trouble holding the match. Oh, that was all she needed, to have someone come across a communication like that one! "Crazy," they'd say. "A crazy woman writing formal letters to herself!" Nor could she go roaming over the hospital, snooping and trying doors.

She must preserve an effect of normality; she dared do nothing else. Any future communication had to depend on the real Mrs. Porter, who, startlingly enough, did not seem unfriendly. And was, at least, alive.

Arthur Crandall turned out to be a grayhaired, stocky, bustling man, with the alert, sidewise glance of a high class horse that has been mistreated. "You're looking well, Mrs. Porter," he said. "Glad to see you so blooming."

"Be honest," she said. "Would you have known me if you'd passed me on the street?"

"Well, maybe not. But the change is all to the good. All to the good. There are many resemblances, naturally. I think I'd know your hands anywhere." He sat down opposite her. "Now, what can I do for you, after all this long while? What's on your mind?"

"Several things. The first is that, since I'm healthy once more, I'd like to leave the hospital."

"That depends entirely on Dr. Lindsay. He's the one who has to discharge you. Naturally we'd be happy to see him do it. There are matters on which we'd welcome your decision."

"I hope you'll say so to him. He won't discuss my leaving with me at all."

"That's because he still has some reservations about you. He didn't tell me what they were. Just said that he had 'em. Medical men are pretty conservative, you know. Have to give them a little time." He slapped his hand down on the arm of his chair. "But if you could see yourself, sitting there, smiling, with pink in your face—you look better this minute than you ever did in your whole life! And I've known you for forty years!"

She smiled her best smile at him. "Thank you, Arthur." A small tremor in his face told her that the first-name basis was new. "I'm very fond of Dr. Lindsay, but you're going to have to find some little ways to pressure him into letting me go. Not bad little ways. Nice little ways. I remember you as a subtle man, Arthur."

He flushed with pleasure. "Oh, I think we can hurry him up a little. Surely by early spring we'll have brought him around. Will that suit you?"

"Yes. You understand that there are things I will never remember because of the surgery. Dr. Lindsay says there's no help for that."

"I understand. Everyone on the board understands."

"Good. Now the next item is Robert. Will he come to visit me? I imagine that he isn't very eager to see me, but I want very much to see him."

"So I was told. Yes, I believe that he'll come. For one thing he's still legally your husband. For another, he isn't a man to hold grudges." He cleared his throat. "As your lawyer I'd be interested in knowing *why* you want to see him."

She spoke simply and directly. "I want to be reconciled to him, if he'll have me."

"My God!" he said. "Mrs. Porter, are you sure? After all those years of our dragging him into court on one contrived pretext or another? I don't think I'll be able to look him in the face, much less talk to him!"

"I'll take all the blame—for everything," she said earnestly, "and you're going to have to help me convince him that I've changed. For instance, settle the Gregory Porter business right away. Give Gregory what he wants, give him *more* than he wants. It's long overdue."

Mr. Crandall's jaw went slack. "But that would mean—mind you, I've always been in favor of settling with Gregory, all we could do was delay him, he was always going to win in the long run—but to settle now, and willingly, knocks the props out of our defense against the suits of about eight other relatives of yours who think they're entitled to—"

"Settle with them, too. I want them off my mind."

"*All* of them?"

"All of them. As the old proverb has it, 'There are no pockets in shrouds.' "

"Well, of course, that's an eminently sensible viewpoint, Mrs. Porter, and, as you'll see when we go over the figures, your finances have never been in better shape. You can afford it."

She smiled. "What I don't want to afford is the time to go over the figures. I'm going to be completely honest with you, Arthur. If Robert will have me back, I intend to give my power-of-attorney to him and turn over the whole boring business to the two of you."

"But—but what will *you* be doing?"

"Enjoying life," she said.

He made gasping sounds for ten minutes, but, in the long run, she thought he was not displeased. She made bold to kiss his cheek before he left. "Dear Arthur, you've put up with so much. Just a few months more and I hope you'll be dealing with a stable Robert instead of an eccentric Ellen."

He was nonplussed, but he was a man who said what he had on his mind. "If you're not sane right this minute, Mrs. Porter, then there's no hope for any of us."

So she had made the right impression on the very important Mr. Crandall, and the results began to appear immediately. The hospital people, always attentive and kind, snapped into something like military precision, and Dr. Lindsay, though friendly as usual, began to look harried. "I've told your Mr. Crandall that he can begin to familiarize you with your business affairs, though I think he's being a bit premature. Don't let him tire you out."

"I won't. Though I don't believe I'll ever be very interested in business things again. I told him I wanted Robert to take care of all that for me."

"I think I should tell you that Robert is not being responsive to the idea of a reconciliation," he said, frowning. "Like Mr. Crandall, I think that he'll come 'round eventually, but I don't want you to build on it and then be disappointed."

She quoted him to himself. " 'I will face reality as honestly and cheerfully as possible.' "

"Good. Plus a touch of rule five."

" 'I will assume that the unhappy are always wrong.' Therefore, I will try to be happy."

"I thought you *were*, you know. Now it seems that you can't wait to get away from us."

"Please, *please* don't think that, Dr. Lindsay. It's not that I'm running *away* from something, it's that I'm running *toward* something else."

His face cleared. "Well, that helps. Now, let's get down to work. Nurse Hanson tells me she's found you sleeping with your lights on three times this week. How do you account for that? Does darkness worry you all of a sudden?"

Every Tuesday afternoon, like clockwork, Mr. Crandall visited her, with eyes that saw everything. "New dress, Mrs. Porter? Beautiful shade of blue. Your sapphires might go well with that." And the next day a messenger from the bank appeared in an armored car with case after case of extravagant blue baubles.

Embarrassed at the display, she chose sparingly and sent the rest back. "We have no security precautions here, Arthur, and I didn't like to risk—but aren't these earrings sublime? Are they really real?"

"Yes. We have a good many facsimiles, but those

are the real thing. I have a theory that it does jewels good to have a lovely woman wear them."

"Thank you. It would be nice to be younger."

"You were not nearly as handsome then as you are now."

"Will Robert think so?"

His mouth tightened. "It has been some time since Robert has favored me with his opinions, Mrs. Porter."

Most of the time, however, it was like having one's own personal genie. One shiver from Ellen-in-a-woolcoat, and Mr. Crandall offered her a warmer one. "Your sable is probably still hanging in the closet at Quercorum. I can get it to you by Friday."

"Tell me," she said, pouring his tea, "are my delphinium still in the garden there? They were so lovely, remember?"

"I—well, I'll inquire. There's no gardener these days, I believe. Only a skeleton staff at any of the houses."

The sable coat arrived promptly. She drew its dark splendor from the pink-enamelled box and saw that there was a note. "Delphinium all present and accounted for," wrote Mr. Crandall. "My office is looking around for some house help, including a gardener. I'm assuming that you plan to spend part of next summer at Quercorum? I always thought you liked it the best of your residences."

At night, her bedlights carefully extinguished, her ears alert for a possible intruder, she lay imagining the scene in the magazine—the great house, the tall blue flowers, the man with the sensitive mouth in the background—with a different woman standing where the embittered Mrs. Porter had stood, a woman who, smiling and serene, reached out a hand to her husband to draw him into the very center of the picture.

Just before Christmas, Robert came to see her. The preparations had been long-drawn-out and ticklish, so she was ready for him, from the tension in her stomach to the bowl of holly on her table to the sapphire earrings that gave her courage. From noon on the appointed day, she sat by her window, watching a snowy stretch of walk that he was almost sure to traverse; and so she saw him before he saw her—a tall, thin man, limping, leaning heavily on a cane, being careful of the slippery walk. The face was still handsome, but so drawn that she was moved nearly to tears.

Because she had found honesty to be the best policy whenever she could afford it, the first thing she said to him was, "I didn't know you limped. Nobody told me."

"It's from the accident. Other people are used to it by now, so they wouldn't think to mention it to you. For a while I was not sure I would walk again."

"Both of us have changed," she said. "Oh, Robert, it was good of you to come." She did not offer to shake hands. Something in his manner made her think it inadvisable.

That first visit was brief, awkward, and the subsequent ones were hardly better. He avoided her eyes, retreated from any proximity, spoke in a constrained way. Sometimes they drove down to the village for lunch—he had to sign out for her permission to go, which seemed to amuse him a little—but he never suggested that he sign her out for a weekend, which he had the legal right to do and which Dr. Lindsay might well have permitted.

None of her conversational gambits worked out well. "Are you staying at Quercorum?" she asked.

"No. I'm staying in a house I bought a few years ago, up near Concord. Have a young married couple to do the chores for me."

"But Quercorum is quite close. Don't you like it there?"

"Under the circumstances, no."

The forbidding tone in his voice always scared her off, and she could think of nothing safe to say, and their visits would end in painful silence.

"Mr. Crandall says the Gregory Porter thing is settled," she told him one afternoon.

"I know. Greg came to thank me, and I told him I had nothing whatever to do with it."

"You did, though. Indirectly."

"I'm glad it wasn't taken to court. We wouldn't have had a good press."

"If things work out as I hope, and if you take full charge of my affairs for me—"

"That would be quite impossible," he said, sharply. "Crandall said something about that, and I refused, unequivocally."

The only hopeful sign was that he kept coming—once a week, twice, three times. "I think you're getting a *little* used to me," she said. "Do I still seem like a stranger to you?"

"You're always charming these days. Which makes you quite a stranger indeed."

"I know I behaved unbearably to you but, thank God, I don't remember a lot of it. Since you haven't the advantage of a bad memory, I can only hope you'll forgive me, eventually."

"I didn't mean to be caustic. I was stating a fact."

"Then I'll state a fact, too. I regret most of the past. Except our marriage. I'll never regret that."

She expected that to please him, but he fell silent and left early again that day.

By the middle of February she was prickly with nerves and hard put to preserve the good-natured outgoing exterior the hospital seemed so fond of. Then, out of a magazine she picked up from her bedside table fluttered the second of the strange notes. The jagged black handwriting stared up at her from the floor until she bent, stiff with distaste, to pick it up.

> Robert's no better than a murderer. It wasn't his fault he had no luck with it. Tell him so.   E.

Carefully she burnt the note in an ashtray. Then she walked out to ask the nurses on the floor whether they had seen anyone entering or leaving her room.

"No, Mrs. Porter. No one's gone by here, and they'd have to, to get to you."

"I think it would be a woman," she said, incautiously. "One of the other patients, maybe?"

"It certainly wouldn't be a patient. This isn't a free floor. Is something missing from your room?"

She saw that their eyes were intent, speculative. "Oh, no, no. Nothing like that. It's only—well, I found a magazine that I didn't recognize, and I thought someone might have left it for me— "

She retreated in a flurry of excuses, but not soon enough. She had earned herself a black mark for the day, and Dr. Lindsay brought the matter up the next morning.

"Are you well enough acquainted with one of our women patients for her to *want* to visit you, Mrs. Porter?"

"Well, no. I speak to some of them in passing, but I don't know their names or anything. I just thought maybe—"

"What magazine was it?"

"Oh. Well, one of those picture magazines, I think."

"You seemed quite certain yesterday. Are you less certain now?"

She felt ill—dizzy, nauseated, a ringing in her ears. She had to summon her forces to be bold. "I am not paranoic, Dr. Lindsay. I made an honest mistake, asked an idle question. To tell you the truth, I'm so upset over Robert's behavior that I don't know which way to turn. It makes me absentminded and foolish, and I'm sorry."

That gave him something new to think about. "What about Robert? He seems quite devoted, to me. He'd come every single day, if we'd let him."

She clasped her hands. "Really? Is that really true?" The joy of it warmed her. The nausea receded. "Oh, Dr. Lindsay, you've made my day!"

"If he's being cautious, you can't blame him. It seems not to have worked out well, before."

"But it will this time," she said, confidently. "Because I know better now, don't you see?"

"*What* do you know? Let's talk about that."

But she could not talk about it satisfactorily without telling him that she was not really Ellen Porter, so she stumbled over his questions and was finally dismissed, feeling like a student who had abjectly flunked an important test.

She went straight to her telephone and asked Robert to come at once. "I'll meet you outside by the fountain near the parking lot," she said. "We can have some privacy there. I have some important questions I *must* ask you. Please prepare yourself to be honest, no matter what. Absolutely honest."

The air was lively with snowflakes, and the day was cold. She waited by the fountain, huddled in her sable, squinting against the wind. A bad setting for a very serious conversation, but it was one that simply must not be overheard—by the real Ellen Porter or anyone else. (For surely one of the things the mysterious notes revealed was that the writer had some method of surveillance.) Robert arrived on the dot, his eyes curious and worried, and she didn't bother to greet him.

"I've run out of time," she said, "so I must ask

these things openly. First, do you think you could ever be—well—fond of me?"

He answered without hesitation. "I'm fond of you now, and I don't in the least want to be. At first I felt nothing because you seemed like a stranger to me, but then I saw that you were being the way you were when you were sixteen, before all the bad temper and money-grubbing set in. I wouldn't have thought you could ever be that way again, but you are."

"Good. Second question. If I had died in that accident, would you have been tried for my death?"

"Yes. I nearly was, anyway. The police tried hard to make a case—at least of manslaughter—but I was laid up for so long, and there were no immediate witnesses, and you *didn't* die—"

"Did you want me to?" she asked, gently. "Was it attempted murder?"

For the first time he looked directly at her, in a long silence. "Yes," he said, steadily. "I meant to kill us both. I hoped you wouldn't remember that, but I'm glad you have. I can't tell you how it's weighed on me all these years."

"I thought we should get that question out of the way. Does anyone else know?"

"I tried to tell Arthur Crandall, but he said he didn't want to listen to it. He said that when two people were angry and fighting each other for the steering wheel, there was no telling who was more at fault. But I know that I aimed us straight at that abutment, and that, if you hadn't managed to turn us the least bit—"

She put her hand over his lips. "Forget about it. It doesn't matter anymore."

"Now you can understand why I felt so guilty, especially when you were being friendly and dear—"

She kissed his stricken face. "We mustn't waste a minute on regret. That's one lesson I've been taught in this hospital. What we should be doing is making plans for the next twenty years or so. Shall we begin by going to Quercorum for Easter?"

He put an arm around her waist, fell into step beside her, his eyes alight. "Better yet, why don't we go down there this weekend? I could ask my young married couple to come along to do the cooking. Remember how beautiful those big oaks were in the winter? I suppose there are still seventy-nine of them. I counted them once, if you recall."

She blinked away tears of happiness. "I'd love to go there. I'd forgotten about the oak trees—"

"But that's where the place gets its name. 'Quercus' means 'oak,' in Latin. Maybe the horses are still there, too. Not that I'll ever be able to ride again—"

In their absorption, they nearly collided with Dr. Lindsay, on his way to the parking lot. "Well," said the doctor dryly. "It looks like an early spring."

They both talked to him at once, about the necessary pass for the weekend at Quercorum, about how wonderful it was that Ellen was so well, about the miracle of being given a second chance at happiness. Dr. Lindsay agreed with them on everything. There was reluctance in his eyes, but he knew when he was outnumbered.

As she and Robert continued their stroll, she was careful, however, to keep a line of trees between the hospital windows and themselves. The real Ellen Porter, seeing her husband thus engrossed, might not be completely magnanimous.

On the spring morning when Mrs. Porter left the hospital for good, holding her husband's arm, talking to the circle of doctors and nurses that attended her, Wally thought she looked great. Very happy. Animated. Beautiful, almost, though that was a funny word to use about a woman who was fiftyish. He traded smiles with her—he had said his own farewells the day before—and then stood back and just watched, out of the way of the fuss the hospital apparently felt it had to make over a member of the Founding Family.

Thus he saw a strange little occurrence that no one else appeared to see. He saw Mrs. Porter, still laughing and talking and without once lowering her eyes from the faces around her, reach into her purse, bring out a small notebook, write something on one of the pages, tear the page from the notebook, fold it carefully, and put pen and notebook away, retaining the folded note in her gloved hand. There was nothing odd about any of that, except her cleverness at writing without looking; but five minutes later, just before she entered her car, she looked down at the folded paper, recoiled as if she'd seen a tarantula, and threw the little piece of paper, still folded, into the gutter.

So I'm imaginative, he thought, I make things up, why would anybody be repelled by something he had just written? And when, after the car had driven off and the godspeed group dispersed, he picked up the folded paper and read it, he was still puzzled. In an angular, black handwriting, the note said: "I am content to remain here, having set you free. You are rid of me for good. Be happy. I never was. E." A strange little note, but not a repulsive one. And, of course, Mrs. Porter hadn't even read it—though, since she had written it, she must know what it said.

Wally, old boy, he told himself, pull yourself together. This note could not possibly have been written by Mrs. Porter, it's a crazy little note and must have been handed to her by another patient; the hand is quicker than the eye, there must have been *two* pieces of paper, and you're mistaken about the whole business.

For a moment he thought of showing the note to Dr. Lindsay, as a psychological curiosity, but it was getting near dinnertime and he was hungry. He pitched the paper into a trash can and walked down the hill toward home, whistling. The days when the sick recovered were the best of days.

The Paintbox Houses
by Ruth Rendell

Elderly ladies as detectives are not unknown in fiction. Avice Julian could think of two or three, the creations of celebrated authors, and no doubt there were more. It would seem that the quiet routine of an old woman's life, her penchant for gossip and for knitting, and her curiosity born of boredom provide a suitable climate for the consideration of motive and the assessment of clues. In fiction, that is. Would it, Mrs. Julian had sometimes wondered, also be true in reality?

She took a personal interest. She was 84 years old, thin, sharp-witted, arthritic, cantankerous, and intolerant. Most of her time she spent sitting in an upright chair in the bay window of her drawing room in her very large house, observing what her neighbors were up to. From the elderly ladies of mystery fiction, though, she differed in one important respect: they were usually spinsters, she was a widow. In fact, she had been twice married and twice widowed.

Could that, she asked herself, after reading a particularly apposite detective novel, be of significance? Could it affect the deductive powers, could it be her spinsterhood that made Miss Marple, say, a detective of genius? Perhaps. Anthropologists say (Mrs. Julian was an erudite person) that in ancient societies maidenhood was revered as having awesome and unique powers. It might be that this was true and that prolonged virginity, though in many respects disagreeable, only serves to enhance those powers.

Possibly, one day, she would have an opportunity to test the Aged Female Sleuth theory. She saw enough from her window, sitting there knitting herself a twinset in dark-blue two-ply. None of that double-knit for her. Mostly she eyed the row of houses opposite, on the other side of broad, tree-lined Abelard Avenue.

There were six of them, all joined together, all exactly the same. They all had three stories, plate-glass windows, a bit of concrete to put the car on, a flower-bed, an outside receptacle to put parcels in, and an outside receptacle to put the rubbish bag in. Mrs. Julian thought that unhygienic. She had an old-fashioned dustbin, though she had to keep a black plastic bag inside it if she wanted Northway Borough Council to collect her rubbish.

The houses had been built on the site of an old mansion. There had been several such in Abelard Avenue as well as big houses such as Mrs. Julian's which were not quite mansions. Most of these had been pulled down and those which remained converted into flats. They would do that to hers when she was gone, thought Mrs. Julian, those nephews and nieces and great-nephews and great-nieces of hers would do that. She had watched the houses opposite being built. About ten years ago now it was. She called them the paintbox houses because there was something about them that reminded her of a child's drawing and because each had its front door a different color—yellow, red, blue, lime, orange, and chocolate.

"It's called Paragon Place," said Mrs. Upton, her cleaning woman and general help, when the building was completed.

"What a ridiculous name! Paintbox Place would be far more suitable."

Mrs. Upton ignored this as she ignored all of Avice Julian's remarks which she regarded as "showing off," affected, or just plain senile. "They do say," she said, "that the next thing'll be they'll start building on this bit of waste ground next door."

"Waste ground?" said Mrs. Julian distantly. "Can you possibly mean the wood?"

"Waste ground" had certainly been a misnomer, though "wood" was an exaggeration. It was a couple of rustic acres, more or less covered with trees of which part of one side bordered Mrs. Julian's garden, part the Great North Road, and which had its narrow frontage on Abelard Avenue. People used the path through it as a short cut to and from the station. At Mrs. Upton's unwelcome forebodings, Avice Julian had got up and gone to the right-hand side of the bay window which overlooked the "wood" and thought how disagreeable it would be to have another Paintbox Place on her back doorstep. In these days when society seemed to have gone mad, when the cost of living was frightening, when there were endless strikes and she was asked to pay 98 percent income tax on the interest on some of her investments, it was quite possible that anything could happen.

No houses, however, were built next door to Mrs. Julian. It appeared that the "wood," though hardly National Trust or an Area of Natural Beauty, was nevertheless scheduled as "not for residential development." For her lifetime, it seemed, she would look out on birch trees and green turf and small hawthorn bushes. When she was not, of course, looking out on the inhabitants of Paintbox Place, on Mr. and Mrs. Arnold and Mr. Laindon and the Nicholsons, all young people, none of them much over 40. Their activities were of absorbing interest to Mrs. Julian as she knitted away in dark-blue two-ply, and a source too of disapproval and sometimes outright condemnation.

After Christmas, in the depths of winter, when Mrs. Julian was in the kitchen watching Mrs. Upton peeling potatoes for lunch, Mrs. Upton said, "You're lucky I'm private, have you thought of that?"

This was beyond Mrs. Julian's understanding. "I beg your pardon?"

"I mean it's lucky for you I'm not one of those council home helps. They're all coming out on strike, the lot of them coming out. They're NUPE, see? Don't you read your paper?"

Mrs. Julian certainly did read her paper, the *Daily Telegraph*, which was delivered to her door each morning. She read it from first page to last after she had had her breakfast, and she was well aware that NUPE, the National Union of Public Employees, was making rumbling noises and threatening to bring its members out over a pay increase. It was typical, in her view, of the age in which she found herself living. Someone or other was always on strike. But she had very little idea of how to identify the Public Employee and had hoped the threatened action would not affect her. She said as much to Mrs. Upton.

"Not affect you?" said Mrs. Upton, furiously scalping brussels sprouts. She seemed to find Mrs. Julian's innocence uproariously funny. "Well, there'll be no gritters on the roads for a start and maybe you've noticed it's snowing again. Gritters are NUPE. They'll have to close the schools, so there'll be kids all over the streets. School caretakers are NUPE. No ambulances if you fall on the ice and break your leg, no hospital porters, and what's more, no dustmen. We won't none of us get our rubbish collected on account of dustmen are NUPE. So how about that for not affecting you?"

Mrs. Julian's dustbin, kept just inside the front gate on a concrete slab and concealed from view by a laurel bush and a cotoneaster, was not emptied that week.

On the following Monday she looked out of the right-hand side of the bay window and saw under the birch trees, on the frosty ground, a dozen or so black plastic bags, apparently filled with rubbish, their tops secured with wire fasteners. There was no end to the propensities of some people for making disgusting litter, thought Mrs. Julian, give them half a chance. She would telephone Northway Council, she would telephone the police. But first she would put on her squirrel coat, take her stick, go out, and have a good look.

The snow had melted, the pavement was wet. A car had pulled up and a young woman in jeans and a pair of those silly boots that come up to the thighs was taking two more black plastic bags out of the back of the car. Mrs. Julian was on the point of telling her in no uncertain terms to remove her rubbish at once, when she caught sight of a notice stuck up under the trees. The notice was of plywood with printing on it in red chalk: *Northway Council Refuse Tip. Bags This Way.*

Mrs. Julian went back into her house. She told Mrs. Upton about the refuse tip and Mrs. Upton said she already knew but she hadn't told Mrs. Julian because it would only upset her.

"You don't know what the world's coming to, do you?" said Mrs. Upton, opening a tin of peaches for lunch.

"I most certainly do know," said Mrs. Julian. "Anarchy. Anarchy is what it is coming to."

Throughout the week the refuse on the tip mounted. Fortunately, the weather was very cold; as yet there was no smell. In Paintbox Place black plastic bags of rubbish began to appear outside the receptacle doors, on the steps beside the colored front doors, overflowing into the narrow flowerbeds. Mrs. Upton came five days a week but not on Saturdays or Sundays. When the doorbell rang at ten on Saturday morning, Mrs. Julian answered it herself and there outside was Mr. Arnold from the house with the red front door, behind him on the gravel drive a wheelbarrow containing five black plastic bags of rubbish.

He was a good-looking, cheerful, polite man was Mr. Arnold. Forty-two or -three, she supposed. Sometimes she fancied she had seen a melancholy look in his eyes. No wonder, she thought, she could well understand if he was melancholy. He said good morning, and he was on his way to the tip with his rubbish and Mr. Laindon's and could he take hers too?

"That's very kind and thoughtful of you, Mr. Arnold," said Mrs. Julian. "You'll find my bag inside the dustbin at the gate. I do appreciate it."

"No trouble," said Mr. Arnold. "I'll make a point of collecting your bag, shall I, while the strike lasts?"

Mrs. Julian thought. A plan was forming in her mind. "That won't be necessary, Mr. Arnold. I shall be disposing of my waste by other means. Composting, burning," she said, "beating tins flat, that kind of thing. Now if everyone were to do the same—"

"Ah, life's too short for that, Mrs. Julian," said Mr. Arnold and he smiled and went off with his wheelbarrow before she could say what she was about to say, that it was shorter for her than for most people.

She watched him take her bag out of the dustbin and trundle his barrow up the slope and along the path between the wet black mounds. Poor man. Many an evening, when Mr. Arnold was working late, she had seen the chocolate front door open and young Mr. Laindon, divorced, they said, just before he came there, emerge and tap at the red front door and be admitted. Once she had seen Mrs. Arnold and Mr. Laindon coming back from the station together, taking the short cut through the "wood." They had been enjoying each other's company and laughing, though it had been cold and quite late, at least ten at night.

And here was Mr. Arnold performing kindly little services for Mr. Laindon, all innocent of how he was deceived. Or perhaps he was not quite innocent, not quite ignorant, and that accounted for his sad eyes. Perhaps he was like Othello who doted yet doubted, suspected yet strongly loved. It was all very disagreeable, thought Avice Julian, employing one of her favorite words.

She went into the kitchen and examined the boiler, a small coke-burning furnace disused since 1963 when the late Alexander Julian had installed central heating. The chimney, she was sure, was swept, so the boiler could be used again. Tins could be hammered flat and stacked temporarily in the garden shed. And—why not?—she would start a compost heap. No one should be without a compost heap at the best of times, any alternative was most wasteful.

Her neighbors might contribute to the squalor; she would not. Presently she wrapped herself up in her late husband's Burberry and made her way down to the end of the garden. On the "wood" side, in the far corner, that would be the place. Up against the fence, thought Mrs. Julian. She found a bundle of stout sticks in the shed—Alexander had once grown runner beans up them—and, selecting four of these, she managed to drive them into the soft earth, one at each of the angles of a roughly conceived square. Next a strip of chicken wire went round the posts to form an enclosure. She would get Mrs. Upton to buy her some garotta next time she went shopping. Avice Julian knew all about making compost heaps—she and her first husband had been experts during the war. Now she felt quite excited by what she had done, though tired.

In the afternoon, refreshed by a nap, she emptied the vegetable cupboard and found some strange potatoes growing stems and leaves and some carrots cov-

ered in blue fur. Mrs. Upton was not a hygienic
housekeeper. The potatoes and carrots formed the
foundations of the new compost heap. Mrs. Julian
pulled up a handful of weeds and scattered them on
the top.

"I shall have my work cut out, I can see that,"
said Mrs. Upton on Monday morning. She laughed
unpleasantly. "I'm sure I don't know when the cleaning'll get done if I'm traipsing up and down the garden
path all day long."

Between them they got the boiler alight and fed it
Saturday's *Daily Telegraph* and Sunday's *Observer*.
Mrs. Upton hammered out a tin that had contained
baked beans and banged her thumb. She made a tre-
mendous fuss about it which Mrs. Julian tried to ig-
nore. Mrs. Julian went back to her window, cast on
for the second sleeve of the dark-blue two-ply jumper,
and watched women coming in cars with their rubbish
bags for the tip. Some of them hardly bothered to set
foot on the pavement but opened the trunk compartments of their cars and hurled the bags from where
they stood. With extreme distaste, Mrs. Julian
watched one of these bags strike the trunk of a tree
and burst open, scattering tins and glass and peelings
and leavings and dregs and grounds in all directions.

During the last week of January, Mrs. Julian always
made her marmalade. She saw no reason to discon-
tinue this custom because she was 84. Grumbling and
moaning about her back and her varicose veins, Mrs.
Upton went out to buy preserving sugar and Seville
oranges. Mrs. Julian peeled potatoes and prepared a
cabbage for lunch, carrying the peelings and the outer
leaves down the garden to the compost heap herself.
Most of the orange peel would go there in due course.
Mrs. Julian's marmalade was the clear jelly kind with
only strands of rind in it, pared hair-thin.

They made the first batch in the afternoon. Mr.

Arnold called on the following morning with his barrow. "Your private refuse operative, Mrs. Julian, at your service."

"Ah, but I've done what I told you I should do," she said, and insisted on his coming down the garden with her to see the compost heap.

"You do eat a lot of oranges," said Mr. Arnold.

Then she told him about the marmalade and Mr. Arnold said he had never tasted homemade marmalade, he didn't know people made it anymore. This shocked Mrs. Julian and rather confirmed her opinion of Mrs. Arnold. She gave him a jar of marmalade and he was profuse in his thanks.

She was glad to get indoors again. The meteorological people had been right when they said there was another cold spell coming. Mrs. Julian knitted and looked out of the window and saw Mrs. Arnold brought back from somewhere or other by Mr. Laindon in his car. By lunchtime it had begun to snow. The heavy, gray, louring sky looked full of snow.

This did not deter Mrs. Julian's great-niece from dropping in unexpectedly with her boy friend. They said frankly that they had come to look at the rubbish tip which was reputed to be the biggest in London apart from the one which filled the whole of Leicester Square. They stood in the window staring at it and giggling each time anyone arrived with fresh offerings.

"It's surrealistic!" shrieked the great-niece as a bag, weighted down with snow, rolled slowly out of the branches of a tree where it had been suspended for some days. "It's fantastic! I could stand here all day just watching it."

Mrs. Julian was very glad that she departed after about an hour (with a jar of marmalade) to something called the Screen on the Hill which turned out to be a cinema in Hampstead. After they had gone it snowed harder than ever. There was a heavy frost that night and the next.

"You don't want to set foot outside," said Mrs. Upton on Monday morning. "The pavements are like glass." And she went off into a long tale about her son Brian who was a police constable finding an old lady who had slipped and was lying helpless on the ice.

Mrs. Julian nodded impatiently. "I have no intention of going outside. And you must be very careful when you go down that path to the compost heap."

They made a second batch of marmalade. The boiler refused to light, so Mrs. Julian said to leave it but try again tomorrow, for there was quite an accumulation of newspapers to be burned. Mrs. Julian sat in the window, sewing together the sections of the dark-blue two-ply jumper and watching the people coming through the snow to the refuse tip. Capped with snow, the mounds on the tip resembled a mountain range. In the Arctic perhaps, thought Mrs. Julian fancifully, or on some planet where the temperature was always sub-zero.

All the week it snowed and froze and snowed and melted and froze again. Mrs. Julian stayed indoors. Her nephew, the one who wrote science fiction, phoned to ask if she was all right, and her other nephew, the one who was a commercial photographer, came round to sweep her drive clear of snow. By the time he arrived Mr. Laindon had already done it, but Mrs. Julian gave him a jar of marmalade just the same. She had resisted giving one to Mr. Laindon because of the way he was carrying on with Mrs. Arnold.

It started thawing on Saturday. Mrs. Julian sat in the window, casting on for the left front of her cardigan and watching the snow and ice drip away and flow down the gutters. She left the curtains undrawn, as she often did, when it got dark.

At about eight Mrs. Arnold came out of the red front door and Mr. Laindon came out of the chocolate front door and they stood chatting and laughing together until Mr. Arnold came out. Mr. Arnold unlocked the doors of his car and said something to Mr. Laindon. How Mrs. Julian wished she could have heard what it was! Mr. Laindon only shook his head. She saw Mrs. Arnold get quickly into the car and shut the door. Very cowardly, not wanting to get involved, thought Mrs. Julian. Mr. Arnold was arguing now with Mr. Laindon, trying to persuade him to do something apparently. Perhaps to leave Mrs. Arnold alone. But all Mr. Laindon did was give a silly sort of laugh and retreat into the house with the chocolate door. The Arnolds went off, Mr. Arnold driving recklessly fast in this sort of weather, as if he were fearfully late for wherever they were going or, more likely, in a great rage.

Mrs. Julian saw nothing of Mr. Laindon on the following day, the Sunday, but in the afternoon she saw Mrs. Arnold go out on her own. She crossed the road from Paintbox Place and took the path, still mercifully clear of rubbish bags, through the "wood" toward the station. Off to a secret assignation, Mrs. Julian supposed. The weather was drier and less cold but she felt no inclination to go out. She sat in the window, doing the ribbing part of the left front of her cardigan and noting that the rubbish bags were mounting again in Paintbox Place. For some reason, laziness perhaps or depression over his wife's conduct, Mr. Arnold had failed to clear them away on Saturday morning. Mrs. Julian had a nap and a cup of tea and read the *Observer*.

It pleased her that Mrs. Upton had apparently burned up all the old newspapers. At any rate, there was none to be seen. But what had she done with the empty tins? Mrs. Julian looked everywhere for the hammered-out, empty tins. She looked in the kitchen cupboards and the cupboards under the stairs and even in the dining room and the morning room. You never knew with people like Mrs. Upton. Perhaps she had actually done what her employer suggested and put them in the shed.

Mrs. Julian went back to the living room, back to her window, and got there just in time to see Mr. Arnold letting himself into his house. Time tended to pass slowly for her on the weekends and she was surprised to find it was as late as nine o'clock. It had begun to rain. She could see the slanting rain shining gold in the light from the lamps in Paintbox Place.

She sat in the window and picked up her knitting. After a little while the red front door opened and Mr. Arnold came out. He had changed out of his wet clothes, changed gray trousers for dark brown, blue jacket for sweater and anorak. He took hold of the nearest rubbish bag and dragged it just inside the door. Within a minute or two he had come out again, carrying the bag, which he loaded onto the barrow he fetched from the parking area.

It was at this point that Mrs. Julian's telephone rang. The phone was at the other end of the room. Mrs. Julian's caller was the older of her nephews, the commercial photographer, wanting to know if he might borrow pieces from her Second Empire bedroom furniture for some set or background. They had all enjoyed the marmalade, it was nearly gone. Mrs. Julian said he should have another jar of marmalade next year but he certainly could not borrow her furniture. She didn't want pictures of her wardrobe and dressing table all over these vulgar magazines, thank you very much. When she returned to her point of vantage at the window Mr. Arnold had disappeared.

Disappeared, that is, from the forecourt of Paintbox Place. Mrs. Julian crossed to the right-hand side of the bay window to draw the curtains and shut out the rain, and there he was, scaling the wet, slippery, black mountains, clutching a rubbish bag in his hand. The bag looked none too secure, for its side had been punctured by the neck of a bottle and its top was fastened not with a wire fastener but wound round and round with blue string. Finally he dropped it at the side of one of the high mounds round the birch tree. Mrs. Julian drew the curtains.

Mrs. Upton arrived punctually in the morning, agog with her news. It was a blessing she had such a strong constitution, Mrs. Julian thought. Many a woman of her advanced years would have been made ill—or worse—by hearing a thing like that.

"How can you possibly know?" she said. "There's nothing in this morning's paper."

Brian, of course. Brian, the policeman.

"She was coming home from the station," said Mrs. Upton, "through that bit of waste ground." She cocked a thumb in the direction of the "wood." "Asking for trouble, wasn't she? Nasty dark lonely place. This chap, whoever he was, he clouted her over the head with what they call a blunt instrument. That was about half-past eight, though they never found her till ten. Brian says there was blood all over, turned him up proper it did, and him used to it."

"What a shocking thing," said Mrs. Julian. "What a dreadful thing. Poor Mrs. Arnold."

"Murdered for the cash in her handbag, though there wasn't all that much. No one's safe these days."

When such an event takes place it is almost impossible for some hours to deflect one's thoughts to any other subject. Her knitting lying in her lap, Mrs. Julian sat in the window, contemplating the paintbox houses. A vehicle that was certainly a police car, though it had no blue lamp, arrived in the course of the morning and two policemen in plainclothes were admitted to the house with the red front door. Presumably by Mr. Arnold who was not, however, visible to Mrs. Julian.

What must it be like to lose, in so violent a manner, one's marriage partner? Even so unsatisfactory a marriage partner as poor Mrs. Arnold had been. Did Mr. Laindon know, Mrs. Julian wondered. She found herself incapable of imagining what his feelings must be. No one came out of or went into any of the houses in Paintbox Place and at one o'clock Mrs. Julian had to leave her window and go into the dining room for lunch.

"Of course you know what the police always say, don't you?" said Mrs. Upton, sticking a rather underdone lamb chop in front of her. "The husband's always the first to be suspected. Shows marriage up in a shocking light, don't you reckon?"

Mrs. Julian made no reply but merely lifted her shoulders. Both her husbands had been devoted to her and she told herself that she had no personal experience of the kind of uncivilized relationship Mrs. Upton was talking about. But could she say the same for Mr. Arnold? Had she not, in fact, for weeks, for months now, been deploring the state of the Arnolds' marriage and even awaiting some fearful climax?

It was at this point, or soon after when she was back in her window, that Avice Julian first began to see herself as a possible Miss Marple or Miss Silver, though she had not recently been reading the works of either of those ladies' creators. Rather it was that she saw the sound common sense which lay behind the notion of elderly women as detectives. Who else has the leisure to be so observant? Who else has behind them a lifetime of knowledge of human nature?

Who else has suffered sufficient disillusionment to be able to face unpalatable facts so squarely?

Beyond a doubt, the facts Mrs. Julian was facing were unpalatable. Nevertheless, she marshaled them. Mrs. Arnold had been an unfaithful wife. She had been conducting some sort of love affair with Mr. Laindon. That Mr. Arnold had not known of it was evident from her conduct of this extra-marital adventure in his absence. That he was beginning to be aware of it was apparent from his behavior of Saturday evening. What more probable than that he had set off to meet his wife at the station on Sunday evening, had quarreled with her about this very matter, and had struck her down in a jealous rage? When Mrs. Julian had seen him first he had been running home from the scene of the crime, clutching to him under his jacket the weapon for which Mrs. Upton said the police were still searching.

The morning had been dull and damp but after lunch it had dried up and a weak watery sun come out. Mrs. Julian put on her squirrel coat and went out into the garden, the first time she had been out for nine days.

The compost heap had not increased much in size. Perhaps the weight of snow had flattened it down or, more likely, Mrs. Upton had failed in her duty. Displeased, Mrs. Julian went back into the front garden and down to the gate where she lifted the lid of her dustbin, confident of what she would find inside. But, no, she had done Mrs. Upton an injustice. The dustbin was empty and quite clean. She stood by the fence and viewed the tip.

What an eyesore it was! A considerable amount of leakage, due to careless packing and fastening, had taken place, and the wet, fetid, black hillocks were strewn all over with torn and soggy paper, cartons and packages, while in the valleys between clustered, like some evil growth, a conglomeration of decaying fruit and vegetable parings, mildewed bread, tea leaves, coffee grounds, and broken glass. In one hollow there was movement. Maggots or the twitching nose of a rat? Mrs. Julian shuddered and looked hastily away. She raised her eyes to take in the continued presence under the birch tree of the bag Mr. Arnold had deposited there on the previous evening, the bag that was punctured by the neck of a bottle and bound with blue string.

She returned to the house. Was she justified in keeping this knowledge to herself? There was by then no doubt in her mind as to what Mr. Arnold had done. After killing his wife he had run home, changed his bloodstained clothes for clean ones, and fetching in the rubbish bag from outside, inserted into it the garments he had just removed and the blunt instrument, so-called, he had used. An iron bar, perhaps, or a length of metal piping he had picked up in the "wood." In so doing he had mislaid the wire fastener and could find no other, so he had been obliged to fasten the bag with the nearest thing to hand, a piece of string. Then across the road with it as he had been on several previous occasions, this time to deposit there a bag containing evidence that would incriminate him if found on his property. But what could be more anonymous than a black plastic rubbish bag on a council refuse tip? There it would be only one among a hundred and, he must have supposed, impossible of identification.

Mrs. Julian disliked the idea of harming her kind and thoughtful neighbor. But justice must be done. If she was in possession of knowledge the police could not otherwise acquire, it was plainly her duty to reveal it. And the more she thought of it the more convinced she was that here was the correct solution to the crime against Mrs. Arnold. Would not Miss Seeton have thought so? And Miss Silver? Would not Miss Marple, having found parallels between Mr. Arnold's behavior and that of some St. Mary Mead husband, having considered and weighed the awful significance of the quarrel on Saturday night and the extraordinary circumstance of taking rubbish to a tip at nine thirty on a wet Sunday evening, would she not have laid the whole matter before the C.I.D.?

She hesitated for only a few minutes before fetching the telephone directory and looking up the number. By three o'clock in the afternoon she was making a call to her local police station.

The detective sergeant and detective constable who came to see Mrs. Julian less than half an hour later showed no surprise at being supplied with information by such as she. Perhaps they too read the works of the inventors of elderly lady sleuths. They treated Mrs. Julian with great courtesy and after she had told them what she suspected they suggested she accompany them to the vicinity of the tip and point out the incriminating bag.

It was quite possible, however, for her to do this from the right-hand side of the bay window. The detectives nodded and wrote things down in notebooks and thanked her and went away, and after a little while a van arrived and a policeman in uniform got out and removed the bag. Mrs. Julian sat in the window, working away at the lacy pattern on the front of her dark-blue two-ply cardigan and watching for the arrest of Mr. Arnold. She watched with trepidation and fear for him and a reluctant sympathy. There were policemen about the area all day, tramping around among the rubbish bags, investigating gardens and ringing doorbells, but none of them went to arrest Mr. Arnold.

Nothing happened at all apart from Mr. Laindon calling at eight in the evening. He seemed very upset and his face looked white and drawn. He had come, he said, to ask Mrs. Julian if she would care to contribute to the cost of a wreath for Mrs. Arnold or would she be sending flowers personally?

"I should prefer to see to my own little floral tribute," said Mrs. Julian rather frostily.

"Just as you like, of course. I'm really going round asking people to give myself something to do. I feel absolutely bowled over by this business. They were wonderful to me, the Arnolds, you know. You couldn't have better friends. I was feeling pretty grim when I first came here—my divorce and all that—and the Arnolds—well, they looked after me like family, never let me be on my own, even insisted I go out with them. And now a terrible thing like this has to happen and to a wonderful person like that . . ."

Mrs. Julian had no wish to listen to this sort of thing. No doubt, there were some gullible enough to believe it. She went to bed wondering if the arrest would take place during the night, discreetly, so that the neighbors should not witness it.

The paintbox houses looked just the same in the morning. But of course they would. The arrest of Mr. Arnold would hardly affect their appearance. The phone rang at nine thirty and Mrs. Upton took the call. She came into the morning room where Mrs. Julian was finishing her breakfast.

"The police want to come round and see you again. I said I'd ask. I said you mightn't be up to it, not being so young as you used to be."

"Neither are you or they," said Mrs. Julian and then she spoke to the police herself and told them to come whenever it suited them.

During the next half hour some agreeable fantasies went round in Mrs. Julian's head. Such is often the outcome of identifying with characters in fiction. She imagined herself congratulated on her acumen and even, on a future occasion when some other baffling crime had taken place, consulted by policemen of high rank. Mrs. Upton had served her well on the whole, as well as could be expected in these trying times. Perhaps one day, when it came to the question of Brian's promotion, a word from her in the right place . . .

The doorbell rang. It was the same detective sergeant and detective constable. Mrs. Julian was a little disappointed, she had thought she rated an inspector now. They greeted her with jovial smiles and invited her into her own kitchen where they said they had something to show her. Between them they were lugging a large canvas sack.

The sergeant asked Mrs. Upton if she could find them a sheet of newspaper, and before Mrs. Julian could say that they had burned all their newspapers, Saturday's *Daily Telegraph* was produced from where it had been secreted. Then, to Mrs. Julian's amazement, he pulled out of the canvas sack the black plastic rubbish bag, punctured on one side and secured at the top with blue string, which she had seen Mr. Arnold deposit on the tip on Sunday evening.

"I hope you won't find it too distasteful, madam," he said, "just to cast your eyes over some of the contents of this bag."

Mrs. Julian was astounded that he should ask such a thing of someone of her age. But she indicated with a faint nod and wave of her hand that she would comply, while inwardly she braced herself for the sight of some hideous bludgeon, perhaps encrusted with blood and hair, and for the emergence from the depths of the bag of a bloodstained jacket and pair of trousers. She would not faint or cry out, she was determined on that, whatever she might see.

It was the constable who untied the string and spread open the neck of the bag. With care, the sergeant began to remove its contents and to drop them

on the newspaper Mrs. Upton had laid on the floor.
He dropped them, insofar as he could, in small separate heaps: a quantity of orange peel, a few lengths
of dark-blue two-ply knitting wool, innumerable Earl
Grey teabags, potato peelings, cabbage leaves, a
lamb-chop bone, the sherry bottle whose neck had
pierced the side of the sack, and seven copies of the
Daily Telegraph with one of the *Observer,* all with
Julian, 1 Abelard Avenue scrawled above the masthead.

Mrs. Julian surveyed her kitchen floor. She looked
at the sergeant and the constable and at the yard or
so of dark-blue two-ply knitting wool which he still
held in his hand and which he had unwound from the
neck of the bag.

"I fail to understand," she said.

"I'm afraid this sack would appear to contain waste
from your own household, Mrs. Julian," said the sergeant. "In other words, to have been yours and been
disposed of from your premises."

Mrs. Julian sat down. She sat down rather heavily
on one of the bentwood chairs and fixed her eyes on
the opposite wall and felt a strange tingling hot sensation in her face that she hadn't experienced for 60
years. She was blushing.

"I see," she said.

The constable began stuffing the garbage back into
the bag. Mrs. Upton watched him, giggling.

"If you haven't consumed all our stock of sherry,
Mrs. Upton," said Mrs. Julian, "perhaps we might
offer these two gentlemen a glass."

The policemen, though on duty which Mrs. Julian
had formerly supposed put the consumption of alcohol
out of the question, took two glasses apiece. They
were not at a loss for words and chatted away with
Mrs. Upton, possibly on the subject of the past and
future exploits of Brian. Mrs. Julian scarcely listened
and said nothing.

She understood perfectly what had happened—Mr. Arnold changing his clothes because they were wet, deciding to empty his rubbish that night because he had forgotten or failed to do so on the Saturday morning, gathering up his own and very likely Mr. Laindon's too. At that point she had left the window to go to the telephone. In the few minutes during which she had been talking to her nephew, Mr. Arnold had passed her gate with his barrow, lifted the lid of her dustbin, and finding a full bag within, taken it with him. It was this bag, her own, that she had seen him disposing of on the tip when she had next looked out.

No wonder the boiler had hardly ever been alight, no wonder the compost heap had scarcely grown. Once the snow and frost began and she knew her employer meant to remain indoors, Mrs. Upton had abandoned the hygiene regimen and reverted to bag and dustbin. And this was what it had led to.

The two policemen left, obligingly discarding the bag on to the tip as they passed it. Mrs. Upton looked at Mrs. Julian, and Mrs. Julian looked at Mrs. Upton, and Mrs. Upton said very brightly, "Well, I wonder what all that was about then?"

Mrs. Julian longed and longed for the old days when she would have given her notice on the spot, but that was impossible now. Where would she find a replacement? So all she said was, knowing it to be incomprehensible:

"A *faux pas*, Mrs. Upton, that's what it was," and walked slowly off and into the living room where she picked up her knitting from the chair by the window and carried it into the farthest corner of the room.

As a detective she was a failure. Yet, ironically, it was directly owing to her efforts that Mrs. Arnold's murderer was brought to justice. Mrs. Julian could not long keep away from her window and when she returned to it the next day it was to see the council men dismantling the tip and removing the bags to some distant disposal unit or incinerator. As her newspaper had told her, the strike was over. But the hunt for the murder weapon was not. There was more room to maneuver and investigate now that the rubbish was gone. By nightfall the weapon had been found and 24 hours later the young out-of-work mechanic who had struck Mrs. Arnold down for the contents of her handbag had been arrested and charged.

They traced him through the spanner with which he had killed her and which, passing Mrs. Julian's garden fence, he had thrust into the depths of her compost heap.

The Mahogany Wardrobe

by John H. Dirckx

I cannot say what it was about the girl's appearance, when she came to my door that foggy night in April, that made me want to take her in even though the house was already full. Maybe it was her unmistakable air of innocence and simplicity. Or it may have been the fact that just then all the neighborhood dogs began to howl. Whatever the reason, I took Alice Weldon in that night, put her wrap and her single piece of luggage in the hall, and told Doris to make up the bed in the studio.

At the outset I must explain that I am a widow of more than ample means with a large house and no children. Without quite intending to do so, I had drifted into the business of boarding and letting rooms to single girls, most of them just arrived in Bradford to make their way in the wide world. We were a simple household, consisting, besides myself, of Jessie Frazer, the cook, whose training as a nurse had sometimes to be put to use; Doris Brewer, the maid; my nephew Arthur, who had lost his parents and served as our man of all work; about six girls in more or less temporary residence; and a cat of obscure antecedents named Etcetera.

The room that we had always called the studio—

the original owner of the house was a professional portrait painter—was on the first floor at the front, and was therefore not very suitable as a sleeping apartment because of the street noises. But it was large and comfortable all the same, with tall arcaded windows to admit the light on three sides, and a fireplace to supplement the furnace in the dead of winter. Among the odd articles of furniture stored there, a bed stood in one corner for the sake of the occasional super-numerary guest. It was in the studio that we placed Alice.

Though she will not remain long on our stage, I must just give a brief sketch of her, since she was the first victim of that reign of terror that drew so much public attention to our formerly placid neighborhood and nearly put my establishment out of business. Alice Weldon had stepped off the bus from Mooreton half an hour before presenting herself on my doorstep and, like so many of my girls, she had been directed to me by a previous tenant. Perhaps, after all, it was that which decided me to take her in.

She was a mere wisp of a girl, barely nineteen, with dark hair and eyes and a sober, self-contained manner. She assured us that she had already had her supper, but gratefully accepted Cook Jessie Frazer's offer of a refreshing cup of tea. All of the girls were home that night, I remember, and they welcomed the newcomer warmly to the oversized dining room that, fitted up with a radio and a record player and a couple of sofas, served as our informal sitting room—a haven in which to relax when the day's toil was done.

Although inclined to be a little reserved at first, Alice soon thawed in the glow of the girls' cordiality and manifest goodwill. She had come to town, she said, with recommendations from her clergyman and the principal of her high school, and she hoped to find a job at the woolen mill which is Bradford's chief industry, and which Bradfordites never call by any other name than "the blanket works."

"You must let me take you to the office," said Jan Talbot, looking up from the jigsaw puzzle with which she had been monopolizing the sideboard for the better part of a week. "I've been in the mail room at the blanket works for six months. We could use another girl, I think—maybe they'll let you work with me."

"That would be nice," remarked Alice shyly.

"If you take my advice," said Jessie Frazer, "you won't tell a soul at the blanket works that you know Jan Talbot. What they don't know, they can't hold against you."

Jan put out her tongue at Jessie and went back to her puzzle.

Our resident cook was a stout, high-spirited girl in her early thirties with a ready smile and a word for everyone—too many words, in fact, for some people's tastes, for now and then her goodnatured chaffing aroused a bit of ill feeling. But she was as generous in deed as in words. When Alice was getting settled down in the studio for the night, it was Jessie who lent her a heavy blue flannel nightgown to keep out the chill that had crept in, along with traces of fog, while Doris was airing the room.

I was up next morning before dawn, as usual, to see that the others were stirring and doing betimes. Mornings were always somewhat hectic and confused at our house, with the girls dashing about to get ready in time for work, begging and borrowing clean shirtwaists, searching for shoes imprudently left in the most unlikely places, and breakfasting on a swallow of coffee and a bit of toast, when their haste permitted them to breakfast at all. Above the hubbub rang Jessie's clear, sharp accents, extolling the virtues of her sausage and waffles, goading the sluggards into wakefulness, and soothing short tempers with her unfailing good cheer.

I had gone first into Polly Gerard's room that morning. Polly was just recovering from a lengthy illness, and I had got into the habit of seeing to her needs in the early morning while Jessie was busy in the kitchen. Polly thought she might try a soft-boiled egg and some toast.

I was surprised not to find Alice Weldon among those huddled round the kitchen table in various stages of undress. She had planned to arise early, I knew, so that Jan could introduce her at the blanket works before reporting for duty herself. I sent Doris to wake her and told Jessie about the egg and toast for our invalid.

In less than a minute Doris was back to report that Alice wasn't in her bed—in fact, didn't seem to be anywhere in the house. "But she can't have gone out, Mrs. Byers," said Doris, "because her wrap is still hanging there in the wardrobe."

Something cold clutched at my heart when I heard those words. On first coming into the kitchen I had noticed, by the gray light of dawn, something lying on the grass between the garage and the back fence. I had thought it must be a scrap of wrapping paper blown into the yard by the wind. Now I rushed to the window for another look and then, without pausing to put on my coat or to speak a word to anyone, I threw open the kitchen door and ran down the steps into the yard.

Alice Weldon was lying all in a heap against the fence, barefoot and in her nightgown, or rather in Jessie's nightgown. A hideous wound disfigured her throat, and there was blood everywhere. Her face wore the pallor of death. My head swam, and I believe I was on the point of tumbling down in a faint beside

her when Jessie brushed past me and bent over the
still form.

With brisk efficiency she felt the limp wrist for a
pulse and brushed the hair back from the girl's brow
for a look at her eyes. "She's just barely breathing,
Mrs. Byers," she said. "Her pulse is like a thread,
coming and going. One of us must call for Dr. Melton
at once."

"I'll call," said I, glad to escape that appalling
scene.

"And do bring a blanket," Jessie called after me.

Dr. Melton lived in our street, though his office was
several blocks away in what our town council rather
grandly calls the commercial district. He had often
been to our house—twice in the past week, in fact, to
see Polly.

I sent Doris out to Jessie with a blanket and hurried
to the telephone in the front hall. My hands shook as
I dialed the familiar number. From the kitchen came
the sound of at least two young women having
hysterics.

The doctor was just on the point of leaving on his
rounds. He advised me to call for an ambulance and
said he would be along in half a minute. It could not
have been much more than that before I caught sight
of his yellow roadster drawn up in the alley behind
the garage and went out to report that the ambulance
was on its way.

"It can't come too soon," he said grimly, kneeling
in the dewy grass beside Alice. "She's in deep shock."
With deft fingers he prepared to give her a hypodermic injection. Two of the girls had come out to ask if
they could help, and he sent one of them along the
alley to his house to fetch more supplies.

"This is a bad business, Mrs. Byers," said the doctor, when he had put away his syringe and adjusted

the dressing at Alice's throat. "Not one of your regular girls, is she?"

"She only came last night."

"What on earth can she have been doing out here in her nightgown? She must have been lying here for hours. She's chilled to the bone and soaked with dew."

"Oughtn't we to move her indoors?"

"No, better not. The ambulance will be here in a few moments and then we'd only have to move her again."

"Will she—"

"She's far gone." His eyes hardened and fixed on some distant point. "This is the work of a maniac," he said. "You didn't find any weapon?"

"Weapon? Why, no—" I suppose that until that moment I hadn't dared to face the fact that some fiend in human guise had done this to Alice. A young woman does not, I now told myself, get her throat cut accidentally in the back yard of a rooming house at three in the morning. Of course there was no weapon in sight. He would have taken that away with him. . . .

As the eerie wail of the approaching ambulance broke in on my reverie, Dr. Melton knelt beside Alice again, gently shouldering aside the vigilant Jessie. He felt for a pulse and then bent lower to use his stethoscope. Very slowly he drew erect.

"There's no occasion for haste now," he said, as if to himself. "The poor child is dead."

Even before the ambulance, its siren stilled, took Alice away to the mortuary, two policemen, very square of chin and stern of eye, arrived. One of them interviewed each of us in turn, asking many pointed questions and writing down our answers in a notebook. The other ransacked the house and went up and down the alley peering into trash cans and probing among dead weeds. He lingered long in the kitchen, examining Jessie's stock of knives with a professional eye.

I handed over the dead girl's small suitcase to the officer who asked the questions, but he made me open it and go through the contents with him. There was precious little to go through. Some plain but decent clothes, a book or two, a few toilet articles, and a pocket purse with twenty-seven dollars and a few cents. That was the lot.

Some other articles of clothing hung in the wardrobe next to the bed. On a table we found a leather case containing Alice's letters of recommendation and a few private papers, one of them bearing her home address in Mooreton.

"I gathered from some things she said last night that she was an orphan," I told the policeman, "but I don't really know that. I believe she was raised by an aunt and uncle."

"They'd be the Pattersons mentioned in those papers."

"I'm sorry I can't be of more help, officer, but I'd barely met the poor girl when she was—"

"That's all right, ma'am," said the policeman stolidly, shutting his notebook and putting it away. "This is just preliminary. A detective from the Homicide Bureau will be around to see you before long."

Was it my imagination, or did his tone imply that the homicide detective would succeed in extracting any information that I had deliberately withheld from him?

The other policeman, the searching one, had poked around our empty garage (we kept no automobile), but to my relief he seemed not to have noticed that there were living quarters above it. Perhaps I should have explained before that my nephew Arthur had made his home there since the preceding autumn. He took his evening meals with us and was often in the house to do odd jobs, but he slept above the garage, and left very early to catch the first bus to the technical college, where he was studying radio engineering.

Arthur's mother, my sister Louise, had died while Arthur was away in military service, and her husband had passed away shortly after. My sister hadn't made a very good marriage, and when Arthur was demobilized after the European armistice he found himself not only without parents but almost without funds. It seemed an act of common decency rather than of charity to install him in my vacant chauffeur's quarters and help him start a life for himself.

Arthur had always been a quiet boy, but since his war experience, of which he seldom spoke, he seemed to have grown more somber and introspective than ever. I don't mean that he was queer exactly, just different. Sensitive, and not easy to talk to. Only Jessie seemed able to get round his shyness and reserve and draw him out a little.

As soon as the police had left, I shooed all of the girls except Polly off to work. They were late, of course, and most were so upset that they might as well have stayed home for all the good they were going to do their employers. Then I went to Arthur's rooms and let myself in with my key.

If you had asked me then what I expected to find, I hardly know what I would have answered. I am sure that I was afraid to ask myself.

Arthur's small apartment was tidy with a masculine sort of tidiness, Spartan rather than cosy. Along the wall next to the bed ran a workbench with a rack of tools and a few electrical appliances. Arthur had always been mechanically inclined. In the last letter I ever received from my sister, she reported with pride his acceptance to army radio school. That was before he was sent overseas.

It would hardly be correct to say that I searched

Arthur's rooms. I may have opened a drawer or two, but not to disturb, much less rummage through, their contents. I left the small, battered secretary alone, though the key was in the leaf.

On a shelf in the closet I saw a dull gleam of metal and knew what I had come to find. I lifted down, and carried to the window, a German bayonet—Arthur always called it "Prussian"—which looked as long as a fencepost and as sharp as a razor. Arthur had brought this grisly trophy into the house once to cut some leather, and another time to pry off the lid of a jar. Had it borne those dark stains the last time I saw it? I wrapped the bayonet in a piece of newspaper and took it away with me.

In the studio stood an old mahogany wardrobe, square and massive, which had come with the house. Some of Alice's clothes still hung in it, but otherwise it was empty except for a secret compartment of which no one knew but me. Under the false floor of the wardrobe there was a cavity as big as an orange crate, which could be opened by simultaneously pressing two catches concealed in the molding at the base. How my late husband came to discover this I don't know— probably by the exercise of that same ingenuity that raised him to the rank of major in Army Intelligence. In any event, he had used the secret compartment as a repository for private documents and, during one dark period, for large sums of money that he dared not entrust to a bank.

Feeling very much like a malefactor, I stole into the studio, opened the compartment at the bottom of the wardrobe, and laid the Prussian bayonet inside it atop a pile of birth certificates, faded photographs, bundled letters, and boxes of miscellaneous mementos. Having completed this task without the knowledge of any of the others then in the house—Polly, the maid Doris, and Jessie—I breathed more freely, and went about my daily routine with a less heavy heart.

Some reporters came around noon, but Doris repelled them with brisk indignation.

None of us made any pretense of eating lunch that day. I was with Polly, trying to coax her to take a little more of the soup for which I myself had no appetite, when Doris announced that a detective was waiting to see me. I asked her to put him in the front parlor, a small, square room off the hall where I allowed the girls to entertain gentlemen callers.

I found the detective sitting in a brown study with his hat on his knee. He rose promptly as I entered and introduced himself as Inspector Franklin.

He was a pleasant-faced man, not very tall, with a quiet but authoritative manner. "Mother was a Franklin," I said, inviting him to resume his seat and taking one opposite him. "I'm afraid that most of the girls have gone to work."

"That's all right, Mrs. Byers. You are the one I particularly wanted to see. It was you who found the murdered girl, I believe."

"Yes. Only of course she wasn't dead when I found her."

"Did she say anything—anything at all?"

"No, she was quite unconscious. 'Comatose' was the word that Dr. Melton used."

He nodded. "I've talked with the doctor. But you saw her first. Tell me how her condition impressed you."

"I was—shocked. I thought she was dead. She never moved, and her skin was as pale as ivory."

"I suppose you've no idea how she came to be outdoors in her nightgown?"

"None whatever. That's as much of a mystery as how she came to be killed."

"Those two mysteries, I fancy, are one," he remarked. "May I smoke?"

I consented politely, fearing that he would proceed to embue the premises with the odor of some rank cigar or sputtering pipe. I was relieved when it was only a cigarette. I noticed with amusement that he kept his matches in his hat.

"I wonder if it's occurred to you," he said, "that Alice Weldon must have gone outside willingly to meet her assailant, unless he was already in the house?"

I shuddered. "Couldn't she have been walking in her sleep?"

"She could, of course," he conceded with an indulgent smile. "But if we postulate that, we must also postulate that she walked barefoot out into the chilly night and chanced to meet a homicidal maniac in the back yard."

"But, surely," I said, "if she went outdoors willingly—I mean, awake—she would be all the more unlikely to go without her shoes or her wrap?"

"But supposing that her going out was a matter of great urgency?"

Something lay hidden in his words that I could not fathom. "I can hardly imagine—"

"Suppose, for example, that she heard, or thought she heard, a child outside crying for help. Would she stop to put on her shoes before rushing out? Would you?"

"No, I don't imagine that I should. But no one else heard anything during the night."

"I understand that the murdered girl slept on the ground floor, whereas the other sleeping apartments are all upstairs."

"Yes, except Polly's."

He unfolded a sheet of paper covered with small,

neat writing and smoothed it out on his knee. "That would be Miss Gerard."

"Yes. She's just come out of the hospital with scarlet fever—without it, I suppose I mean. The doctor said she wasn't to use the stairs during her convalescence, so we moved her, bed and all, into what used to be the serving pantry. But it would take an earthquake to rouse her during the night because she gets a bromide at bedtime."

He had a curious gesture, a trick of running the tip of his little finger round the rim of his ear from the top down to the lobe. Later on, I was to know that gesture well. Whether it betokened concentration or bafflement, I could not then be sure. "Turn it around," he said. "Suppose the girl ran outside to get away from something."

"Something in the house?"

"Or someone."

"You said before that the murderer could have been in the house. Surely you don't mean—"

"She might have admitted him herself."

"Really, inspector. A young woman doesn't admit a stranger to her rooming house in the dead of night."

"Oh, I didn't say it was a stranger. A murderer isn't often a total stranger to his victim. Just how much do you know about this girl?"

"Very little, I'm afraid. I went through her things with the policeman this morning—"

"I've been through them, too," he said. "I mean, did she say anything about her personal affairs? Any mention of an engagement broken off, or of any sort of trouble at home that might have caused her to leave?"

"Oh, no, nothing like that. She spoke of her aunt and uncle, affectionately I thought, and of her plan to apply for a job at the blanket works. She paid a week's rent in advance."

"She didn't seem restless or frightened?"

"Not in the least. Just shy. Of course the police have been in touch with her family?"

"The aunt and uncle, yes. Her parents are deceased. The Pattersons are arriving this evening. They'll take the body back to Mooreton for burial."

"Do you really suppose she might have let someone into the house during the night—someone who had followed her from home?"

He did not reply at once. "Let's say, Mrs. Byers, that that's the most likely explanation. This morning you were perfectly certain that the front and back doors were securely locked at bedtime last night, and that they remained so until you went out to Alice Weldon in the back yard this morning. Has anything occurred to you since to shake that conviction?" He was so soft-spoken that at times his words actually became inaudible, only the movement of his lips showing what he meant to say.

"No, nothing. And the police officer and I went round the whole house to examine all of the window fastenings on this floor and in the basement."

He nodded. "Nothing open, and no sign of an entry having been forced."

"If the murderer was inside the house," I asked, choosing my words carefully, "why would he take Alice outside to—do what he did to her? There wasn't a trace of blood in the studio—that is, in Alice's room—or anywhere else in the house."

Inspector Franklin stood up and went to the window. It commanded a view of the side yard, but not that part of it where Alice had died. "We come back again to the question of the relationship between murderer and victim. Who has a key to this house besides yourself?"

"Why, everyone. All of the girls have keys, and Doris and Jessie. And, of course, Arthur."

He returned to his seat and consulted his notes. "Who," he asked, "is Arthur?"

"Arthur Sims, my nephew." I tried to make my tone sound natural. "He lives above the garage."

His hand went up at once to his ear. "He wasn't here this morning, was he?"

"No, he'd already gone out. He's studying radio engineering at the technical college, and he has to catch an early bus."

"Doesn't he come into the house for breakfast?"

"No, he gets his breakfast at a lunch counter at the college. He comes in to stoke the furnace on cold mornings, but we haven't needed the furnace for the past three days."

"How long has your nephew made his home here with you?"

"About six months." I told him as much of Arthur's history as seemed pertinent.

"I'd like to interview your nephew as soon as possible," he said. "What time does he usually come home?"

"At half past four, or a little later."

He considered. "I hadn't planned to trespass on your hospitality for so long as that," he remarked. An inspector in the Homicide Bureau talking of trespassing on one's hospitality! I was beginning to like him. "I'll probably stop back this evening. Does your nephew lead an active social life?"

"If you mean will he likely be out for the evening, the answer is no. Arthur is a quiet, studious boy, very keen on doing well at college. He practically exists on charity here, and it's obvious that he yearns for independence. I expect he'll break away as soon as he can."

"No particular lady friends?"

"None that I know of."

"An attachment to one of the girls in the house, perhaps?"

"Oh, no. I don't think so."

He fell silent for a time and appeared to be studying the pattern of the wallpaper with intense concentration. At length he referred to his notes. "May I ask you to give me a thumbnail sketch of each of the girls presently living here? How long they've been with you, any traits of character that strike you as outstanding . . ." His voice trailed off into silence again.

"Well, I've mentioned Polly already. She's a bright, vivacious girl when she's well, but just now she's pretty low. She's lived here for about a year, and until her illness she was employed in the design department at the blanket works. Iris Crane and Mary Dockerty are cousins from Shelbyville who room together. They're both teachers at the elementary school three blocks away on Market Street. They've been with me since last August, and sometimes I think they plan to stay for the rest of their days."

"Not the marrying kind, then?" suggested the inspector shrewdly, ticking off the names on his list with a pencil.

"Not like Beverly Lamb," I said with a smile. "Beverly is attending art school, but I'd say the odds are against her finishing before the wedding bells ring."

"Lots of gentlemen callers?"

"Telephone callers, mostly. She doesn't get much company here. You see, Beverly comes from a wealthy family in Avondale. She's been staying with me since January because I knew her mother at school, but the decor here and the neighborhood don't suit her idea of proper surroundings for a young lady of culture and—prospects. So she contrives to meet her friends in town."

"Contrives?" He caught at the word. "To me that suggests something furtive—devious."

"Then I've misled you. Beverly is a good girl at heart, just spoiled. She shares a room with Gussy Warren, who has nothing, and whom she contrives—that word again!—to keep well supplied with nearly new stockings and other nice things. Gussy works at the German bakery on State Street. She's supporting an aged mother and a younger brother who live out in Hartley beyond the end of the streetcar line. She spends her Sundays with them. She came to me just before Christmas."

"And Janet Talbot?" he prompted, almost in a whisper.

"Jan has lived here for about six months. She's a steady, sensible girl. She sorts mail orders at the blanket works, but I shouldn't be surprised if one day she were running the company. The other two members of the household besides myself are fixtures. Doris Brewer has been with me as a maid for seven years—since before my husband's death. Her father is a Baptist minister in Mississippi, and he is the only male in creation for whom she has a good word. Jessie Frazer came to stay with me four years ago, when I had just two other girls. She's a practical nurse and had taken a job at the hospital. Then came the first wave of wounded soldiers when the military hospitals began to overflow, and it was just too much for her. I lost my cook at about that time, and Jessie stayed on in her place."

"What do you make of the fact that Alice Weldon was wearing a nightgown of Jessica Frazer's when she was murdered?" asked the inspector.

"Why, nothing at all. The room where we put Alice to bed was chilly because we'd opened the windows to air it out. It seemed terribly late to call Arthur in to lay a fire in the studio, so Jessie lent Alice a heavy flannel gown for the night."

"You think it unlikely that someone mistook Alice for your cook?"

"Yes, I do. Jessie would make two of Alice. And no one but the members of the household would know that Jessie sometimes wore a dark blue flannel nightgown."

"I realize that," he said mildly.

"But you can't think that one of us—"

"What about girls who have left you in the past few months? Might any of them have had a feud with Jessie Frazer? Did any of them perhaps go away 'under a cloud,' as the saying is?"

"No, certainly not. I assure you, Inspector Franklin, that no one who has lived under this roof in my time is capable of doing what someone did last night to Alice Weldon."

His little finger sought the rim of his ear. "Your nephew, you say, lives above the garage—"

"Inspector!" My voice grew shrill in spite of, or perhaps because of, my determination to remain calm. "Did you think I was playing with my words? Arthur hasn't killed anyone—"

"Have you ever asked him that? He was in France, you said—"

"As a radio operator."

"As a soldier, Mrs. Byers. A soldier's business is to kill. His own survival may depend on it."

"But what has that to do with Alice Weldon?" I was smoldering with indignation and he knew it.

"I will tell you. Alice Weldon was killed from behind by a right-handed person who used a large, heavy knife and held her head against his chest, covering her mouth with his left hand. She may have bitten that left hand, by the way—"

"Well?" I demanded, still not seeing the connection with Arthur.

"Soldiers are taught to kill in exactly that way."

"Surely not with a knife! Even in the Middle Ages they could do better than that."

"Better?" he asked, with a wistful smile that was almost a reproof. "Yes, bombs and shells and machine guns are better, I suppose, if you don't like to look your enemy in the face—to hear his screams of fear and pain, and find his blood on your hands afterwards—"

I must have turned pale at that, for he broke off and picked up his hat from the floor. "I'm sorry if I've upset you," he said. "I wonder if I might see the room where Alice Weldon slept last night?"

Without a word I led him to the studio.

He examined the windows and the fireplace, and spent some time studying the bed, which the police had ordered us to leave unmade. He knelt on the floor and peered under the bed with the aid of a pocket flash. When he had looked over Alice's few poor garments hanging in the wardrobe, he shut its heavy door and put his back to it, letting his eyes roam searchingly round the room, and now and then fixing me with a glance that seemed to probe my deepest thoughts— thoughts just then straying to Arthur's bayonet, which lay hidden within his reach.

I often think of that scene, Inspector Franklin leaning against the mahogany wardrobe, I peevishly refusing to meet his gaze, and neither of us suspecting that the solution to the mystery of Alice's death was there in the room with us.

The inspector was preparing, I think, to leave when I heard Arthur's voice in the hall. As we came out of the studio, we found him at the foot of the back stairs, still in his coat and hat, getting the story of Alice Weldon's murder from Jessie. He appeared pale and shaken. I introduced him to the inspector.

"I heard it on the radio at lunch," said Arthur. "I thought there must be a mistake because I'd never heard of the girl. But they gave your name, Aunt Vi, and the address. I tried to telephone several times, but the line was always busy."

"That was Doris's doing," I said. "She left the telephone off the hook because reporters kept calling."

"You didn't see or hear anything unusual last night or this morning, then, Mr. Sims?" asked the inspector.

"Not a thing. I left before seven. It was still dark then."

"Would you mind stepping out and showing me how you go in the mornings—since you still have your hat and coat on?" He went into the front hall and got his own coat.

Arthur led him through the kitchen and out the back door. I fought down an urge to slip on my coat and follow them. Arthur would be all right, I told myself. I'd already done enough to protect him from needless harassment. Perhaps too much. Would he miss the bayonet at once and tell the inspector about it himself?

From the kitchen window I watched them pacing side by side along the driveway, deep in conversation. Later they went up the outside stairs to Arthur's apartment. They were there a long while. I felt sure the inspector managed to get a good look at Arthur's left hand, and probably to search his quarters pretty thoroughly, too, without appearing to do so.

By the time Arthur came in for dinner, most of the girls were home. I was surprised to learn that the inspector had gone away without coming back into the house.

Dinner was a somber meal that night, eaten in almost complete silence—the silence that reigns when each person is lost in his own thoughts. Even Jessie's spirits seemed to have been damped by the events of the morning.

Dr. Melton came to see Polly that evening, and

afterwards he held a long conference with Jessie in the kitchen. I supposed that they were talking about Polly's condition and began to grow concerned when the minutes passed and the indistinct tones of his voice still droned on, nearly drowned by the clatter of Jessie's typically energetic dishwashing.

Jessie was pouring the doctor a second or third cup of coffee when I went into the kitchen and asked him whether our tragedy had set back Polly's recovery.

"Not exactly, Mrs. Byers," he replied.

He slipped his pipe surreptitiously into his pocket, as if its aroma had not already penetrated to the front hall and beyond. "She's rallying nicely, but she's begun having nightmares again. I believe she can move back upstairs. In fact, I think it advisable."

"Yes, I shouldn't care to sleep alone down here myself. I'll have Arthur take her bed up."

"Arthur's gone out, Mrs. Byers," said Jessie. "He went to get some lecture notes he missed by coming home early. But I can move Polly's bed up for you."

"I daresay you can, Jessie," nodded Dr. Melton. Then, turning to me, "I understand you've had a detective from Homicide here this afternoon."

"Inspector Franklin."

"What's his theory?"

"I'm not in his confidence," I said. "I don't know that he has a theory yet."

"I'm something of a detective myself, Mrs. Byers— have to be, in my line. I've seen some grim sights in my day.

"What strikes me about this girl's death is that there was only a single wound, and that scarcely a fatal one."

"*Scarcely* fatal?" I said, moving round to the stove and helping myself to coffee.

"Why, the girl was still alive when you found her, and she must have been lying there for hours. It was exposure that killed her, as much as that wound—bad as the wound was."

"And what is your theory?" I asked him.

"That I shall keep to myself for the time being," he said, adopting a little of his pompous sickroom manner. "I must be going—three more calls to make." He retrieved his coat and his bag from a chair in the breakfast nook. "Keep on with the nightly bromides, Jessie, and try a bouillon cube in her eggnog."

I regretted not having taken a bromide myself that night as I lay awake listening to the noises of the old house and thinking of poor Alice Weldon lying stiff and cold at the mortuary. Thinking, too, of that horrid weapon at the bottom of the mahogany wardrobe. I wasn't prepared to believe that I was nursing a viper in my bosom, or that my sister's son was a callous murderer of strange young women, military training or not. But I saw hard days ahead for Arthur unless Inspector Franklin found some more likely suspect in the case, and I prayed that I had done right in concealing that weapon.

Next afternoon Alice's aunt and uncle came to the house to collect her things. They seemed decent enough people, well on in years and evidently not prosperous.

Mrs. Patterson became somewhat noisy in the accusative case, suggesting I know not what dark things about my rooming house. But her eyes were dry and hard, and she seemed to think of Alice Weldon as an investment gone astray rather than as a child who had died.

"We thought she was planning to stay at the Y.W.C.A.," said her husband. I believe they were the only words I heard him speak. I felt sorry for him. His reticence was a surer token of grief than her peevish ranting.

For a day or two the newspapers made much of us,

as newspapers will. We grew hardened to the sight of the curious and the morbid-minded gawking at us from the sidewalk at all hours and trooping through the alley for no other reason than to view the spot where Alice Weldon had lain dying.

There was an inquest, of course, which Jessie and I were required to attend, but no new evidence was submitted and the inevitable verdict was murder by some unknown person.

That evening things seemed to be getting back to normal at our place. Polly Gerard appeared at the supper table for the first time in weeks, and the buzz of conversation was as lively as ever. Afterwards, when the table had been cleared and the room transformed once again into a sitting room, the girls took up their regular activities as if Alice Weldon had never come into their lives. Jan was back at her jigsaw puzzle, while Beverly nodded over a novel, and our two teachers, Iris and Mary, sat on opposite sides of the table correcting papers. Gussy Warren worked at knitting a cardigan for her brother when she was not fiddling with the dials of the radio.

It was that evening that I overheard a curious conversation between Arthur and Jessie. I had no intention of eavesdropping, but having heard a few words as I passed through the back hall, I found I could neither advance nor retreat without hearing more.

Arthur seldom invaded our sitting room after dinner, but he would often sit in the kitchen with his coffee and chat with Jessie as she did the washing up. When there was leftover dessert to be begged, he would even take up a dishtowel and help.

"Who's got a key to my place besides me?" he was asking.

"Just your Aunt Vi, I'd say," answered Jessie. She rinsed something at the tap and laid it on the drainboard.

"What about before I moved in? Wasn't there somebody else living up there for a while?"

"Not recently. About three years ago your aunt rented the apartment to a navy recruiter, Ensign Coles, and his wife. But they only stayed a couple of months."

"Did they have a key to the house?"

"Oh, no. I'm sure they didn't. Mrs. Coles cooked their meals on a hotplate, or they went out." I missed a few words while she scraped out the stewpan into the cat's dish. Our tabby Etcetera streaked past me on her way from the sitting room to the kitchen.

"Inspector Franklin seems to think whoever killed Alice Weldon got into the house somehow, dragged her out into the yard, and then killed her," said Arthur.

"It gives me the shivers, thinking of somebody prowling around inside the house and none of us knowing it. Just leave those—they go under the sink."

"It's a good thing none of you did know it; otherwise you might be as dead as Alice Weldon."

"You don't think he broke in meaning to kill her, then?"

"I don't think he broke in at all. The police didn't find any indication that he did."

"You think it's somebody with a key to the house, don't you?" I could almost feel her shudder through the wall. "You ought to tell your aunt. She could have the locks changed."

There was a long silence. "I don't think that would be of much use," said Arthur at last. How accurate that statement would prove in the light of later events!

A week to the day after the murder, Inspector Franklin paid us another call. Jessie and I had gone marketing together, as we often did. On our return Doris informed me that the inspector was waiting in the front parlor. I asked Jessie to put on a pot of coffee, and went myself to invite him to come back into the sitting room.

"It's more comfortable here," I said, adjusting the Venetian blinds at the east window.

He nodded in his quiet way, and when I placed an ashtray at his elbow, he smiled appreciatively and drew out a packet of cigarettes.

He seemed strangely reluctant to open the interview, perhaps remembering that matters had become strained at our first meeting.

"Are there any new developments?" I asked at length.

"None, I'm afraid. We've checked up very thoroughly on the dead girl's past, her family background and her connections in Mooreton. There isn't the slightest indication that she had an enemy in the world. No one besides her came to Bradford that night by train. The last Greyhound from the direction of Mooreton arrived at two o'clock in the afternoon."

"Her killer could have preceded her. Her plans were no secret."

"Good for you. But I only said the Greyhound arrived. I didn't say anyone got off."

"So you've come back to us for another look at the scene of the crime? And I thought by now that we'd all been exonerated." I do not know what led me to bait him so—perhaps it was the bright spring sunshine that flooded the room that morning, chasing away shadows physical and mental and making the death of Alice Weldon seem very remote and scarcely real.

His hand was at his ear, carrying with it a cigarette that threatened to singe his hair. "No one will be exonerated," he said simply, "until the true murderer is known."

"You're still not satisfied about Arthur?"

"It's my opinion that Arthur knows more about the murder than he has told. I hope you've had no further unpleasantness here?"

"Not since the Pattersons left," I remembered ruefully.

"I understand that your invalid is much better."

"Polly is fine," I assured him, wondering where he had obtained his information. The mystery was solved later when I learned that he had quizzed a reluctant Doris at length before my return home.

Jessie brought coffee then, and he invited her to stay, but she declined politely, saying she had to put away the meat. When she had gone, Inspector Franklin rose and, to my surprise, closed the kitchen door behind her.

"Seems a sensible enough girl," he remarked quietly, not resuming his seat but prowling slowly round the room with his coffee cup in one hand and his saucer in the other. "Not given to idle imaginings or groundless frights?"

"Certainly not. Why do you ask?"

"Are you aware that Jessica Frazer has been to the police and made a statement regarding curious happenings in the house? No? I thought not."

"What curious happenings?" I demanded in astonishment.

"Sounds during the night. Objects unaccountably moved in the studio where Alice Weldon slept and, I believe, in this room."

"But I know nothing of this. When is it supposed to have happened?"

"On the third and fourth nights after the murder."

I drew myself up and was turning in my seat to call Jessie back into the room when he raised his hand in a peremptory gesture of prohibition. "Let her tell you in her own good time," he said. "It may be only her imagination, after all. But I shall have to look into it."

Gone was the bright optimism of a spring day, driven out by a chill blast of fear. "But, inspector, what does all of this mean? Are we to have a second murder before the police have solved the first one?"

He seemed taken aback by the asperity of my tone. "I sincerely trust not. But we are up against something inexplicable here. On the one hand we have a killer who strikes apparently without motive and disappears. On the other, a house full of people which someone seems able to enter at will in spite of locked doors."

I remembered Arthur and Jessie's conversation. "Do you think I should have the locks changed?"

"I was going to suggest it. And you ought to have bolts put on, too."

"Oh, very well. That will mean that someone will have to get up and let Arthur in when he has to stoke the furnace, but the cold weather is nearly over, anyway."

He stopped opposite the sideboard and stood pondering Jan's jigsaw puzzle, which was still far from complete. After a minute he tried a piece and found that it fitted. "Amazing, isn't it," he said, "how looking at a puzzle from a new angle sometimes provides an immediate solution?"

"My husband was a great worker of jigsaw puzzles."

"And a great solver of them, I don't doubt," he replied. "I had the honor of knowing Major Byers slightly."

"You didn't tell me that the other day."

"You didn't invite me into your sitting room the other day and give me coffee."

I hardly knew what to say to that, so I said nothing. He stepped back a pace from the puzzle and seemed to go on studying it, though I was sure his thoughts were elsewhere. "Do you know the hardest kind of piece to place in a puzzle?" he asked suddenly, and gave me no chance to answer. "The one you don't know about." He stooped and picked up a piece that had fallen to the floor, holding it up between two fingers for me to see before replacing it on the sideboard.

He spent a great deal of time in the studio, and later I heard him rummaging in the basement. That day he came and said goodbye to me before leaving.

In the afternoon a locksmith replaced the locks on the front and back doors, and added sliding bolts that gave the place the look of a prison or a fortress. But I felt more secure when I went to bed that night than I had since Alice's death.

I awoke to black darkness, or rather half awoke, and was turning over to resume my slumber when I felt Etcetera curled up on the covers at my feet. I came fully awake then with a start of horror, for I had put the cat out myself before locking up, and no one had had any occasion that I knew of to go out afterwards.

I do not know how long I lay there motionless, drenched in an icy sweat, listening for the slightest sound. None came but the sighing of the wind, the ticking of my alarm clock, and the familiar rasp of Mary Dockerty's snoring from across the hall. But at length I decided that I must get up and investigate.

I switched on the lamp beside my bed and noted that it was not quite five o'clock. Etcetera yawned and stretched and turned her head away from the light, resenting the interruption of her nap. I put on my robe and slippers and got a flashlight from my bureau drawer so as not to awaken the whole house by turning on the hall lights.

Once in the hall I turned instinctively toward the rear of the house. The front stairs were exposed on too many sides. Anyone going down them with a flashlight would be plainly visible not only from all parts of the lower hall but from the front parlor and the studio as well. I shone my flash briefly down the length of the back stairs and, finding nothing more sinister than a dustpan out of its proper place, I descended quickly in the dark.

It was so cold in the lower hall that I felt sure the back door must be open. No sound came to my strain-

ing ears. I reached round the frame of the kitchen
door and pressed the light switch, drawing courage
from the answering flood of light. A glance at the
back door showed that the bolt was still in place. But
in the next instant I recoiled against the icebox, cow-
ering in terror at what I had seen on the floor.

Jessie Frazer lay crumpled before the stove in her
nightgown, robe, and slippers. Her contorted features
wore a bright flush, and her eyes were open and staring. I did not need to go closer to know that it was
the police I must call, and not the doctor.

I went round the downstairs putting on light after
light before going to the telephone. Even then I kept
looking over my shoulder down the bright, cold,
empty hall, and I spoke in such a faint whisper that
the man at police headquarters had to ask me to talk
louder. I didn't know what had happened to Jessie
exactly, but I felt certain that if she had been murdered, the murderer must still be in the house, for the
front door was still as securely bolted as the back one.

After hanging up the telephone I slumped down
where I was and wept silently. I do not think I have
ever felt so alone and afraid as I did then. Alice Weldon had been practically a stranger, but in Jessie I
had lost a bosom friend and loyal companion. I did
not move until I heard the police knocking at the front
door.

Then in an instant everyone in the house was up,
and the whole place erupted in a fresh storm of horror
and hysterics. The police searched the house with a
thoroughness bordering upon indecency, but found no
intruders.

Inspector Franklin appeared shortly, an unshaven
Inspector Franklin looking very gray and haggard in
the garish electric light. He spent some time in the
kitchen with the police officers and then sought me
out. I told him all I knew.

"He's got round us, hang it all!" he exclaimed, hammering his fist into his palm. "I thought the bolts would keep him out, but—"

"Then it is murder?"

"Murder made to look like suicide. We found a hypodermic of cyanide under the table in the kitchen. Her fingerprints are on it, but they're the wrong way round. It's murder, all right."

"Dear God! Why? Who did it? If you know, it's your duty to tell me."

"If I knew, Mrs. Byers, I wouldn't be here wringing my hands like a milk maid."

"Do you suppose that, after all, Jessie was his intended victim when he killed Alice—that he was misled by the nightgown?"

But he was in no mood for hazarding theories.

Someone had gone across the yard and roused Arthur, and presently he appeared in our midst, blinking and shaking his head. One of the policemen made coffee, for no one else would set foot in the kitchen. And no one thought of complaining that it was too strong as we huddled numbly round the sitting room, watching the first streaks of dawn as on that dreadful morning a week before.

I sent Doris with a cup of coffee for the inspector, but she came back with it saying that he was nowhere in the house. Yet a few moments later he stepped out of the studio into the hall. He seemed somehow altered, more in command of himself. A cigarette was in his mouth, but he had forgotten to light it.

"Come in here a minute, will you, Mrs. Byers?" he said, drawing me into the studio. "I'm going to show you something about your house that you don't know yourself."

He went to the window next to the fireplace, pulled up on the broad wooden sill as if it had been a trunk lid, and then thrust outward. At once the entire window, frame and all, swung away almost noiselessly like a huge door, leaving a yawning gap in the wall.

"This explains a lot, I think," he said. He pulled the window shut again.

"It explains how that mahogany wardrobe got in here," I said. "A furniture mover once assured my husband that it must have been made in this very room, since it wouldn't go out through the door."

"It also explains how the murderer came and went. I barely touched the frame of the window just now from the outside and it swung right open."

"But why should anyone build such a contrivance into a house?"

"Just the thing for a studio, to bring in blocks of stone and take out the finished sculptures."

"It was a painter's studio."

"Finished canvases, then. This ought to be closed up at once. Tell you what—I'll have a builder here this morning. But first I want my man to go over these painted surfaces for fingerprints."

No one went out to work that day. Even Arthur stayed home. Before lunch Iris and Mary came to tell me their mothers insisted that they move out of the house immediately. There would not have been time for their mothers, away in Shelbyville, to learn of what the papers tritely but inevitably called the "Second Nightgown Murder" unless one of them had called her mother long-distance to report it.

Inspector Franklin was as good as his word. By mid-afternoon the carpenters had come and gone, leaving behind them no trace of their work except the clean smell of freshly sawed pine. After supper I shut myself in the studio and opened the secret compartment at the bottom of the wardrobe. It was empty!

I felt I had to discuss this new development with someone at once—but how admit to Arthur that I had spirited away his bayonet? How explain to Inspector

Franklin the complicated motives that had led me to do so? I decided to confide in Dr. Melton, who had for years been a trusted family retainer. He had already shown an interest in our troubles—had, indeed, been involved in them from the first.

I put on my coat, and without telling anyone where I was going, I walked down the alley to the doctor's house. His yellow roadster stood in the open garage. My knock at the back door was answered by Mrs. Melton.

"Is it a professional call, Mrs. Byers?" she asked, with the slight sneer that seemed never to leave her face. I had often felt the doctor was not particularly happy in his home life.

She led me to his cramped, smokefilled study, where he was reading at his desk by a green-shaded lamp. He put away his book and motioned me into a leather armchair. He listened in silence to my tale, nodding sagely from time to time and puffing furiously at his pipe.

"You haven't said anything about this to Inspector Franklin, then?" he asked when I had finished.

"No. I did what I did to spare Arthur the torment of being questioned about that bayonet. If I tell the inspector about it now, it will go all the harder for Arthur."

"But you'll want to recover the family papers that were taken."

"That's a mere inconvenience. It's the bayonet that I'm worried about now. It may have been the weapon that killed Alice. It probably has Arthur's fingerprints on it. It certainly has mine."

He pondered that for a long while, toying with the articles on his desk. "Mrs. Byers, my advice to you is to make a clean breast of it all to the police. That's the soundest policy after all, and you'll see it will all come right in the end. Tomorrow will do. The inspector needs his rest like everybody else. Do you know what I'd advise you to do tonight? Move that nephew of yours into the house. He's a stout lad, but he can't do you any good away in the top of that garage."

"Then you think we're still in danger?" I told him about the closing up of the false window in the studio.

"Danger is a hard thing to measure before the fact," he said sententiously, hammering the ashes from his pipe into a battered brass bowl at his elbow. "Get the boy into the house with you. Has he got a revolver?"

"Not as far as I know."

I thought he was on the point of lending me one, but he did not.

Arthur readily agreed to sleep in the studio, but it was very late, almost eleven, before he carried in a few things in a suitcase and I bolted up the house for the night.

I could not sleep that night. Several times I put on the light to look at the clock, and the last time I remember it was about half past two. Shortly after that I thought I heard a creaking sound from the front stairs, as if someone were coming slowly and stealthily up from the front hall.

I suppose the events of the past few days had strung my nerves nearly to the breaking point. At another time I should probably have assumed that one of the girls had gone down to get a glass of milk, but on this occasion I was convinced that an intruder had managed yet again to enter the house.

Resisting an impulse to bury my head under the covers, I slipped out of bed and, without turning on the light, went to the door of my room. "Is that you, Arthur?" I asked, in a voice meant to carry only to the stairs.

"Yes. Are you all right, Aunt Vi?"

"I suppose so. You gave me a fright just now, coming up the stairs in the dark."

"There's something I want to show you in the basement."

"What is it? Can't it wait until morning?" I felt rather than saw him moving along the stair rail toward me.

"No, it can't. I've found a box of pictures and letters hidden in the furnace."

"In the furnace!"

"You'd better come and see."

"Why don't you put on the lights?"

He switched on a flashlight then, and waited in the hall while I put on my robe and slippers before leading me down the back stairs and through the kitchen. At the basement door he stood aside and let me pass, shining his flash down the stairs instead of switching on the light. As I reached the foot of the stairs, something happened. His flash abruptly went dark, and I no longer heard his step behind me.

"Arthur?" I said sharply. There was no answer.

I wanted to rush back up the stairs and switch on the electric light, but I sensed that someone or something was there crouching motionless on the stairs above me in the dark. Stifling a scream of terror, I retreated into the basement.

Have you ever noticed how familiar places and objects become strange and inimical in the dark? I dashed against laundry tubs that seemed to lean at an angle to their customary position, and furnace pipes reached down silently from between the joists to brush my hair.

"Arthur?" I called again. Suddenly I heard someone near me, behind me. I started to turn but in an instant I felt a strong hand clapped over my mouth, drawing my head up and back against a heaving chest. I clawed and beat frantically at the arm that held me, but in vain. A chilling sensation of despair came over me as unable to cry out, I waited a seeming eternity for the plunge of a knife into my throat. My head swam. I thought I heard hammering overhead, followed by a crash. Lights shone somewhere. I was dragged back into darkness and then, just when my nerves seemed unable to endure more, a fearful explosion burst over me, and I sank back into merciful oblivion.

I awoke many hours later in a hospital room with my head bandaged and a nurse in a starched white uniform and cap reading a book by the window. She looked up as I stirred, and then I dropped off again to sleep.

It was nearly dark when I awoke next, and the first face I saw was Inspector Franklin's. He sat leaning forward in a chair drawn up next to my bed, his elbows on his knees. "How are you feeling, Mrs. Byers?" he asked, with what seemed an excessive degree of solicitude for a police detective.

"My head hurts," I said, in a voice that sounded thick and drunken. "Where is Arthur?"

"Your nephew," he said, setting his teeth for the task, "died a hero's death."

"Arthur is dead?" I tried to sit upright but fell back as though I had been struck.

"Don't distress yourself unduly, Mrs. Byers. Arthur has been dead, as nearly as we can tell, for about a year. We believe he was killed by enemy fire near Verdun. The young man you have been entertaining in your home since September is an impostor named Charles Lawrence Beale."

"But that's impossible! I've known Arthur since he was an infant. There is some mistake."

"Fingerprints never lie, Mrs. Byers. I assure you there is no mistake. I believe it had been about seven years since you'd seen your nephew when Charles Beale came to live with you."

"At least that. My sister lived in Des Moines, and they couldn't afford to travel much."

"There you are, then. Any differences between Arthur Sims and Charles Beale you would put down to your nephew's passage into manhood and his military experience."

"But there *were* no differences! Have you seen photographs of my nephew as a boy?"

"Yes, several, and I agree there is a striking resemblance. Indeed, that seems to have been what induced Beale to change places with Arthur Sims."

"Change places! For what reason?"

"For two reasons. First, because Charles Beale was about to be court-martialed and very likely executed for a crime that needn't concern us. Second, because he knew that Arthur Sims had a wealthy aunt with no children."

"Do you mean to say that this Charles Beale killed Arthur?"

"No. He's admitted killing Alice Weldon and Jessica Frazer, but he steadfastly maintains that Arthur was killed in action. Beale and your nephew went to radio school together. The officers were continually getting them mixed up. They went to the front together, too, and it was there that Arthur learned that both of his parents had died. Somewhere along the way he told Beale about his rich, widowed, childless Aunt Vi and her mahogany wardrobe with a secret compartment full of documents and money."

"Money? There's been no money in it for years."

"It was the documents he was after, to help establish his identity and his claim to your estate after—"

"Go on, say it, inspector. After he'd killed me."

"Beale claims he only got the idea of impersonating Arthur after Arthur was killed. He was in serious trouble with the authorities, and he thought if he weren't killed by a shell he'd probably be shot by a firing squad. Then nearly his whole division was wiped out in a night raid. He switched papers and dogtags with Arthur and—burned Arthur's hands to prevent identification. But the body was never found, and Beale was reported missing in action. Meanwhile he'd taken up Arthur's identity among people who had hardly known Arthur. Later he remembered about you and the compartment in the wardrobe. After his discharge, as Arthur Sims, he got in touch with you. You know the rest."

I lay quite still, trying to take it all in. The inspector fidgeted in his chair and I knew that he wanted a cigarette but wasn't going to allow himself one.

"I never thought Arthur knew how to open that compartment," I said after a time.

"Apparently he didn't. It was several months before Beale found a way to get into the studio at night. He discovered the false window frame when he took down the storm windows just a few days ago. But the first night he slipped into the studio through the window, he couldn't get the compartment open. The second time he took along his bayonet to pry up the lid, unaware that Alice Weldon was sleeping in the room. She awakened and surprised him at his work, and with a soldier's instinct he seized her, dragged her into the yard, and—you know what he did.

"When he found next day that the bayonet was missing, he thought at first that the police had it. As time went on he became convinced we didn't, since he hadn't been arrested or questioned about it. It was the piece of the jigsaw puzzle that I didn't have, remember? Then something that Jessica Frazer said led him to believe that she was a danger to him. She'd seen and heard things, and he believed it was only a matter of time before she deduced his guilt. He even thought she had the bayonet.

"Perhaps if he'd known she'd already gone to the

police he'd have left her alone. But she told no one in the house about that, and so he killed her. He arranged for her to let him into the house that night after midnight, saying he had some new information to discuss with her. That wasn't hard to manage—Beale says she was sweet on him—"

"I'm sure her feelings toward him were purely maternal."

"However that may be, they cost her her life. He tried to get her to talk about her suspicions, but she wouldn't. That convinced him that she suspected him, and he killed her with an injection of cyanide he'd prepared."

"But where did he get it, and the hypodermic syringe?"

"He stole them from a laboratory at the technical college. After killing Jessie he went up and searched her room. Then he attacked the wardrobe, managed to force open the secret compartment, and emptied it. He bolted the doors and made his exit by the false window, thinking that we'd conclude either that Jessica Frazer had died by her own hand, or that the murderer was someone living in the house.

"He got a shock, of course, when he found that bayonet in the secret compartment of the wardrobe. That pointed to you as the greatest danger to his safety, and he altered his program, moving up the date of your death to the present."

"The date of my death," I repeated with a sigh. "It very nearly was, too. Who—rescued me? I seem to remember someone tramping down the basement stairs—"

"It was Dr. Melton's warning that saved you—that and the fact that we found fresh fingerprints on the false window frame belonging to a man who was supposed to have been killed in the war. We put things together pretty quickly after that, and came down with a warrant for Beale's arrest in the middle of the night.

Only he wasn't there. We broke into his place and found a cache of family documents he'd taken from the wardrobe. We never dreamed he was inside the house at that time. But we met the doctor patrolling the alley, very uneasy for your safety, and when we compared notes and he told us 'Arthur' had moved into the house, we didn't waste any time getting in ourselves."

"Then it was you who rescued me?"

His little finger made a beeline for the rim of his ear. "The doctor and a couple of policemen and I."

I put my hand to my throbbing and thickly bandaged head. "What—what happened to me?"

"I'm afraid I must take full credit for that," he said. "When we rushed into the cellar, Beale had that bayonet at your throat. It was no time for talk, and the light was bad—I snatched up a washboard and swung it at him and—"

"And missed."

"Indeed I did not miss. Beale has more than thirty stitches in his scalp. You have only seven."

"Thank you very much." We fell silent after that, as the shadows thickened in the room. A nurse came and took my temperature and pulse, and asked a number of banal questions such as only a nurse could think of. At least she didn't drive my visitor away.

"And so Arthur didn't come back after all," I said thoughtfully. "Probably he wasn't so handy with a rifle or—or a bayonet. It scares you to think what kind of people survive a war, inspector."

"My son," he said, in that deathly quiet voice of his, "is buried in the Ardennes."

"I am so sorry. It's not for us to fix the blame, but one likes to understand. What does it mean, all this killing, and when will it end?"

"God knows, Mrs. Byers," he replied, with something like a shudder. "I don't."

The Plum Point
Ladies

by Henry T. Parry

The hand protruded from the water, the wrist caught
in the yellow nylon line that slanted from the buoy to
a vanishing point in the black sea. Eddie Morse saw
it when he reached with the gaff to snag the line and
leaned over the side for a closer examination. Deciding that its present mooring was sufficiently secure
until he could return with help, he pushed the throttle
forward and headed back through the harbor mouth
toward the town dock, leaving the hand to ride gently
in the swell among the buoys over the lobster ledges.

He found Pursell Small in the one-room police station, the telephone hunched between shoulder and
ear, listening with raised-eyebrow patience to a com-
plaint about outboard-motor noise near a private
dock.

"I found her, Purs."

"Who?"

"You got any other prominent member of the summer colony who's been missing two weeks except Mrs.
Turner?"

"Where?"

"Off Plum Point. There's a body snarled up in the
line of one of my lobster traps. I didn't look close

165

enough to identify her for sure. I figured you'd be the one to pull her out of the water."

"I bet you did, Eddie, I bet you did. Well, let's get on out there. Wait till I get Earl from the filling station to help."

"I'll get the reward, won't I, Purs? Seems I should. I'm the one found her."

"How do I know, Eddie? I suppose so. Mrs. Wright's the one who put up the reward, so I guess she'll decide."

"I'll take you out there in my boat, Purs. And Purs—"

"Yes?"

"You think the town will pay for the gas? All three trips, that is?"

Laura watched him file through the arrivals gate at the island airport, the suitbag containing his one suit slung over his shoulder and in his hand the plastic shopping bag that contained whatever else he remembered would be needed for his visit. It was unlikely that Alex would have been mistaken for any of the other men arriving with him, trim casual men from Boston law firms and austere Philadelphia banks. He was about to pass through a social examination, in an environment as different from his and Laura's September-to-June world at the Music Institute as a prehistoric Abenaki village on the Penobscot. She looked forward to his comments on the ways of the tribe that had been coming to Spruce Island for a hundred summers.

"Was it hot in the city?" she asked, and immediately wished she could withdraw the question. She knew it had been ninety-two degrees, and after waiting weeks to see him she wanted to talk endlessly and not about the weather.

"The big news in Spruce Harbor," she said as she

edged the car into the highway traffic, "is that Mrs. Turner's body has been found."

"Who is Mrs. Turner?"

"She's a member of one of the old families who have been coming to Spruce Harbor since 1890. One grandfather was Vice President and another was one of the biggest vote buyers in Boston. She led a rather quiet life up here, with her friend Marion Blake. She was the president of the Plum Point Ladies Club this year but that was only because it was her turn. She was very fond of clothes and she dressed beautifully."

"I brought you a present but I left it on the plane. It was a Bartok score."

"I appreciate the thought—and considering how little I've played this summer, I appreciate your leaving it on the plane even more."

"Tell me more about Mrs. Turner."

Laura explained that her mother and Mrs. Turner had been children together at Spruce Harbor and that their houses were near each other on Sound Road. The *Harbor Times* reported that Mrs. Turner had excused herself during a picnic of the Plum Point Ladies Club and had not been seen again. Her car was found near the gate to the club property where everyone else had parked. Nothing was learned for two weeks until a lobsterman named Eddie Morse found her body in the sea. In the absence of local relatives, official identification was made by a friend, Mrs. C. Taylor Wright. Mrs. Wright had also offered a reward for information concerning Mrs. Turner's disappearance.

"Didn't anyone at the club see anything?"

"Apparently not," Laura said. "Sit back while I tell you about the ladies who belong."

The Plum Point Ladies Club, she went on, was a state of mind. There was no clubhouse, golf course, or swimming pool. Many years ago Mrs. Turner's grandmother and the other ladies who summered in

Spruce Harbor got together for a yearly picnic. The picnics were always held on Plum Point, a low wooded bluff that jutted into the sea at the harbor's mouth. From these meetings the present club had evolved. At first there was only one requirement: a member must be a summer person who owned property in Spruce Harbor. Residence in the other three villages on the island, Gull Harbor, French Harbor, and Eastworth, was not recognized. Fifty years later another requirement had been added. To become a member, a person must be descended from one of the original Plum Point Ladies. Men might be invited for special picnics—on the Fourth of July, for example—but they were not normally included in the routine get-togethers. One member had purchased the entire point and given it to the club, and a fence was built from water's edge to water's edge, with gates that were kept locked. After years of discussion, a cottage was built on the property.

"The food at the picnics isn't exactly remarkable," Laura said. "Just sandwiches and tea and, of course, clam chowder."

"Ah, ritual consumption of sacred native food to ward off evil spells cast by day-trippers."

"Right," Laura said, and went on. "The only other structure on the property is a decaying summer house out at the edge of the rocks overlooking the sea. It was there long before the Plum Point Ladies organized themselves."

"And there in the long-ago dusks," Alex suggested, "girls in long white dresses and young men in white flannel boaters played mandolins and sang romantic songs. What else do the ladies do in this club except eat together?"

"Nothing."

"I wonder what an anthropologist would make of it. A social organization whose entrance requirements can only be satisfied by one's ancestors and which does nothing but meet occasionally on what has become highly desirable shorefront property and consume clam chowder."

"I suppose we maintain the organization," Laura said, "out of a half-humorous, half-serious sense of obligation to the past and to the people, many of them dearly loved people, who formed that past here in Spruce Harbor."

" 'We?' Are you a member?"

"No, but Mother is."

"When I was twelve," Alex said, "the greatest privilege of my life was to belong to the Rodney Street Rangers. We had a clubhouse over the garage of one of the members. I remember what pleasure it gave me to blackball applicants for memberships. Except one of the kids I voted against caught me alone on the street and gave me a black eye."

"On the way home we're supposed to drop in at a cocktail party the Mrs. Wright I mentioned is giving to mark the beginning of the Founders Day celebration. When I tell you that the celebration isn't going to occur until next year, Spruce Harbor's two hundredth anniversary, it will give you an idea of Mrs. Wright's dedication."

"Who is she anyway?"

"Only the prime mover and shaker-up of the island. She came here at a time when it showed signs of exhausting whatever social credit it had built in the early years of the century. The tourists were closing in, and with them all the establishments that cater to tourists—restaurants decorated with waterfront fakery, cheap bars, plastic motels. She bought the old Palmer place on Sound Road and set to work improving the community. She pushed the adoption of zoning ordinances and fought all the way to the state supreme court to make them stick. She headed a group that

got the waterfront rebuilt to look the way it had a
hundred years ago. She prevented the construction of
a causeway from the mainland to the island. If it had
been built, not even she could have saved Spruce
Harbor.

"If they ever erect a statue to the person who has
done the most for Spruce Harbor, that person should
be Mrs. Wright," Laura said.

"I presume the Plum Point Ladies approach her on
bended knee, bearing offerings of clam chowder."

"She isn't a member because her grandmother
wasn't. Mother says this rankles Mrs. Wright more
than she lets on because she wants so much to belong.
She says Mrs. Wright is always trying to get the heri-
tage rule changed so that she can become a member."

"It defies any reasonable explanation, doesn't it,"
said Alex, "that a competent, powerful leader of the
community like Mrs. Wright should want to belong to
a little group of ladies who meet every now and then
in a little cottage on a fenced-off reservation and eat
clam chowder? Or that the ladies should refuse to
change the rules and keep her out? From what you
say she has done more for the community than all the
ladies put together."

"Oh, she has, but that's just the point. Keeping her
out of their organization is the ladies' way of saying
that even though Mrs. Wright gets things done that
they are too ineffectual or too indifferent to do for
themselves, there are still some aspects of life here
that she can't dominate, some innerness that she can't
invade."

"The Rodney Street Ranger syndrome," Alex said.

They passed a highway sign reading "Spruce Harbor." Fifty feet farther on where a propped-up sign
suggested they "Stop At Paul's," the shoulder of the
road was lined with crates displaying ears of corn, jars
of jelly, crude containers of wild flowers, and plastic

jars of a violent-purple liquid described as Spring Water Grape Drink. The proprietor was a boy in jeans, T-shirt, and a long-billed tan cap, whose eyes had a peering quality as though he were straining to see farther than anyone else was seeing.

"Come look at this," Laura said, stopping the car. "This kid is the island merchant. Last year he specialized in livestock, guinea pigs, hamsters, and, as he called it, a genuine, live, stuffed python. He's a genuine con artist.

"How's business, Paul?" she asked as they stepped out of the car. "Where did you get corn this early in the season?"

"Oh, I get it around. Say," he said, "do you want to buy something special? Look at these."

He tilted a tall can toward them to show three lobsters sprawled on a fibrous mattress of seaweed, and poked them to demonstrate that they were still alive and edible.

"Where did you get them?"

"From my own traps. Me and Chokey—he's my partner but he had to go home and eat—we set some off Plum Point. We're going to put out some more and maybe go into lobstering and give up all this kid stuff."

"How much are you charging for them?"

When he told her, Laura laughed. "That's only about twenty-five cents more each than they would cost in the village."

"How about you, mister?" Paul asked. "Would you like to try a glass of genuine Spring Water Grape Drink? Fresh this afternoon."

"Only if the water came from the fountain of youth," Alex replied.

"Sorry, Paul," Laura said, "we have to push on. I hope you get rid of the lobsters while they're still fresh."

Back in the car Laura told Alex, "Paul is known as Paul the Peddler. He's been selling one thing or another along this road since he was six years old. His grandfather has a chain of supermarkets hundreds of miles long. Apples don't fall far from the tree."

The cars ahead of them slowed down at a point where a man in civilian clothes wearing a policeman's cap separated the traffic between the main stream and those cars that were turning into a private driveway.

"Hi, Laura. How's the musically talented, rich city kid?"

"Fine, Purs, and how's the poor country cop? Making a dollar out of Mrs. Wright's cocktail party?"

"The more dollars, the less poor," he said.

"Is there anything new on the Turner case or are you sworn to official secrecy?" Laura asked.

"Official secrecy, hah! Any time I want to know what's going on on this island I only got to stop at two places. Earl Jenkins' filling station and Mrs. Barnes at the library—though my wife says the Elite Beauty Parlor is better than both. At the filling station they tell me the coroner's report says that Mrs. Turner was dead from a skull fracture before she was put into the water. Sorry, Laura, if you're going to turn into Mrs. Wright's driveway, you better do it. The natives behind you are restless."

"So instead of a missing-persons case," Laura persisted, "what you've got is—"

"Murder, seems like."

The house was wide-windowed, with numerous dormers in steeply pitched roofs that seemed unable to agree on a common level, its shingles faded from brown to streaked grayish tan. Rhododendrons reached to the roof of the deep porch that ran across the front, accentuating the depth and coolness of the house. Set into the base of one of the stone pillars at the foot of the steps was a masonry slab with "Limberlost" carved on it. To the right of the house a wide lawn ran down to a grassy point where a flagpole stood silhouetted against the water. The wide double doors were thrown back, the decibel level of the voices within indicating that the party was well under way.

A young maid with a serious face directed them across the gloomy entrance hall.

" 'My heart leaps up when I behold—' " Alex quoted.

Mrs. Wright greeted them before a tall fieldstone fireplace. Her tanned face bore an expression of impassivity that was augmented by her high-bridged nose and intense dark eyes that looked searchingly at those to whom she addressed herself as though focusing on them her entire strength and assurance. Her clothes, as Laura commented later, were obtained either from a men's tailor who had been requested to make them feminine or from a ladies' tailor who had been asked to make them masculine.

"Laura, how nice to see you." Alex had expected a booming voice to match the woman's powerful presence, but it was instead low and controlled. "I'm sorry you can't serve on the Founders Day committee. We could use some young people." She turned to Alex. "And how nice to meet you," she said with a lesser note of engagement.

"Weighed and found wanting, that's me, kid," he said to Laura as they moved on to the next room.

Laura guided Alex toward a woman who stood in the corner of the room inspecting a print, as though finding the picture more interesting than the people.

"Marion, this is a friend of mine from school, Alex Sartaine. Alex, this is Marion Blake. She is the Henry Moore of Spruce Harbor. When I was fourteen she immortalized my head in bronze. She is one of the reasons I studied music. I spent a lot of summers watching her break rock and I decided that, whatever I was going to be, it wasn't a sculptor." She turned serious. "I haven't been able to express my sympathy to you about what happened to Mrs. Turner," she said to Marion Blake.

The woman was square, with steel-rimmed glasses and the pudding-bowl haircut of a medieval serf. Her eyes were absorbed with some interior question and the expression on her face was both firm and uncertain. She laid a blunt, work-hardened hand on Laura's arm and after a pause in which she seemed to be dispelling a natural reticence said:

"All the talk here about poor Eleanor. I wish I hadn't come but I'm involved in this Founders Day business. I guess you know that I've got an entry in the contest for a suitable memorial. But I'm really in no state, Laura, in no condition to be out on my own."

Her left hand joined her right in its grasp upon Laura's arm as she addressed herself to Alex.

"As Laura knows, Eleanor Turner found me dying, literally dying, in the mental wing of a hospital in the city. I was desperately ill, and not just mentally. I had worked hard at my art for years. I was approaching middle age and had absolutely no recognition for it whatsoever. Eleanor changed all that. She brought me up here with her and nursed me back to health. She gave me a place to work and live and, most of all, she gave me back my confidence in myself and in my capacities."

"What motive would anyone have for killing Mrs. Turner?"

"The motive, in my opinion, was robbery. They didn't say anything about it in the news but Eleanor had stopped off at the bank on the way to that picnic and had taken out several thousand dollars in bearer bonds. That means that anybody who holds them can cash them. She was flying home the next day and was going to give them as a present to her niece's first baby. She went from the bank to the Plum Point Ladies' picnic, directly as far as anyone knows.

"But what I am saying to you, Laura," she went on, "is that I'm convinced they think I had something to do with her death. They will find out that I have a history of mental illness, they will learn that at times I was violent—"

"But you had everything to lose by the death of Mrs. Turner," Laura said. "She was your best friend. You lived in her home. You had nothing to gain."

"Not quite. There's something that nobody but me knows and it's certain to come out.

"I am due to inherit her entire estate."

The next morning, low swift-riding clouds covered the island and a steady gray rain fell.

"Let's go over to Rockhaven on the mainland," Laura suggested. "We can leave the car in the parking lot and take the ferry. There's a maritime museum, a couple of bookstores, some junk shops, and some second-hand stores that are putting on airs and calling themselves thrift shops. And on the pier there's a place called Squeamish's where we can get lobster rolls for lunch."

"Go over that part about lobster rolls again, leaving out the name of the restaurant, and I'm your man. And maybe in the thrift shops I can pick up material for my new article."

"What on?"

"Pre-electronic popular music in the United States between 1890 and 1920. Sheet music for piano is what I'm looking for."

"I know one place you should try," Laura said. "The Try Again Thrift Shop. We'll go there."

As they entered, a bell, activated by the opening of the door, jangled over their heads. A round rosy lady in a flowered smock beamed at them through jewelled glasses. "My, the weather has turned nasty, hasn't it?" she said.

"It has," Alex said and asked if the shop carried turn-of-the-century sheet music.

"We don't get that kind of thing," the woman said. "Mostly we take items that will sell fairly soon. We give the people who bring them in one-third of what we sell them for and the other two-thirds goes to the local hospital. We buy clothes, dishes, furniture— things like that."

As Laura and Alex turned back to the door Alex's elbow swept from the counter a wicker basket which held the outgoing mail awaiting pick-up. He scooped the half dozen envelopes together and replaced them in the basket.

"Look," Laura said, picking up the letter on top. The address read Eleanor Turner, Sound Road, Spruce Harbor, and the return address was that of the thrift shop. She turned to the woman and asked her if she'd read of Mrs. Turner's death.

"Oh, I had no idea it was *that* Mrs. Turner," the woman said. "I never connected the two names when I addressed that envelope. That is a driver's license I found in a handbag that was left with us to sell. When the person who originally brought the bag in came back for her share of the sale money, we forgot to give her the driver's license."

"When was this?"

"About ten or twelve days ago, I should think. It sold quickly because it was an expensive bag. French manufacture. I think we got thirty-five dollars for it. It must have cost two hundred and fifty new."

"Do you know who brought the bag in?"

"No." A guarded note entered the woman's voice.

"You realize, I'm sure," Laura explained, "that you don't have to tell us anything. But a serious crime has been committed and the victim is someone I know. Can you tell us what she looked like? I assume it was a woman who brought it in."

"It was. She had an elaborate hairdo that was beginning to come apart. She was short and heavy-set. Her hair was an unbelievable yellow and she wore a short skirt just above the knees and high white boots that almost dislocated her kneecaps. She said her boss had given her the bag and told her it was left behind by a customer who never came back for it. She said—and I couldn't agree with her more—that every time she carried the bag it made the rest of what she was wearing look crummy, so she figured she might as well get a few dollars for it. My guess is that she's a waitress."

"Did she sound like a local person?"

"Well, I've never seen her before but I'd guess she's from around here all right. She came in and left by the back door. There's a small parking lot in the back that the summer people don't know about but the locals do. She was driving a beat-up foreign car that had a piece of a bumper sticker that said 'Guns Don't—' If it had had out-of-state plates, I think I would have noticed."

"Do you often find things in handbags that you get to sell?"

"It happens all the time. Once we found three hundred dollars tucked under a torn lining. This bag we're talking about now had at least eight or ten compartments so it would be easy for the girl to overlook one of them."

"Do you pay people by check?" Alex asked.

"We usually take their names and addresses and when the items are sold, we mail them a check for their share. But not everybody wants the money sent to their home. In that case we give them a numbered receipt and when they come in again, if the article has been sold, we give them cash."

"Do you remember to whom you *sold* the bag? Maybe if we could recover it—"

"There were two ladies in here from Boston. One of them bought it. I don't see much chance of tracing them, do you?"

After suggesting that the manager mail the license with a letter of explanation to the Spruce Harbor police, Alex and Laura moved on to Squeamish's. At their table by a window they sat looking down through the clear water at the pavement of beer cans on the bottom.

"What do we know?" Alex asked. "Or rather, what don't we know?"

"We don't know if Eleanor Turner left that bag behind her in a restaurant," said Laura. "We don't know if it was lost or stolen before she disappeared. We don't know if she had it with her the day she disappeared. But Marion Blake might know." Laura put her own bag on the floor. "I'll be right back."

Alex watched as she left the table and went to the phone booth on the pier. And we don't know, he thought, who it was that brought the bag into the thrift shop to be sold. But it's highly unlikely that, if the bag is in any way associated with the disappearance and murder of Mrs. Turner, it would have been brought in for sale. More than likely it would have joined the beer cans on the bottom of the harbor.

"Marion Blake checked through Eleanor's things and says the bag is missing," Laura reported. "She doesn't know if she was carrying it the day she disappeared. Marion says Eleanor bought it in Paris about a year ago and used it often. She's certain she didn't lose it in a local restaurant because she never ate in restaurants here. Marion also looked for the driver's license and couldn't find it."

"All we know then," Alex said, "is that the bag was brought to the thrift shop by a woman who might be a waitress, who drives a foreign car that carries a fragment of a gun propaganda sticker and has in-state plates. She is probably a native but is unlikely to live here in Rockhaven or the thrift-shop lady would know her."

"But we can't go up and down the coast looking for her in every restaurant we see," Laura said.

"Where is the biggest concentration of restaurants around here?" Alex asked.

"On the island, definitely. Let me get the telephone directory and we can count them."

The directory listed fifteen restaurants in the island's four communities—two each in Eastworth and Gull Harbor, three in Spruce Harbor, and eight in French Harbor.

"The ferry to the island leaves in five minutes," Laura said. "Should we catch it and check out the restaurants or stay and have lobster rolls?"

The restaurants in Eastworth, Gull Harbor, and Spruce Harbor revealed nothing. Laura drove across the island to French Harbor and parked in the town lot.

"Let's split up the restaurants," Alex suggested, consulting the list. "I'll take Windjammer, Santoro's, Anchor, and Mainsail. Huh, some names. Why don't they call themselves Deep Fat Fry or Fifty Frozen Foods? Or an Indian name which, when translated, means 'Would-You-Folks-Like-to-Wait-in-the-Bar-and-When-You-Have-Spent-Some-Money-There-a-Table-Will-Be-Available'? After we check the cars in their lots, we'll go in and take a look at the waitresses. If they try to seat you, just tell them you're looking for

a friend, a certain James G. Blaine. I'm only trying
to coach you as an innocent city kid, me being a wily
musician full of guile."

"When I stop shaking with laughter I'm going to
suggest that whoever gets back here first should check
the cars here in the lot."

An hour and a half later they met at the car with
nothing to report.

"Nothing in the restaurant parking lots," said
Laura, "and every waitress I looked at resembled the
woman Madame Le Thrift Shop described. And nothing in the town lot here either."

"The restaurants I checked had nothing but fresh-
faced pretty college girls working for the summer. It's
in the eye of the beholder, they say."

What had seemed like a light-hearted digression, an
essay at amateur sleuthing, was revealing itself to require what all detection is based on—patient routine
slogging. In a subdued mood they drove home to
Spruce Harbor.

"What about a place like that?" Alex asked, pointing to a cabinlike structure made of logs of an unreal
irregular plastic perfection. In one window a beer sign
flicked on and off, unsynchronized with the curly neon
that crept along the ridge of the roof, flashing the
name "Down East Bar."

"That's Chucky Logan's place. It's patronized
mostly by locals but some summer people go there to
stare at what they think are real live lobstermen. What
they're really seeing are real live boozers. Pursell
Small tells me that the police get two-thirds of their
business from Chucky's place, winter and summer."

"Would it have cocktail waitresses?"

"I don't know. In the summer they might. I've only
been in the place once and that was when I was in my
teens and was demonstrating how free and indepen-
dent I was. They don't serve much in the way of food.

Let's just check the cars parked there anyway, as long as we're going by."

Laura swung the car into the parking lot and skirted the rear of the pick-up trucks and panel vehicles whose drivers were able to bring their working day to an early conclusion. They found one foreign car of the type they were looking for but it bore out-of-state plates and a sticker authorizing the use of Harvard University parking facilities.

"Let me just take a look around the back," said Laura. "Maybe an employee would park so as to leave the front lot for the use of the customers."

She got out of the car and disappeared around the back of the building. Moments later she reappeared and motioned for Alex to join her. Parked before a rank of garbage cans was a small foreign car, its front end showing rusted dents and its bumper wearing a torn sticker reading "Guns Don't—" Alex wrote the license number down and said:

"This is the point where we should turn this over to your school chum, Pursell Small."

"Maybe so, but let's check inside. Think how patronizing I can be to Purs if we hand him a real hot lead."

At the far end of the bar where it turned at right angles, they saw a short heavy-set woman who waited while the bartender placed drinks on a tray. She wore a black dress of midthigh length, a patch of white apron, and high white boots with tassels at the top. Her face showed an aggrieved dissatisfaction and had the wary, surface-involvement-only look of one who dealt at length with the public and had found it not rewarding. Alex and Laura made their way through the beer-and-tobacco fumes to a dimly lit booth along the wall. They ordered beer and when the waitress had served them Alex asked:

"May we ask you a personal question?"

"In this job, mister, I get a lot of personal questions, but they're all the same one."

"We're trying to trace a handbag that belonged to a friend."

"Did she leave it here? You could ask Chucky if anything's showed up."

"We think it was last seen at the Try Again Thrift Shop in Rockhaven. Do you know the place?"

"Sure I know the place," she answered, her voice quick with resentment and suspicion. "Are you trying to say that maybe I know something about this bag?"

"That foreign car parked in the back. Is that yours?"

"Yeah. So what?"

"The bag we're looking for was left for sale at the thrift shop by someone who drove a car like that."

"There's a million cars like that, mister, so don't go trying to pin anything on me."

"We're not. It's only that you may not know that this bag belonged to somebody who was involved in a serious crime. It belonged to that lady whose body was found off Plum Point. Maybe you heard—"

"Well, don't come snooping around me," she said, "I don't know anything about it. You summer people make me sick. You don't *know* what it's like living up here! You don't know anything! You're a bunch of amateurs!"

She swept off with an unsteady gait, clutching her tray, her boot-top tassels flouncing. Laura and Alex stared at each other.

"She's right," said Alex, revolving his beer glass on the cigarette-scarred surface of the table. "We're playing at detection, knowing the responsibility for solving this belongs to someone else and that we can quit whenever we want. What right do we have to ask people questions?"

"But facts are facts," Laura said, "and they don't

need official discovery to make them so. We did find out that Eleanor Turner's bag was sold."

"That doesn't mean it was connected to her murder," Alex said. "She may have lost the bag weeks before she died."

"And she may have had it with her the day she disappeared."

"But even if this waitress does know something about the bag," Alex said, "she won't tell us—and she probably won't tell the police. And we have put her on her guard for when the police do question her."

"Well, we've done everything we could," said Laura. "Let's get out of this depressing place and go and tell Purs what we've learned—or not learned."

When they returned to the parking lot they found the waitress waiting for them, pacing, her arms folded and shoulders hunched.

"Look," she began, a note of reluctant ingratiation in her voice, "maybe I was too quick in there. I been thinking. Why should I cover for that cheapskate and maybe get the cops on me when I haven't done anything?

"He promised me everything, sure, but when I asked for some money to make up the rent, you know how much he gave me? Six dollars! Six dollars! And a handbag that was found along the road, that fell out of somebody's car! He said I could get something for it, so I took it into that place in Rockhaven and they sold it and gave me twelve dollars. Now you tell me that it belonged to that dead lady.

"Now I hear he's running around with some floozy from French Harbor half his age who thinks she's going to get some of the reward money."

"Reward money?" Laura asked.

"The reward for finding the dead lady. I heard there was a reward."

"Who do you think is going to get it?"

"The guy I'm talking about. Mr. Eddie Tightwad Morse. Beer and hamburgers in some cheesy joint like this, that's what she'll get. He's the one who give me the bag. It's a good thing the bag didn't look like it was ever wet or I'd wonder if Eddie didn't find it in the water when he found the body."

"Did this Eddie Morse act as if he'd come into any sudden money?" Alex asked.

"Him? He could pull up his lobster traps every day and pour diamonds out of them and you'd never know it. His mouth is just like the rest of him. Closed. That guy's still got his first blueberry-picking money.

"And that's all I know about it," she went on. "Look, you look like decent folks that would give a girl a break. Don't tell anybody where you learned what I told you. I don't want to get into any more mess with Eddie. I got enough trouble as it is. Today I heard that Chucky is looking for somebody younger."

The mailbox at the edge of the highway read "E. Morse." In the rutted driveway the tops of the weeds were grease-stained from brushing the engine pans of cars. The trailer-type dwelling rested on columns of gray cinder block and provided shelter beneath for nondescript items of rusting equipment. At the end of the driveway lobster traps were stacked in a neat wall, their precisely coiled lines and straight slatted sides giving an incongruous sense of order.

The man who answered Alex's knock on the aluminum door examined him unhurriedly through the glass, taking a pull from the beer can in his hand and staring at him with veined brown eyes. He pushed the door open a few inches with his beer-can hand. In the dim interior Alex could see the flickering heat lightning of a television set and hear the measured maniacal bursts of sound-track laughter.

"Something you want?"

"Mr. Morse, I wonder if we can talk with you about a handbag that you're supposed to have found?"

"Just a minute, let me turn that set off. No use it being on if nobody's watching."

When he returned he came outside, closing the door behind him, and stood looking at Laura and Alex with tight-lipped resentment.

"Ida Jean's been running off at the mouth about me again. She's a great one for bad-mouthing a guy. You give her a couple of drinks and she can go on all night, especially about her husband. I don't blame the guy for clearing out."

"But did you find that bag?"

"I found a bag. I don't know if it was Mrs. Turner's like you say or whose. I found it down at Plum Point, outside those chain-link gates where they park when they're using the grounds."

"When was this?"

"A Friday. It'll be three weeks this coming Friday, just before dark."

"That would be the day after the Plum Point Ladies had their picnic, the day after Mrs. Turner disappeared," Laura said.

"I had a couple of bags of garbage in the car," Eddie Morse went on, "and I stopped there to heave them into the bushes by the fence. Figured nobody would know, place is so overgrown."

Laura and Alex refrained from exchanging glances. Eddie Morse may or may not have been guilty of murder, but if he were to be convicted of defacing the landscape within Spruce Harbor, the sentence, if left to its citizens, might approach that for a capital crime.

"I saw this handbag lying in with the blueberry bushes at the edge of the parking space. There wasn't anything in it so I figured somebody had stolen it or found it, cleaned it out, and threw it away. So I give it to Ida Jean. I thought she might get a couple of bucks for it because it looked like it might have cost a lot new. I never connected it with Mrs. Turner and I don't see why I should have."

Eddie Morse dipped his head to the beer can and took a long swallow. "And you can tell Pursell Small that I'll tell him all about it, and the state detectives too if they're still around, when I come uptown tonight. Don't see what call you got to come messing in it anyway.

"Seems to me," he called after them, "that if you folks want to get mixed up in this business you might start by seeing when I'm going to get the reward for finding the body!"

"What about Mrs. Turner's car?" Alex asked.

"It was found in the parking area near the gate, where Eddie Morse says he found the bag. Marion Blake came out and drove it home."

"It's possible that the bag could have fallen out of the car when Mrs. Turner got out or when Marion Blake got in."

"But what happened to those bonds? Somebody got them."

"There is that. Rationally, though, it defies probability that one person should independently and by accident discover two separate facts relating to this murder. In the course of getting rid of garbage, Eddie Morse finds the victim's purse. In the course of pulling up his lobster traps, he finds the victim's body."

"Logically, it's possible for both to happen to the same person."

"Another point in his favor," said Alex, "is that he talked to us. He wasn't exactly a fount of information but he could have told us nothing. Why did he talk to us at all?"

"Because he knows he is innocent, that would be

my guess," said Laura. "We're passing the Plum Point property now. That fence is the boundary."

"Let's stop at the parking place and take a look."

The parking area, barely a car length in depth, was a cleared section between the edge of the highway and the dense undergrowth at the base of the fence.

"Show me the blueberry bushes Eddie Morse referred to."

"Most of the growth along the bottom of the fence is blueberry."

Alex left the car and walked through the undergrowth along the fence for fifty yards on either side of the clearing.

"What were you looking for?" Laura asked when he returned.

"Garbage. Why would somebody who could dump garbage a reasonable distance out at sea go to the trouble of driving down here and dumping it on club property?"

"What did you find?"

"When Leif Ericsson or whoever it was who first discovered Spruce Harbor arrived, he couldn't have found it cleaner. I found nothing."

"I'm a coarse type. Instead of the apple tree, the singing, and the gold; give me sun, a bottle of wine, and a pretty girl," Alex said, leaning back against the rocks and turning his face to the sun. "Not in that order, of course."

"Dispensing with the required book of verse and loaf of bread, I see. Well, the first thing people in the arts must learn is to do without."

"Until this moment. Look how lovely it is here. Blue sea, white sails, dark-green shores, old gray rocks to remind you of your mortality."

"It is a beautiful spot. You can see why the Plum Point Ladies let the summer house remain standing.

Not only because of the view but as a reminder of a gentler day."

"It reminds me of the bandstands you sometimes see on the village greens in some old towns."

"They say that at least two generations of Plum Point Ladies have been proposed to in that summer house. Oh, we're going to have a visitor."

An outboard curved in toward the snaggled row of pilings that marked the remains of the old dock and bobbed alongside. A boy leaped out onto the decaying stringers, moored the boat, and picked his way along the dock.

"That's Paul the Peddler," Laura said, and waved for him to join them. "Who's watching the store, Paul?" she asked.

"My partner Chokey. I came out to see if there are any lobsters in our traps and maybe to set a couple more traps."

He pointed offshore where several orange-and-white buoys floated fifty yards off the rocks along with a dozen or so yellow plastic balls. "Oh, thanks, Miss Laura," he said, accepting a sandwich, "and thanks," he added, reaching for the lemonade that Laura held out.

"It won't be as good as Spring Water Grape Drink, but you ought to keep in touch with the competition," said Alex.

"That's right," agreed Paul, "but we don't make as much selling that as we do with the lobsters. So I'm going to put down some more traps. Mom bought a whole bunch of old traps and buoys to use in decorating for a party at the club. Afterwards, me and Chokey brought them out here and stashed them in that summer house there."

"Do you mind if I come up with you and see what it is you use?" Alex asked. "I'm a landlubber and I don't know anything about trapping lobsters."

They climbed the rocks to where the summer house stood between vegetation and rock. The structure was hexagonal, open-sided, its floors resting on masonry columns to which fragments of lattice clung, with elaborate scrimshaw scrolls and fretwork brackets on the posts and railings. Piled on the rickety bench that ran around the inside of the railing were a half-dozen slatted lobster traps, semi-cylinders with concave ends. The buoys, which were designed to float above the ledges where the traps lay, were homemade and bullet-shaped, with short broomstick handles and heavy iron straps bent stirrup-like around the pointed ends. Twenty inches in length, and weighing six or seven pounds, the buoys resembled crudely whittled bullets with potato-masher handles.

"Now if you were doing a paper on how the machine has driven out the folk crafts, these would be an example," said Laura. "They don't use homemade buoys like this anymore because the plastic balls are better. Some even use the plastic containers that cleaning compounds come in. The homemade ones were usually painted for identification and visibility."

"Yeah, we painted ours with orange handles and a white body," said Paul. "But I don't guess that anybody is going to mistake ours for those yellow balls out there. They belong to Mr. Morse. He's a pretty mean guy. We think he cuts our buoys loose."

"You mean that the lobster traps lying out there beneath the yellow buoys belong to Eddie Morse?" Alex asked. He looked speculatively at Paul, and asked:

"Would you take us out there? I'd like to look at some of Eddie Morse's lobster traps."

"Man, that's the worse thing you can do up here," said Paul, "fool around with some guy's traps."

"He's right, Alex," said Laura.

"All right, I'll tell you what. Paul, would you rent us your boat? For five dollars?"

"Well, yes, I guess so, though maybe I ought to get seven-fifty."

"Seven-fifty is a deal. Laura, can you run Paul's boat?"

"Yes, but we better have Paul start the engine. But why?"

"You'll see. Paul, here's your money. You come down and start her up and wait for us. That way, you won't be involved at all."

They climbed down the rocks to the dock where Paul started the engine and cast off the mooring line. Laura eased the boat away from the dock and headed it toward the buoys.

"Stop at that first yellow buoy, or whatever you do in a boat. Heave to or something."

At the first buoy Alex reached with the gaff and snagged the line leading from the buoy to the trap below. He hauled on the line, surprised at the weight of the trap, and slowly brought it up to the gunnel where he balanced it. He picked off streamers of kelp, looked briefly into the trap, and dropped it back into the water.

"Next buoy."

"I hope you know what you're doing."

"Of course I don't know what I'm doing. I just had a thought, that's all."

He pulled up three more traps, one of which held a lobster, examined them, and let them drop back over the side.

"Go to the farthest buoy out and we'll work our way back."

When he had examined the next trap, he swung it inboard and extracted from it a glass jar sealed with a rubber ring and a screw cap. He dried his hands on his shirt, twisted off the cap, and, inserting two fingers into the jar, withdrew a stiff, official-looking document that had ornate numerals printed diagonally across its topmost corners. He handed the paper to Laura.

"This is a five-thousand-dollar Treasury bond!" she said. "But how did you know to look here?"

"Just a minute and I'll explain, but first, just in case Eddie Morse gets out here before we can take the proper steps, let's put the empty jar back in the lobster trap and drop it back where it came from."

"But what made you think of looking into the lobster traps?"

"An association of ideas based on something you said the other day after we had stopped at Paul's roadside stand. You pointed out that Paul's grandfather was the head of a vast mercantile organization and that Paul with his stand showed the truth of the old saying that the apple doesn't fall far from the tree."

"So?"

"Consider Eddie Morse. He found the body. He was in possession of the bag. This bond was in the bag when he found it, or when he took it. Since he can't cash it in for a long time, what would be a better hiding place than a lobster trap, especially one that nobody but Eddie Morse is ever going to haul up off the bottom? If you accept that this bond is the apple, it's likely that Eddie Morse is the tree it wouldn't fall far from. I know it's not rational, but we did find the bond."

"What do you propose we do now?"

"First, we don't say anything to Paul the Peddler. It might occur to him to sell the story to a newspaper. After he leaves, we make our way back across the Plum Point Ladies property to where your car is. Then we look up your chum, Pursell Small, and present him with some hard evidence that makes it look very much as if Eddie Morse is guilty of the murder of Mrs. Turner."

"When I hear it expressed in those words," said Laura, "it makes me wish we had never gone to that thrift shop, that we had nothing to do with this. Up to now we were trying to solve a problem. Now someone is going to get hurt."

"Someone has already been hurt. And, anyway, what alternative do we have, Laura? If no man is an island, surely no man's death is an island."

It was not until the next morning that Laura and Alex were able to track down Pursell Small and present him with their findings. "Let's go down and talk to Eddie before we do anything official," Pursell said.

Eddie appeared at the door of his trailer in answer to Pursell's knock, giving a snort when he saw Laura and Alex.

"I see you brought some Junior G-men, Purs."

"Eddie, I want to talk to you off the record but since I don't know at what point this might get to be official I got to tell you that you don't have to—"

"Yeah, yeah, Purs, I don't need no lawyer. You want to hassle me about that handbag. Like I already told these two-bit sleuths, I found it. I can't help it if I found it, can I? There ain't no law against finding things that I know of."

"Eddie, those lobster traps with the yellow buoys off Plum Point, are they yours?"

"Purs, you know they're mine. What about them?"

Without crediting its discovery by Laura and Alex, Pursell told Eddie about finding the bond.

"You don't know what you're talking about, Purs!" Eddie cried. "Those traps are passed by fifty boats a day! Everybody knows I use yellow buoys—you can't prove that I put the bond there! For all you know, they—" he jerked his head toward Alex and Laura "—planted it there themselves!"

"Look, Eddie, this is worse than finding Mrs. Turner's bag with the bond in it, or even stealing the bag. Here's a guy who finds the victim's body, a guy who admits that he had the victim's bag in his possession but didn't know whose it was. And then a five-thousand-dollar bond the victim was carrying when she disappeared suddenly turns up in this guy's lobster trap. I don't know about you, but if I was on a grand jury and that was all that was presented, I might vote an indictment. For murder, Eddie."

"Now, Purs, I've known you ever since you were born. Your dad and I served in the Navy together. You don't think that I'd be mixed up in anything like murder?"

"Eddie, one of the advantages of knowing somebody all your life is that you get a pretty good idea of what they would and wouldn't do. In your case, I'd say no, you wouldn't have anything to do with murder." He paused. "But if you thought you could make a buck—"

"Look, Purs, I know you want to make a good showing in front of these summer people here, but why don't we let them get back to their yachts or something, and you and I can talk this out like good neighbors. Just the way your dad and I might have talked about it if he was alive."

When Pursell replied, there was no change in his voice nor in his expression, but Laura knew from the slight withdrawing movement of his head that, maybe soon, maybe late, Pursell Small would make Eddie Morse pay for having equated himself with Pursell Small's father.

"Let me point out something that maybe you haven't thought of, Eddie," Pursell went on. "If you admit you did what I think you did, and plead guilty, there won't be any long expensive trial. Now I'm not suggesting plea bargaining—that's up to the district attorney—but if you decide to fight this, then they'll try for an indictment and conviction on what's been turned up so far. If you *are* indicted, which seems likely, and go to trial, you're going to need some awfully high-priced lawyers to get you out of this. Even if they don't get you out of it you'll go to jail a mighty poor man."

Eddie gave them a startled look and walked away from them through the grease-stained grass to the end of the driveway where he stood with his back to them, studying the wall of lobster traps. When he returned he spoke in the aggrieved tone of a man subjected to unreasonable demands.

"All right. All right. I can't afford no high-priced lawyers. Here is how it was."

They listened without interruption and when he had finished Pursell sniffed and uttered a rude word. Indicating by a glance that Laura and Alex were to precede him in their car, he said: "O.K., Eddie, let's get out there right away and make another unofficial visit. But I can tell you right now, I think you're lying."

They heard running footsteps within the house and the door was violently snatched open. Mrs. Wright's maid was panting, her face frightened and her voice tense and trembling with fear.

"Oh, come in, come in, you're just in time! There's a terrible row going on! Miss Blake is here! I think she's crazy!"

As the maid led the way across the entrance hall to the closed door of Mrs. Wright's study, Laura and Alex heard Marion Blake's voice pitched high in hysterical indignation.

"How can you do this? You promised me! You said there was no entry that even approached mine. You told me to turn down that other commission in order to be free for this one!"

Mrs. Wright's reply showed a controlled irritation, the stern but kind parent whose patience is being tested. "Come, Marion, get a grip on yourself, you're losing control."

"It's all very well for you to talk. But I need that commission!"

"Of course, Marion, but there will be other opportunities. And haven't you always been provided for up here?"

"But they're saying you gave the commission to that man from Boston because he's a friend or relative of Eleanor Turner's and she gave a lot of money to your Founders Day fund."

"Nonsense, Marion, he's not a relative of poor Eleanor's nor of anybody else up here. She probably never heard of him. You're nursing an illusion to cover up your disappointment. You're fantasizing. The model you entered in the competition, indeed all your recent work, though admirable in every other respect, was thought by some, not by me mind you, to be somewhat dated whereas his is in a more modern idiom. So the committee decided against you."

"But what you tell the committee to do, they do, everybody knows that. *You're* the Founders Day committee."

"Oh, Marion, come now, that's not true. I have a vote like everyone else. They thought that your concept, and the model you submitted for the memorial, was not in keeping with the times."

"But you must know the work and the pure agony it took for me to come up with my entry. The promises you made to me were what kept me going. Oh, I'd like to hammer and smash until I can be myself again, until I can be clean again!"

"Marion! Put that down!"

Laura threw open the door and they saw Marion Blake leaning across Mrs. Wright's desk, her face contorted and tearstained, in her eyes the fixed gaze of one who is in the grip of committing an act she is fearful of carrying out but is powerless to refrain from. In her hand was a stone she had picked up from Mrs. Wright's desk, a grapefruit-sized piece of granite rolled by countless tides into a nearly perfect sphere. When she saw Laura and Alex she let the stone fall with a crash upon the desk and covered her face with her hands. Laura and the maid guided her to a chair where she sat, clasping and unclasping her hands, her head bowed. A long silence prevailed until finally Mrs. Wright spoke, her voice calm with a certain detachment.

"Your arrival was certainly providential," she said.

"Mrs. Wright, we came out here to tell you a strange story that a man named Eddie Morse is telling. He and Pursell Small are following behind but they must have been delayed. While we're waiting, I could give you the message that Mother gave me to give you at the cocktail party the other day. She asked me to tell you that the Plum Point Ladies felt rather embarrassed about not informing you sooner."

"You needn't be so hesitant about telling me, Laura. The Ladies were going to vote on a change of rules governing admission, primarily so that I could be admitted, which was very handsome of them."

"Mother was delegated by the others to tell you what happened. She finds it a bit awkward at this late—"

"No need to be diplomatic, Laura. The motion to change the rules was defeated eleven to ten, wasn't it? Was that your mother's message to me?" A weary note of exasperation crept into her precise speech.

Alex saw the flash of recognition sweep across Laura's face, to be replaced by a familiar expression, the absorbed watchfulness of a musician counting the beats until it is time for him to resume. Before she could speak, Alex broke in:

"Mrs. Wright, we think you should hear Eddie Morse's story. He's going to face some serious charges and maybe you could clear up some things right now."

"But I don't understand what possible connection I could have with anything this Morse man may be charged with. He's the man who found Eleanor's body, isn't he?"

They heard the slam of two car doors, followed by a knocking at the main door of the house. In a few moments the maid brought Pursell and Eddie Morse into the study and, at a nod from Mrs. Wright, left the room. After Laura had introduced them, Mrs. Wright waved them all toward chairs.

"I am due at a committee meeting in half an hour," she said. "I should appreciate it if you would be brief. Now, how can I help you?"

"O.K., Eddie, give us your story," said Pursell, "again."

Eddie bent forward in his chair, squeezing his wrists between his knees, his eyes fixed on the floor a few inches away from Mrs. Wright's gleaming feet.

"I was in my boat off Plum Point tending to my traps when I saw these two kids climbing down the rocks from that rundown old summer house that sits on the rocks there. They had a couple of lobster traps and buoys that they took out in their outboard and baited and dropped over. It made me kind of mad to see kids, more than likely summer kids, messing with lobsters, so I went over after the kids had gone up harbor and snagged their lines. I cut their buoys loose and tied on my own buoys. Then I got thinking, wait a minute, maybe they got more gear in that old summer house and better I should bust it up right now. So I tied up at that old dock and went up to the summer house and, sure enough, there were three, four more traps and buoys. I figured maybe I could use the traps and had just picked one of them up when I saw this lady coming down that path through the trees. I remembered that this was private and posted land and I didn't want to explain anything to anybody—not that I had done anything wrong."

"Don't get too pure, Eddie," said Pursell. "On you it don't set right. The charge against you isn't likely to be trespassing."

"Well, I didn't want her to see me so I jumped down on the other side of that summer house and crawled underneath. I figured she was just taking a walk and would look around for a couple of minutes and then go. The floor was high enough off the ground so I could sit there behind the latticework without anyone likely to see me. I heard her come up the stone steps and walk across the floor just over my head. She walked back and forth a couple of times and then I guess she sat on the bench that ran around the place, then got up and walked some more. After about maybe five minutes, I heard her call to someone. I heard another person come up the steps and walk across the floor.

"This second person said she didn't see any reason why they had to meet there, that they could just as well have talked over the phone.

"The first lady said that she had had a special reason, that she had wanted the second lady to be the first to know about the plans she had for the club, and that she wanted the second lady to take her back to the picnic where she, the first lady, would tell all the others about her plan now that they had voted to change the rules on getting in and she was already as good as a member.

"The second lady said something about not doing anything yet but the first lady went on saying how in honor of her becoming a member she wanted to tell how she was going to build a regular clubhouse and get rid of that ridiculous little shack they had there now. The second lady said something about how the cottage had worked out O.K. all these years and the first lady stopped her again. This time she seemed to be getting mad.

"But, the second lady said, they hadn't elected her a member yet because they hadn't changed the rules about admission yet.

"The first lady kind of snorted and said something about all she had done for the people up here and that all she had ever asked in return was to belong to a little group of women who had never really done anything, just happened to have grandmothers who summered here. She was getting pretty excited by now and I could hear her walking back and forth. How had they voted, she asked?

"The second lady sounded scared but she said the ladies at the picnic voted by writing yes or no on little squares of paper. She said she took them off to count because it made her nervous to count votes in front of that many people. She said that she had counted the ballots three times and the vote was ten to ten.

"Well, the first lady told her, you were president, why didn't you vote and break the tie?

"I did, the second lady said—I voted against changing the rules.

"The first lady screeched. I heard feet stomping and about half a dozen thuds. It stopped for a second and then, just like the last wave is sometimes the biggest and highest of all, I heard one solid whack, just like an axe hitting wood. Then nothing moved.

"Later I heard footsteps going down the steps. Through the lattice I saw the first lady hurrying back toward that path in the woods. I sat where I was until she was gone and then I crawled out and looked through the railing. The other lady was sitting sort of sideways on the bench and leaning against the railing as if she was looking at something on the ground just below the railing. And while I was looking at her she leaned sideways some more and kind of slid to the floor. Right near her head was one of them home-made buoys. It was easy to see what it had been used for. The lady was dead."

"Why didn't you go for a doctor?" Laura asked.

"Because I got a record, that's why. Purs knows that. Once you got a record the cops try and hang everything on you. I did two years in Thomaston for fencing stolen cars. Those two years taught me one thing: I was never going to be inside again. So I just walked down to the dock, took my boat and went up harbor."

"Now who do you say the first lady was?" asked Pursell.

"Purs, I already told you. It was that lady there."

Mrs. Wright stood motionless, her dark eyes cold and purposeful. So might a French aristocrat, Alex thought, have regarded a hostile peasant witness in the Revolutionary courts.

"That night," Eddie went on, "I was sitting at the bar in Chucky Logan's place having a couple of beers and I got thinking. I got a chance for real money, steady money, because I could put the bite on that lady for the rest of her life. And then I parlayed that into an even better idea. Suppose this second lady didn't turn up for a couple of weeks. There was sure to be a reward. What could be more likely than for me to find her body floating in the harbor, then go collect?

"So I had a lot more drinks that night and just before dawn I took the boat down to Plum Point and took the body out to where I had my traps and secured it to one of the buoys, fixing it so it would stay underwater. I had searched all around that summer house to be sure there wasn't anything left and that's when I found the bag. I took it along in the boat and was going to drown it but it seemed a shame to do that because it looked kind of new and expensive. I threw all the stuff that was in it in the water and that was when I found that bond. I had a screw-cap jar in the boat, so I put the bond in that and pulled up one of my traps and hid the jar there. I thought nobody but me would ever haul up those traps. A couple of days later when Ida Jean was after me for some dough I give the bag to her and told her I found it along the road. I figured she could get maybe a couple of bucks for it in one of them second-hand stores."

"This is nonsense," Mrs. Wright broke in. "If any of this is repeated beyond this room, be assured that my lawyers will file suit. It will cost someone a great deal of money over a considerable period of years."

"But I didn't! I didn't!" Eddie repeated. "I did all that other stuff but I never killed her!"

"Doesn't it come down to the word of someone with the highest standing in the community against the word of someone with a prison record?" Mrs. Wright asked.

"I think Eddie is telling the truth," Laura said, "because one thing he says he overheard ties in. When we first came in here, you said that you knew the motion to change the rules of admission had been defeated by an eleven-to-ten vote. Eddie says he heard Mrs. Turner tell you how the vote came out. My mother was present at the picnic when the voting took place. She said that everybody marked her vote on a scrap of paper and gave it to Mrs. Turner. She took them all outside the cottage to count them. And that was the message I was supposed to convey from my mother but which I forgot. None of the members ever knew the result of the voting. Mrs. Turner never came back."

Mrs. Wright stood with her back to the door, her hands clasped loosely behind her, chin up, lips parted as if waiting for the noise in the committee room to die before beginning her report. Then she whirled, opened the door, slammed it, and turned the key in the lock.

Pursell slowly hoisted himself from his chair and went to the telephone. After dialing and giving instructions he hung up and turned back to them. "Where can she go?" he asked. "This is an island. There's only the ferry and the airport."

He looked at Eddie Morse. "I don't know, Eddie," he said. "You would have been home free if you had been satisfied with what you had. The five-thousand-dollar bond, the reward, and maybe the blackmail payments for the rest of your life. But you blew it all for the sake of ten or fifteen bucks from a thrift shop for that handbag. Ten or fifteen bucks you didn't even collect for yourself.

"Let's go, Eddie," he said. "It looks like pretty soon you're going to have a reunion with your old buddies at Thomaston. But don't worry, the town will pay for the gas this time too."

Laura and Alex drove Marion Blake to Mrs. Turner's house and when Laura had seen that she was taken care of, they returned to the car.

"The shock wave that is going to hit the Plum Point Ladies will go right off the Richter scale," Laura said.

"There *is* a consolation that will occur to them though," Alex said.

"Consolation?"

"Well, justification then. I mean how right they were all along in refusing membership to Mrs. Wright. It's obvious that she just wouldn't do."

"Speaking of consolation, let's take the first step in

putting all this behind us. Let's drive down to the village, get some sandwiches and a bottle of wine, and then go find a rock in the sun somewhere directly above the sea."

"Wonderful," Alex said. "And if you continue to deserve it, I may introduce you to the initiation rites of the Rodney Street Rangers."

"Do you think I could ever be admitted?" she asked, switching on the ignition. "My grandmother wasn't a Rodney Street Ranger."

White Wings

by Elizabeth Goudge

Fairhaven, the little town where Miss Syringa and Miss Gloria lived, was built beside the river where it widened to the sea. It was an old town, whose sons had been sailors for generations, and boats and fish and the weather were, and had always been, the chief preoccupation of the people, gentle and simple, who lived there. The very names of the streets and houses echoed the thoughts of the men and women who tramped up and down on the cobbles and sat behind the geraniums in the narrow windows: Fish Street, Nelson Square, Ship Hill, Trafalgar Place, Harbour View, the Moorings.

The town was built on the side of a hill, and all the streets fell steeply to the harbor, as though in a hurry to see how fast they could get there and look out across the smooth, sun-dappled water to the ever-changing shores across the estuary that were now blue, now green, now lilac-colored, but always beautiful; or to the haze of smoke that hung over the big town to the north, or the bar of white across the river to the south that showed where it met the sea. A good deal of traffic went up and down the river: pleasure steamers, tramp steamers, big yachts belonging to rich people that made their way arrogantly downstream to the sea, and little yachts painted red and blue and green whose white woven wings darted about like those of butterflies, and the houses of the little town were all built very high so that they could look over each other's shoulders at the excitement down below. Flights of steep stone steps led up to the front doors under the curiously carved triangular porches that sat on them like hats, the tiled roofs were weather-stained and irregular, and over the crooked chimneys the smoke was always dancing in the wind from the sea.

The High Street was the glory of the town, containing as it did the church, the Town Hall, the lovely bow-windowed shops, and four public houses. You could buy all the necessaries of life in the shops; fishing rods, soap, sardines, and sunbonnets; and the beer at the Mermaid Inn, the Crab and Lobster, and the Anchor was the purest of the pure. The High Street, like all the other streets, ran downhill, and on each side of it was a pavement raised high above the sloping street, with rails like the rails of a ship to prevent pedestrians falling over into the sea of traffic below. The traffic changed with the centuries, sedan chairs and coaches giving place to dogcarts and victorias, and they in their turn to bicycles and motors, but the high pavements and the old rails remained the same.

Miss Syringa and Miss Gloria had seen a good deal of change in the fifty years that had passed since they and their father, the Admiral, first went to live at Harbour View, the beautiful house at the top of the hill. They had been lovely young girls in those days, though even then rather old fashioned in their ways, and the Admiral had been very fond of them so long as they did not cross him in any way. He had married young, and lost his wife a few years after marriage, so that he had brought up his daughters himself, with the help of a succession of strait-laced governesses, and was proud of the fact. He had been one of those men who consider that a woman should be in everything a man's opposite; he himself had had an adventurous life, allowing himself perfect freedom in all matters of manners and morals, so he had kept Syringa and Gloria shut up in Harbour View as in a box, dressed in white muslin with blue ribbon at the waist, pruned their manners vigorously, and stormed for an hour if they so much as peeped over the geraniums in the parlor window at a man across the way; he whose language had been in his heyday unequaled for its richness and who had had a sweetheart in every port. . . . But he had loved them. . . . He had allowed them unlimited supplies of white muslin with blue ribbon and had showed the door to the various young men who aspired to be their husbands, for no man in his eyes had been worthy of either of them.

But youth is a guest who does not stay long, and death is a restless traveler whose hand knocks at one door after another, sparing none, and Miss Syringa and Miss Gloria were old women when the Admiral died, and as unfitted as they could be to face the world outside the doors of Harbour View and the poverty that drove them into it. For the Admiral had been one of those arrogant men who are unable to think of death in connection with themselves, or of misfortune in connection with their children. Other men died, other men's children had to face not the perfect life that parents dream of for their children but life as it is, yet he had apparently thought that neither death nor life would dare to lay violent hands on him or his. He had lived for the moment only, with his fine yacht upon the river, fine food and drink upon his table, and priceless treasures filling the rooms of his lovely house, and when his debts had been paid there was next to nothing for Miss Syringa and Miss Gloria to live upon.

Mr. Pepper, the old lawyer who had helped the Admiral mismanage his affairs for fifty years, was at a loss as to what to do with Miss Syringa and Miss Gloria. Obviously they could not teach, for anything they had ever known they had now forgotten; nor could they be companions to rich old ladies because there were at the moment no rich old ladies in Fairhaven, and Miss Syringa and Miss Gloria flatly refused to leave their beloved town; nor could they be housekeepers, for economy was the last thing for which the Admiral's wild extravagance had fitted them. Old Mr. Pepper was frankly nonplussed, and Miss Syringa and Miss Gloria, overwhelmed with grief as they were, gave him no help.

It was not only the Admiral's death that had upset them, though of course they missed his cherry oaths and his stamping feet about the house and mourned for him most sincerely, but even more the thought of parting from Harbour View and the treasures that were in it.

If fate had never allowed them to leave their home it had in compensation given them a burning love for it that was almost fanatical. The house itself, with its mellow red brick walls, the bow windows and wide front door and old fashioned garden, seemed to them a paradise, and the treasures that filled it were as dear to them as their children would have been. . . . How was it possible to part from the beautiful Sheraton furniture, the four-poster beds, the Bristol glass, and the Chelsea and Rockingham china that were their very life! Yet old Mr. Pepper assured them that these things must be sold if they were to move to the lodgings that were all he could think of for them if they could not, as obviously they could not, hope for professional work.

"Live in lodgings!" exclaimed Miss Syringa in indignation. "My dear young man, I would sooner keep a shop!" She did not realize any more than did Miss Gloria, that time passes, and old Mr. Pepper, now so bald and withered, was still to her the diffident young man they had patronized so kindly when they first came to Fairhaven. "I would sooner," she iterated, "keep a shop!" Nothing, she felt, could be so lowering to their family as the descent to trade.

"Well," said Miss Gloria, "why not keep a shop?"

The spectacles fell from the noses of Miss Syringa and old Mr. Pepper, and they gazed at her in speechless horror. The three of them were sitting in the beautiful parlor at Harbour View. On the mantelpiece were the charming Chelsea figures of shepherds and shepherdesses, and on a table against the wall were the Rockingham lambs, the little china dogs with blue ribbons round their necks, and the loveliest treasure of all, a slender ship modeled in silver, that had been their mother's, a beautiful thing with silver sails like the wings of a bird. On the walls hung miniatures and watercolors, some of them of value, and every piece of furniture in the room was a work of art. . . . Miss Gloria looked round at all these things, and her great idea began to take form in her mind.

"What I mean," she said, brandishing her knitting needles, "is this. If our lovely things must be sold, why not sell them ourselves? Why not keep what they call an antique shop here in Fairhaven? We get lots of visitors here in the summer, and people on holidays are always in a mood to spend money."

"My dear Gloria," said Miss Syringa, when she could speak, "have you gone mad?"

Old Mr. Pepper, on his hands and knees on the floor retrieving his spectacles from under the sofa, looked up at Miss Gloria with admiration. . . . He had not known she had it in her. . . . She was the younger, and she had always seemed the meeker of the two sisters; a little mouse of a woman with smooth gray hair strained back from a girlish little face, and pale blue eyes blinking in a bewildered way behind her glasses; yet here she was coming out with what was positively a bright idea.

"Gloria," said Miss Syringa, "I am ashamed of you."

Miss Syringa had always seemed to Mr. Pepper a more decided character. She was as fragile and as pink and white as Miss Gloria, and had the same pale blue eyes and smooth gray hair, but she had in addition the Admiral's hooked nose, and the prominence of this feature gave to her countenance a look of force that had always alarmed Mr. Pepper. . . . Quite unnecessarily.

"Why?" said Miss Gloria. "If our darlings must be sold in any case, would it not be best for us to sell them ourselves? We should at least be able to see who bought them and give instruction for their care, and we should lose them only gradually." At this she choked a little, and her blue eyes, fixed on the Rockingham lambs, filled with tears.

Anyone would have thought that the lambs were creatures of flesh and blood who could feel physical pain; and it is possible that Miss Gloria thought they were, for she washed them with her own hands every Monday morning and was always careful to see that the water was not too hot and the soap did not get in their eyes.

"I think," said old Mr. Pepper, "that Miss Gloria has had a very good idea. A very good idea indeed. A little capital will be required, of course, but the sale of the house will bring us that. . . . I congratulate you, Miss Gloria, I do most heartily congratulate you."

Miss Syringa burst into floods of tears but she was nevertheless vanquished. . . . Her nose was quite misleading.

Harbour View was sold, and of what Miss Syringa and Miss Gloria suffered when they saw it pass out of their hands into those of a retired publican it is better not to think. They themselves were established by Mr.

Pepper in a beautiful little house in the High Street, with a charming parlor behind the bow-windowed shop and an airy, raftered bedroom above that was really beautiful. There was a small garden, too, but there was no view of the river and the ships either from the garden or from any of the windows of the house, and Miss Syringa and Miss Gloria pined and withered.

But they nevertheless showed a courage that Mr. Pepper would not have expected of them and threw themselves wholeheartedly into the management of their shop. He was surprised at their energy. He did not know that it was mostly directed toward displaying in the window the things that they cared for least and hiding their special treasures well out of sight. "In case," whispered Miss Gloria to Miss Syringa, "just in case the Unexpected should happen and we should return to Harbour View."

What this Unexpected could be she did not specify. She did not know herself. It was just that something, rose-tinted and lovely and waiting just round the corner, that every normal human being believes in so ardently and lives for with such hope.

So they put the heavy pieces of Sheffield plate in the window, and the rather garish tea service that they had never really cared for, but they put the lovely ruby Bristol glass in the shadows, and as for the Rockingham lambs and the silver ship, they hid them away altogether.

The shop was a success. The beauty of Fairhaven attracted more and more summer visitors as time went by, and not the least of Fairhaven's attractions was the old antique shop filled with genuine treasures and kept by the two charming old ladies in their dove-gray dresses. Outwardly Miss Syringa and Miss Gloria were prosperous, and greatly envied, but inwardly they suf-

fered torment as one by one their treasures left them
and the Unexpected did not happen.

Customers were amused at what they called "the
unbusinesslike methods" of the little old ladies.

"Are you sure you can afford it, dear?" Miss Gloria
said to a girl who held between her fingers the long
chain of amber from the Adriatic that the Admiral
had given Gloria on her twentieth birthday. And the
girl, noting the anxiety in the blue eyes behind the
spectacles and mistaking its reason, laughed and was
all the more eager to possess those strung globes of
clotted sunshine. . . . And Miss Gloria, as she packed
up the amber with trembling fingers, remembered the
line of a poem, "And each tear gleams a drop of
amber." The yellow globes were not drops of sunshine
to her, but the unshed tears of her heart.

"But have you anywhere to put it?" Miss Syringa
said to a young man who had taken a violent fancy to
the Admiral's favorite toy, a small brass telescope that
he had had placed on the table beside him when he
was dying, so that from his bed he could watch the
ships go up and down the estuary. "I wouldn't like
you, just for a passing whim, to burden yourself with
a bulky oddment whose purchase you may afterward
regret."

The young man had been in two minds as to
whether to get the telescope or not, but the little old
lady's apparent concern for his welfare touched him
deeply. Laughing, he plunged his hands in his pockets
and brought up two handfuls of jingling change.

"Be careful of it," Miss Syringa adjured him as she
packed up the telescope. "Do you know some competent woman who would dust it for you? Don't, I im-
plore you, dust it yourself."

Very few visitors came to Fairhaven in the winter,
and this was a source of grievance to the tradespeople,

and to the sailors who owned and let out for hire the little colored yachts with their white woven wings, but to Miss Syringa and Miss Gloria it was a source of happiness. The cold winds swept up from the sea and rattled the ill-fitting windows of their old house, the drafts crept under the doors like knives, and they could not afford really satisfactory fires, but they did not care, for their treasures were safe. . . . The ruby Bristol glass could bloom like roses in the shadows, and no one would see it and pluck it away, the Chelsea shepherds could play their pipes to the Rockingham lambs, and the china dogs could skip and run all round the shop and back again, and the music and the skipping would attract no birds of prey. . . . And as for the silver ship, Miss Syringa actually dared sometimes to bring it out of hiding and put it on the table, so that in the fleeting winter sunshine its sails gleamed white as the wings that danced up and down on the river in the summer.

And then one night the Unexpected happened. It was not at all the sort of thing that Miss Gloria had been expecting, but being the Unexpected it naturally couldn't expect to be. The important moments of life never arrive with a fanfare of trumpets; they slip noiselessly out of the dark and the rain and scratch at the door so softly that their coming is at first neither seen nor heard.

"What was that, Syringa?" said Miss Gloria, as they sat one evening in November before their parlor fire, with their skirts turned back on their knees, their knitting in their hands, and the cat asleep at their feet. They were quite alone because Mrs. Barnes, who "did" for them by day, had gone home.

"What was what, Gloria?" snapped Miss Syringa. . . . Miss Gloria had spoken so suddenly that she had dropped a stitch.

"That knocking," said Miss Gloria.

Miss Syringa listened, but the wind was roaring in the chimney and the rain pattering against the windowpanes, and she could hear nothing.

"There!" said Miss Gloria, raising an apprehensive finger.

There came a lull in the storm, and then Miss Syringa could hear it: a gentle knocking at the street door.

"Now, Gloria, don't get flustered!" said Miss Syringa, dropping a whole bunch of stitches, knocking her spectacles crooked, and kicking the cat. "There is nothing whatever to be alarmed about. . . . Keep calm."

"I am not flustered," said Miss Gloria, and she straightened her sister's spectacles and soothed the cat before walking quietly down the passage to the street door.

But she had hard work not to be flustered when the flickering light from the street lamp revealed the very spirit of the storm standing upon her doorstep. A black cloak streamed in the wind, and a pair of fierce eyes were fixed on her.

"My goodness me!" she exclaimed, and recoiled a few steps backward upon the cat. . . . But only a few steps because Miss Gloria was a courageous woman.

"Excuse me, mum," said the apparition.

She breathed again. This was a man, not a ghost, and Miss Gloria was seldom afraid of natural things, only supernatural, and although a tramp upon one's doorstep is not pleasant, it is in no way unusual.

" 'Ave ye such a thing as a shed or summat out the back where a poor man could spend the night, mum?" inquired the tramp. "Cleaned out, I am, my last bob gone."

A strong aroma of beer filled the little passage, suggesting where it had gone to, and Miss Gloria drew herself up with considerable dignity, her hands severely folded at the waist. "My good man," she said, "the place for you is the workhouse."

"Maybe," said the tramp, "but I'm not fond of the 'ouse. I don't fancy the company I meet there."

There was hint of arrogance in his tone that reminded Miss Gloria of the Admiral. His fierce eyes, too, under their bushy brows, were strongly reminiscent of the Admiral, and his burly broad-shouldered figure. She bent forward and looked at him more attentively. A torn old oilskin cloak covered his ragged clothes and the remnant of an oilskin hat was jammed down on his head. He had a rosy, weather-beaten face with a fringe of gray whiskers and beard round it, and a disarming, toothless grin.

"You are an old sailor," said Miss Gloria, and the warmth in her tone caused the tramp to place one booted foot firmly over the doorstep.

"I am, mum. Sailed the seven seas, I 'ave. But I'm getting on in years, mum, and I can't seem to get another ship."

There was no whining in his tone, but he had placed the other foot over the doorstep and was standing beside Miss Gloria in the passage, hat in hand, before she had realized it.

"We have a little shed at the bottom of the garden. We keep the firewood there."

She had not meant to say this, but to her intense surprise she distinctly heard herself saying it.

"I knew I'd struck lucky, mum," said the old sailor. "When I saw that pretty ship I knew it was an Omen."

"What ship?" asked Miss Gloria.

"That silver ship on the table. . . . When ye shut up shop tonight, mum, ye forgot to lower the blinds. . . . That ship, mum, is the very spit of the one I sailed in when I was a boy. When I saw it I knew it was an Omen right enough."

Deep called to deep. Miss Gloria with her belief in

the Unexpected, and the sailor with is faith in Omens, both belonged to that company of the ever-young-at-heart to whom life at its grayest still holds the promise of a fairy tale.

"Come this way," said Miss Gloria.

"Thank ye, mum," said the sailor simply. "My name's 'Erbert Jenks."

But on their way down the passage they encountered Miss Syringa, issuing all of a twitter from the parlor.

"Gloria!" she gasped. "What on earth are you doing?"

"This is Jenks," said Miss Gloria. "He is spending the night in our woodshed. Just move, dear, will you, so that we can get by?"

Miss Syringa felt a little faint and groped with her hand for the wall behind her. "But didn't he see the notice on the door, 'No hawkers, no circulars'?" she whispered.

"Jenks," said Miss Gloria, "is neither a hawker nor a circular. He is an old sailor. Just step aside, dear. That's right. While we're gone, you might be looking for the frying pan, and there are rashers in the larder. Jenks would like a bite of supper, I dare say."

She was gone, Jenks following her, and Miss Syringa was left clinging speechlessly to the door handle.

Herbert Jenks had always known a good thing when he saw it, and by next morning he knew that the woodshed was a good thing. He decided that what the old ladies needed was a handyman about the place. It took him five minutes to get Miss Gloria to see eye to eye with him, two days to get Miss Syringa to give in against her better judgment, and five days to convince Mrs. Barnes, the daily woman, that it was not a scrap of use her arguing any longer and she might as well keep her mouth shut, but by the end of the week they were all four in at least outward agreement. With an oil stove, a scrap of carpet, and some old rugs, together with a few oddments culled from neighboring dustbins, he had the woodshed shipshape in no time and dug himself in as though he meant to stay forever. . . . And indeed Miss Gloria hoped he would, for he was incredibly useful. . . . He scrubbed the floors, cleaned the windows, ran errands, looked after the garden, and did all the thousand and one odd jobs that, added to the daily routine work of the house, seem to a woman just the last straw. He was hardworking, good tempered, sober more often than not, and Miss Gloria vowed that he was honest.

But Miss Syringa had her suspicions, founded on his passionate affection for the silver ship.

"He knows it to be a thing of value," she said one day to Miss Gloria. "Believe me, Gloria, I came into the shop this morning, when Jenks should have been polishing the floor, and there he was standing beside the ship stroking its sails with his finger." She shut her mouth with a snap and re-perched her glasses on her aquiline nose with some severity.

"Ah, dear Jenks!" said Miss Gloria, and a sweet mist of affection obscured her sight for a moment. "He loves that ship, dear, because it reminds him of a ship of his boyhood, and because it was the Omen that led him to this quiet haven of peace."

"Pooh!" said Miss Syringa.

All through that cold and stormy winter Jenks seemed utterly contented, thankful for a roof over his head and good food in his stomach, but when the spring came he seemed to get restless. He showed an increasing tendency to leave his work undone and slip off down to the harbor, where he would sit in the sun on the harbor wall smoking his old clay pipe, watching the ships go up and down and talking to the old ferryman and to all and sundry who were wise in the ways of the sea. Finally he spent so much time absenting himself from his labors that Miss Gloria was obliged to waylay him in the garden and remonstrate with him.

He was penitent as a chidden child. "Ye're right, mum," he declared. "I've been a proper waster lately, so I 'ave. . . . The fact is mum, I'm 'ungering for the sea."

"Ah!" said Miss Gloria with deep sympathy. "I thought that was it, Jenks." Then she swallowed hard and made a suggestion of the utmost nobility. "Should you hear of any other employment, Jenks, something of a seafaring nature more suited to your tastes, you must not hesitate to leave us."

"I couldn't get a ship now, mum, not at my age, but if I was to save a bit of money—" He paused and spat ruminatively; the one thing that Miss Gloria disliked was his habit of spitting; but she could not bring herself to ask him not to. It was such an indelicate thing to have to mention, and there was no doubt that the habit helped him to formulate his thoughts.

"Yes?" she encouraged.

"I could buy part share in a fishing boat, mum. I come from Yarmouth way, and there's many an old pal up there would be glad to take me into partnership if I 'ad a bit of money." He paused, straightened himself, and smiled his engaging toothless smile. "But there ye are, mum, I 'aven't, and ain't likely to. And I'm grateful to ye, mum, for your kindness, and ye won't find me neglecting me work in future."

Miss Gloria beamed on him and went indoors to arrange with Miss Syringa about the raising of his wages. . . . But she did not repeat their conversation.

Summer came, and the visitors returned. The last beloved treasures filled the shop window, while the Rockingham lambs retired back again into the dark corners and the silver ship was hidden away under a soup tureen.

The behavior of Jenks was once more exemplary, and even the heart of Miss Syringa warmed to him at last; indeed it was to Jenks that she ran in distress when she discovered that the George the First teapot had disappeared. Miss Gloria was out, and she rushed down the garden to him all of a twitter, with her spectacles awry on her Roman nose and her pretty little mouth pouting in childish distress.

" 'Oo's bin in the shop, mum?" demanded Jenks at once, flinging down his spade and spitting vigorously upon his hands as though ready instantly to wring the neck of the thief.

"A party of tourists," twittered Miss Syringa.

"Did ye leave 'em alone there?" demanded Jenks.

"Yes," cried poor Miss Syringa. "But only for a moment, Jenks, while I fetched my spectacles."

"Ah!" said Jenks, and there was so much kindly rebuke in his tone that tears sprang to Miss Syringa's eyes.

"Only for a moment, Jenks," she pleaded, "and you know I can't see the price tickets without my glasses."

"And the teapot was there when ye left the shop?" asked Jenks.

"Yes—no—at least—yes, I'm sure it was," stammered Miss Syringa. The reproach in Jenks's eyes quite unnerved her, and she couldn't really feel sure of anything.

"I'll go for Barnes," said Jenks, and went off at the double.

Barnes was the husband of Mrs. Barnes and the very largest of the Fairhaven policemen. There were not many policemen in Fairhaven, because it was such a law-abiding place, and Barnes was bigger than all the rest of them put together.

Barnes came at once, even though it was his dinner

hour and he had taken no more than three mouthfuls of beefsteak pudding and one draft of stout, indeed he came so fast that the High Street rocked beneath his tread. . . . Like everyone else in Fairhaven he was very fond of the old ladies.

He stood in the shop, with his head touching the ceiling and his elbows all but touching the walls on either side, and took copious notes in his notebook while Miss Syringa and Miss Gloria (who had now returned) stood by answering questions and ready to move their treasures quickly out of the way of his feet if he made a movement. He took endless trouble over his notes, sucking his stumpy pencil loudly and enthusiastically between each entry and breathing stertorously through his nose, indeed he took so long over them that, by the time he had finished, the charabanc that had brought the tourists to Fairhaven was thirty miles away in no one knew which direction. . . . So the George the First teapot was not recovered.

A week later an old snuffbox was missing, but it was not until a month had gone by that the silver ship disappeared.

It was as though there had been a death in the family. Miss Syringa cried till her Roman nose was scarlet and she could scarcely see out of her eyes, but Miss Gloria did not cry at all. "Its wings were white when the sun shone on them," was all she said, but she aged ten years in a night.

The old ladies were too stricken to take steps, and it was Mrs. Barnes who told Barnes of the bereavement. . . . He whistled. . . . There had been several other losses in Fairhaven lately; Major Stone had missed a valuable shooting stick, left by him for only one moment outside his front door, and General Grey's gold cigarette case, lost by him while fishing at the harbor, was not returned to the police station in answer to the "Reward" notice posted outside; people

began to pass remarks about the corpulency and ineffi-
ciency of the Fairhaven police and Barnes's blood was
up.

The next day, when Jenks was out on an errand and
Miss Syringa and Miss Gloria were busy in the shop,
Barnes spent a considerable time prowling about at
the back of the house.

And the next day was early closing day. When the
shop was shut, Jenks went off as usual to spend his
afternoon fishing at the harbor and Miss Syringa and
Miss Gloria went upstairs to array themselves in their
best to drink tea with the rector's wife. The folds of
their shabby gray dresses were just shaken out and
adjusted and their cameo brooches pinned in the lace
under their chins, when Mrs. Barnes knocked at the
door.

"You're wanted at the station, m'm," she said
through the keyhole.

"The police station?" gasped Miss Syringa and Miss
Gloria.

"Yes, m'm. At once, m'm. You'll find Barnes
there."

Barnes was there, seated behind a table and swollen
by satisfaction to twice his usual size, and beside him,
in the grip of the second-largest Fairhaven policeman,
stood Jenks. . . . On the table before Barnes was the
silver ship.

A wave of faintness swept over Miss Syringa; she
sank to a chair and fumbled in her reticule for her
smelling salts. But Miss Gloria remained in a vertical
position, and her gaze met the gaze of Jenks. . . . No
eyes had ever looked at her as his were doing except
the eyes of a lost dog she had once encountered in
the High Street.

"Now, m'm," said Barnes, perching his pince-nez
on his nose and wetting his forefinger preparatory to
turning over the leaves of his notebook. "I want you

to identify this 'ere ship as your property. Just a matter of routine."

Once again the eyes of Miss Gloria and Jenks met, and the bond that was between them, that bond that links the ever-young-at-heart to whom life never ceases to be magical, tightened and held.

"What a pretty ship!" said Miss Gloria.

"Yes, m'm," said Barnes with some impatience. "Just identify it as your property, m'm, if you please."

"That is not my ship," said Miss Gloria.

Miss Syringa choked, tried to speak, and could not.

"Not your ship, m'm?" bellowed Barnes in sudden ire.

"No," said Miss Gloria.

"No?" roared Barnes.

"No," said Miss Gloria. "It is Jenks's own ship. I gave it to him."

But Miss Gloria did no good by that first lie of her life, for the general's cigarette case had not yet left the keeping of Jenks, and in his contrition and his misery he confessed to the George the First teapot, the snuffbox, and the shooting stick. . . . He was tried, sentenced, and imprisoned. . . . But he sent back the silver ship to the old ladies with the request that they would keep it for him.

"The cheek!" said Miss Syringa through a tempest of tears. "The appalling cheek!"

"No," said Miss Gloria gently. "It just means that one day he will come back."

"He won't dare to come back!" stormed Miss Syringa.

"I hope so," said Miss Gloria, and she carried the silver ship upstairs and put it away in her long drawer under her best gray dress.

But Jenks did not come back. When the term of his imprisonment was over Miss Gloria expected him, but he did not come. Time passed, and the treasures in the shop slipped away one by one, taking each of them a little of the old ladies' vitality with them. . . . For they never ceased to love their possessions as their children, and they never ceased to ache and pine for the house on the hill.

It had fallen now into the hands of people who seemed not to care for it at all. The beautiful garden was a mass of weeds, the paint cracked and dim, and many of the old rose-red tiles on the roof had slipped out of place. Miss Syringa never went to look at Harbour View now. . . . She could not bear to. . . . But Miss Gloria went often, moved by the instinct that makes one hang the portrait of someone dead upon the wall, the instinct of courage that places a sorrow where it can be faced and faced again, till the continual recognition of it breeds more courage.

She was returning from one of these visits on a summer evening. The sun had slipped away behind the distant hills but had left behind him a glory of soft molten gold that poured over the world like a benediction; a light less pitiless than that of the full sun, a kindly light that drew a veil over ugly details in street corners and revealed the beauty of old roofs against the sky and fishing boats sharp and black on the shining water. Miss Gloria paused in the High Street, just on the brow of the hill where she could see a bit of the estuary between the tumbling roofs of the houses above the harbor, a patch of water that shone like a sheet of gold hung between one roof and another. As she watched a little sailing ship drifted across it, making for home, its white sails seeming to her fancy to droop a little like those of a tired bird.

Miss Gloria turned away with a sigh and suddenly found herself staring at a glaring poster stuck up outside Brown's, the stationer's. "Sensational Surprise. White Wings Wins the Derby." Miss Gloria never looked at posters, for she thought them vulgar, and it is unlikely that she would have noticed this one had she not just been watching those other white wings crossing the golden sea, and even now she thought little of it.

"Dear me," she thought, "that will mean fortunes lost and won. How wicked this betting is. Dear me." And she went home.

Yet as she and Miss Syringa were eating their supper of bread and milk, with a few stewed prunes to follow, she said to Miss Syringa, "White Wings has won the Derby, dear."

"My dear Gloria," said Miss Syringa, "What's that to us? Betting is very wicked."

"Yes, dear," said Miss Gloria. "The sugar, dear, if you please."

That radiant summer was succeeded by a winter of bitter cold, and everything seemed to get too much for Miss Syringa and Miss Gloria. Their little house was damp, and they suffered from rheumatics. Then the shop was not going too well, for their stock was getting low and they had to buy to replenish it. Poverty pinched them hard, and they had to deny themselves the little comforts that meant so much to them. Miss Syringa cried incessantly, and her Roman nose became permanently red and her shoulders bowed. Miss Gloria remained the same, except for a slight deepening of the shadows under her eyes and a whitening of her hair, but then, said Miss Syringa petulantly, Gloria did not feel things as she did. Miss Gloria smiled at Miss Syringa's petulance and was glad that what she felt inside did not show outside; that had always been one of her objects in life; to have perfect control of the front she presented to the world.

But she had black moments in the middle of the night when she wondered for how much longer they would be able to carry on. She felt sometimes that ruin and decay were creeping upon them, as they were creeping over the house on the hill.

For Harbour View had been for sale for a long time now and no one seemed to want to buy it. It was old fashioned, of course, with inconvenient kitchen regions and no hot water laid on upstairs, and it fronted straight on the street, but even then Miss Gloria could not understand how anyone could resist the appeal of its old red roof and gracious bay windows and view of harbor and estuary.

Almost every day now she crept up to the old house and mourned over it; laying her hand upon the cracked front door as though in consolation and peering in through the dirty windowpanes at the empty parlor beyond. In her imagination she furnished it with the treasures that were now gone, the chairs and pictures and china, and saw herself and Miss Syringa sitting there as they used to do, dressed in lavender silk and pouring out tea from the George the First teapot that Jenks had stolen.

"Ah, Jenks!" thought Miss Gloria one shadowy evening, as she turned sadly away from the parlor window. "He has never come back. I fear I was mistaken in him."

The evening was so still that her sigh was audible and she herself, in her gray cloak, looked like a visible sigh, a small regretful ghost flitting in the shadows. She turned back for a last look through the window and then stole away, with many a backward glance of love and compassion. All that she felt about the house would have been perfectly obvious to any watcher.

And that particular night there was a watcher, a burly broad-shouldered man who had come up to look at the view and who stood just behind the bushes at the corner of the street. He was dressed in a loud check suit a size too large for him and a bowler hat two sizes too small; the costume of a poor man who has come into money and who regards his clothes objectively, as possessions that would give him just as much pleasure under a glass case as upon his back, rather than subjectively in relation to himself. . . . He regarded Miss Gloria with fixed attention all the time she was there, and when she was gone he stood for a long time lost in thought, chewing the cud. It was quite dark when at last he came to, spat, and went down the hill for a drink at the Crab and Lobster.

It was not long after, on a night of wind and rain, that old Mr. Pepper came cantering up the High Street in his old fashioned ulster, with his scarlet muffler knotted around his throat and his large green carriage umbrella erected over his head; upon which, most incongruously, he wore his Sunday top hat. It was obvious that old Mr. Pepper was under the influence of strong excitement, for one end of his muffler trailed upon the ground and the wearing of his top hat upon a weekday, together with carpet slippers upon his feet on a wet night, was unlike Mr. Pepper. And the way that he flung himself upon the street door of the antique shop, thumping on it with his fists and kicking it with his carpet slippers, was also unlike him.

"My dear Mr. Pepper!" exclaimed Miss Gloria when she opened the door. "My dear young man!"

She stared in astonishment. Was Mr. Pepper drunk? Of course she knew this failing was sometimes to be met with in high-spirited young men, and she hoped she was a tolerant woman, but all the same. . . . She recoiled a little, and her legs shook beneath her.

Mr. Pepper pranced by her without a word, shedding his outer garments as he went, and disappeared into the parlor, his arrival being greeted by Miss Syringa with a small scream. Miss Gloria followed, having first picked up the discarded ulster, top hat, and scarf and hung them up on the pegs in the passage, for even in moments of dismay Miss Gloria had a tidy mind.

Back in the parlor she discovered that though Mr. Pepper had undoubtedly been celebrating some happy event with several glasses of his priceless old brandy, he was not so much drunk as wildly excited.

"My dear girls!" shouted Mr. Pepper, using a familiarity of address he had never yet presumed upon in all the years of their acquaintance. "My dear girls, you have been left a fortune!"

Miss Syringa and Miss Gloria were incapable of speech, and Mr. Pepper flung himself into a chair, dragged toward him the little table upon which Miss Syringa had placed her knitting, spilled the knitting upon the floor, pulled out a bundle of papers from his pocket, and cast them before him on the table as though they were the entire contents of the Bank of England, and he Sir Montague Norman himself in an expansive mood.

"Scarcely a fortune, perhaps," he amended at the top of his voice. "But documents regarding the purchase of Harbour View, making it yours for life, and a nice fat annuity for the two of you!"

He brought both his hands down upon the documents with such a crash that the two old ladies leaped in their seats.

"Best bit of news I've had for many a day," boomed Mr. Pepper. "Congratulate you, my dear girls, congratulate you!" and jumping up he wrung the old ladies by the hand.

"But who? What?" gasped Miss Gloria, while Miss Syringa felt in her reticule for her smelling salts and swayed upon her chair.

"Here you are," said Mr. Pepper. "If you don't believe me, look for yourselves," and taking up a handful of papers in each hand he cast them upon their laps.

Neither of the old ladies had ever at any time been able to make head or tail of a document, and they could not do so now, but holding the papers in their shaking hands, and staring at them with blurred sight, they noticed that they had seals to them and were written in the beautiful clear writing that always seems to mock at the ambiguity of legal phrasing. . . . They were real things, not figments of the imagination.

"But who?" gasped Miss Gloria again.

"A friend," said Mr. Pepper. "Just a friend who wishes to remain anonymous for the present." And he took a large pinch of snuff to clear his head and sneezed triumphantly and gloriously.

Miss Syringa and Miss Gloria had no very clear idea as to how the rest of the evening passed. They signed their names on the documents where Mr. Pepper's pointing finger directed, and at his suggestion they opened the very last bottle of the Admiral's claret and joined him in just a thimbleful each, drunk out of three ruby Bristol glasses, all that was left now out of the set of a dozen. At least Miss Syringa and Miss Gloria drank just a thimbleful each, but Mr. Pepper obligingly finished the bottle. . . . "By way of celebration, dear girls. . . ." And so happy was he that the tears stood in his eyes.

But the evening was over at last, and the old ladies found themselves in bed, lying with their nightcapped heads upon the pillows and their eyes staring into the dark.

"It can't be true," murmured Miss Syringa.

"It is quite true," said Miss Gloria. Now that she had really taken in what had happened, she found that she was not in the least surprised. She had always expected the Unexpected to happen. In her very darkest hour she had never lost her belief that in the drab weave of life there runs a gold thread of fairy-tale magic. You may see it or you may not see it, but it is there.

"We still have three of the Bristol glasses," said Miss Syringa out of the darkness.

"And the Rockingham lambs," said Miss Gloria.

"And one of the Chelsea figures," said Miss Syringa. "The one with the pansies on her petticoat."

"And the silver ship," said Miss Gloria softly.

"But who is this friend?" asked Miss Syringa for the hundredth time.

"I don't know, dear," said Miss Gloria.

But here she told her second lie, for she knew quite well.

"Ye see, mum," said Jenks, "when I saw there was an 'orse running called White Wings I 'ad to back it. . . . It was an Omen. . . . I remembered the white wings bobbing on the estuary, mum, an' the white wings of your pretty ship. I put my last bob on the 'orse."

The spring sunshine was pouring in through the bow window and flooding the parlor at Harbour View. The room had been repainted and papered, and if it was more sparsely furnished than in the old days, there was not a thing in it, from the Rockingham lambs on the mantelpiece to the silver ship on the table by the window, that was not beautiful.

And Miss Syringa and Miss Gloria, in new lavender silk, looked beautiful too, for their happiness illumined them with a radiance that was almost wonderful. Mr. Herbert Jenks, who was drinking tea with them, could perhaps hardly be described as a beautiful figure, but in his loud check suit, with a bunch of primroses in his buttonhole and a large green handkerchief tucked under his gray fringe of beard to protect his mustard-colored waistcoat, he was nevertheless a sight to gladden the eyes. . . . In himself he had not changed at all; he was just as he used to be, sturdy and strong and cheery, with his eyes under their bushy brows so like the Admiral's and his heart as young as ever it was. There would have been no shadow upon the old ladies' joy had it not been that they appeared to owe their prosperity to the evil of betting.

"But Jenks," quavered Miss Syringa, "betting is very wicked"

"Yes, mum," said Jenks, pouring his tea into his saucer and absorbing it loudly and happily. "And now that I've made my little pile I aint' goin' to 'ave no more to do with it."

"That's right, Jenks," said Miss Gloria approvingly. "Take another piece of plum cake and tell us all about it."

"When I come out of quod, mum," said Jenks, "I 'ad a bad time."

"Dear! Dear!" sighed the old ladies.

"I 'ad to take to the road again, mum, I 'ad indeed, an' I'd be there now but for a bit of luck I 'ad."

"Luck?" queried the old ladies.

"Yes, mum. A picnic party was 'aving a bit of a beano beside the road, someone's birthday I shouldn't wonder, with bottles of beer to celebrate it, an' when they went off in their car I just 'ad a look to see if they'd left any fags be'ind, an' there, mum, lying in the bracken as modest as you please, was a fine gold-mounted leather case with ten quid in it."

"Quid?" queried Miss Syringa.

"Yes, mum. Ten pounds. That was the beginning of my luck, mum."

"But Jenks," said Miss Gloria in horror, "you should have taken the case to the police station."

"There weren't no police station, mum, not within ten miles."

"Then, Jenks, you should have left the case where it was."

"I did, mum," said Jenks indignantly. "I'm not the man to steal a gold-mounted leather case. I've turned over a new leaf, I 'ave, since I came out of quod."

"But—" said Miss Gloria, bewildered.

"But I didn't leave the ten quid in the case, mum," said Jenks, and lowered his eyes modestly as he took a large bit of plum cake.

"Yes, mum," he went on, since the old ladies seemed incapable of speech. "And so I took to putting a bit on an 'orse 'ere an' there, an' it was wonderful 'ow the money came rolling in. There seemed, mum," said Jenks solemnly, "a blessing on all I did."

The old ladies shook their heads in some distress of spirit, but Jenks went imperturbably on.

"An' when I saw White Wings was runnin' in the Derby, I put the 'ole blinkin' lot on 'im, even though 'e weren't the favorite, not by any means. . . . It was an Omen, mum."

"Yes?" queried Miss Syringa faintly.

"An' after that, mum, I went on winning steady. I 'ad my losses now an' again, o'course, but they weren't nothin' to what I gained. I vowed to meself, mum, that I wouldn't leave off till I'd got enough cash to—to—" He paused and his eyes met those of Miss Gloria. "To show ye, mum, as I wouldn't never forget that lie ye told for me at the police station."

His voice turned suddenly husky, and whipping his green handkerchief from his mustard-colored waistcoat he blew a trumpet blast upon his nose to hide his emotion. . . . But over the top of the handkerchief his eyes again met Miss Gloria's and he tipped her the suspicion of a wink. . . . And she smiled back, for she was not offended; how should she be when there was between them that bond that links the ever-young-at-heart to whom life never ceases to be magical?

"But I do hope, Jenks," broke in Miss Syringa

somewhat severely, "that your—er—theiving—is a thing of the past?"

"Yes, mum," said Jenks. "I've seen the error of my ways. I'm going back to Yarmouth way, where I come from. I've purchased a share in as smart a little fishing boat as ye ever saw, mum. Part owner of 'er I am."

"That's right, Jenks," said Miss Gloria. "That's what you always wanted."

"Yes, mum," said Jenks. "And now it's to be 'oped I'll keep straight. . . . I always did say, mum, that there ain't no difficulty in it once ye get what you want."

When he had gone, the old ladies sat for some time in silence, partly rapturous, partly uneasy.

"It seems to me, Gloria," said Miss Syringa at last, "that we are living upon the wages of sin."

Miss Gloria glanced round her at the lovely sun-lit room, at the bright wood fire in the grate, at the soft folds of lavender silk that billowed round the leisured, rested bodies of herself and her sister Syringa, at the Rockingham lambs prancing on the mantelpiece and the precious silver ship sailing before a fair wind, and her mouth curved in a roguish smile.

"Yes, dear," she said. "But never mind."

Sanctuary

by Agatha Christie

The vicar's wife came round the corner of the vicarage with her arms full of chrysanthemums. A good deal of rich garden soil was attached to her strong brogue shoes and a few fragments of earth were adhering to her nose, but of that latter fact she was perfectly unconscious.

She had a slight struggle opening the vicarage gate which hung, rustily, half off its hinges. Some of the chrysanthemums fell to the ground. Mrs. Harmon bent to retrieve them with an ejaculation which was not quite in keeping with vicarage standards. A puff of wind caught at her battered felt hat, causing it to sit even more rakishly than it had before. "Bother!" said Bunch, toning down her language.

Christened by her optimistic parents "Diana," Mrs. Harmon had become "Bunch" at an early age for somewhat obvious reasons, and the name had stuck to her ever since. Retrieving the chrysanthemums, she made her way through the lich-gate to the churchyard, and so into the church.

"Br-r-r-rh!" said Bunch. "I'd better get on with this quickly. I don't want to die of cold."

With the quickness born of practice she collected vases, water, flower holders. I wish we had lilies, she thought. I get so tired of these scraggy chrysanthemums.

Her nimble fingers arranged the blooms in their holders. There was nothing particularly original or artistic about the decorations, for Bunch Harmon herself was neither original nor artistic, but it was a homely and pleasant arrangement. Carrying the vases carefully, Bunch stepped up the aisle and made her way toward the altar.

As she did so, the sun came out. It shone through the east window of crude, colored glass, mostly blue and red—the gift of a wealthy Victorian churchgoer. The effect was almost startling in its sudden Oriental opulence. Like jewels, thought Bunch. Suddenly she stopped, staring ahead of her.

On the chancel steps was a huddled dark form.

Carefully putting down the flowers, Bunch went up to it and bent over it. Just for a moment she thought it might be an old coat or a bundle of clothes, but she now saw that her first impression had been correct.

It was a man lying there, huddled over on himself.

Bunch knelt down by him and slowly, carefully, turned him over. For a moment she had thought that he was dead, but she realized now that he was still alive. Her fingers went to his pulse—a pulse so feeble and fluttering that it told its own story, as did the almost greenish pallor of his face.

There was no doubt that the man was dying.

He was about forty-five, dressed in a dark shabby suit. She laid down the limp hand she had picked up and looked at his other hand. This was clenched like a fist on his breast, the fingers closed over what seemed to be a large wad or handkerchief. All round the clenched hand there were splashes of a brown fluid which, Bunch guessed, was dry blood. She sat back on her heels, frowning, as she wondered in her usual slow, common-sense way what was the best thing to do.

Up till now the man's eyes had been closed, but at this point they suddenly opened and fixed themselves on Bunch's face. They were neither dazed nor wandering. They seemed fully alive and intelligent. His lips moved and Bunch bent forward to catch the words, or rather the word. It was only one word that he said. "Sanctuary."

There was, she thought, just a very faint smile as he breathed out this word. There was no mistaking it, for after a moment he said it again. "Sanctuary."

Then, with a faint sigh, he closed his eyes. Once more Bunch's fingers went to his pulse. It was fainter now and more intermittent. She got up with decision.

"Don't move," she said, "or try to move. I'm going for help."

The man's eyes opened again, but he seemed now to be fixing his attention on the colored light that came through the east window. He murmured something that Bunch could not quite catch. She thought, startled, that it might have been her husband's name.

"Julian?" she said. "Did you come here to find Julian?"

But there was no answer. The man lay with eyes closed, his breathing coming in slow, shallow fashion.

Bunch turned and left the church rapidly. She glanced at her watch and nodded with some satisfaction. Dr. Griffiths would still be in his surgery. It was only a couple of minutes' walk from the church. She went in, without waiting to knock or ring, passing through the waiting room and into the doctor's surgery.

"You must come at once," said Bunch breathlessly. "There's a man dying in the church."

Some minutes later, Dr. Griffiths rose from his knees after a brief examination.

"Can we move him from here into the vicarage? I can attend to him better there—not that it's any use."

"Of course," said Bunch. "I'll go and get things ready. I'll get Harper and Jones, shall I? To help you carry him."

"Thanks. I can telephone from the vicarage for an ambulance, but I'm afraid—by the time it comes . . ."

Bunch said, "Internal bleeding?"

Dr. Griffiths nodded. "How on earth did he come here?"

It was about five minutes later when Dr. Griffiths put down the telephone receiver and came back into the morning room where the injured man was lying on quickly arranged blankets on the sofa. Bunch was moving a basin of water and clearing up after the doctor's examination.

"Well, that's that," said Griffiths. "I've sent for an ambulance and I've notified the police." He stood, frowning down on the patient who lay with closed eyes. His left hand was plucking in a nervous, spasmodic way at his side.

"He was shot," said Griffiths. "Shot at fairly close quarters. He rolled up his handkerchief into a ball and plugged the wound with it to stop the bleeding."

"Could he have gone far after that happened?" Bunch asked.

"Oh, yes, it's quite possible. A mortally wounded man has been known to pick himself up and walk along a street as though nothing had happened, and then suddenly collapse five or ten minutes later. So he needn't have been shot in the church. Oh, no. He may have been shot some distance away. Of course, he may have shot himself and then dropped the revolver and staggered blindly towards the church. I don't quite know why he made for the church and not for the vicarage."

"Oh, I know that," said Bunch. "He said, 'Sanctuary.' "

The doctor stared. "Sanctuary?"

"Here's Julian," said Bunch, turning her head as she heard her husband's steps in the hall.

The Reverend Julian Harmon entered the room.

His vague, scholarly manner always made him appear much older than he was.

"Dear me!" said Julian Harmon, gazing in a mild, puzzled manner at the surgical appliances and the figure on the sofa.

Bunch explained with her usual economy of words. "Do you know him, Julian? I thought he said your name."

The vicar looked down at the dying man. "Poor fellow," he said, and shook his head. "No, I don't know him. I'm almost sure I've never seen him before."

At that moment the dying man's eyes opened once more. They went from the doctor to Julian Harmon, and from him to his wife. The eyes stayed there, staring into Bunch's face.

Dr. Griffiths stepped forward. "If you could tell us," he said urgently.

But with his eyes fixed on Bunch, the man said in a weak voice, "Please—please—"

And then, with a slight tremor, he died.

Sergeant Hayes licked his pencil and turned the page of his notebook. "So that's all you can tell me, Mrs. Harmon?"

"That's all," said Bunch. "These are the things out of his coat pockets."

On a table at Sergeant Hayes's elbow were a wallet, a rather battered old watch with the initials W.S., and the return half of a ticket to London.

"You've found out who he is?" asked Bunch.

"A Mr. and Mrs. Eccles phoned up the police station. He's her brother, it seems. Name of Sandbourn. Been in a low state of health and nerves for some time. Depression. Recently come back from abroad, I understand. He's been getting worse lately. The day before yesterday he walked out and didn't come back. He took a revolver with him."

"And he came out here and shot himself?" said Bunch. "Why?"

"Well, you see, he'd been depressed—"

Bunch interrupted him. "I don't mean that. I mean, why here?"

Since Sergeant Hayes obviously did not know the answer to that one, he replied in an oblique fashion. "Come out here, he did, on the bus."

"Yes," said Bunch again. "But why?"

"I don't know, Mrs. Harmon," said Sergeant Hayes. "There's no accounting. If the balance of the mind is disturbed . . ."

Bunch finished for him. "They may do it anywhere. But it still seems to me unnecessary to take a bus to a small country place like this. He didn't know anyone here, did he?"

"Not so far as can be ascertained," said Sergeant Hayes. He coughed in an apologetic manner and said, as he rose to his feet, "It may be as Mr. and Mrs. Eccles will come out and see you, ma'am—if you don't mind, that is."

"Of course I don't mind," said Bunch. "I wish I had something to tell them."

"I'll be getting along," said Sergeant Hayes.

"I'm only so thankful," said Bunch, going with him to the front door, "that it wasn't murder."

A car was drawing up at the vicarage gate.

Sergeant Hayes, glancing at it, remarked, "Looks as though that's Mr. and Mrs. Eccles come here now."

Bunch braced herself to endure what, she felt, might be an ordeal. Anyway, she thought, I can always call Julian in to help me.

Exactly what she had expected Mr. and Mrs. Eccles to be like, Bunch could not have said, but she was conscious, as she greeted them, of a feeling of surprise.

Mr. Eccles was a stout, florid man whose natural manner would have been cheerful.

Mrs. Eccles had a vaguely flashy look about her. She had a small, mean, pursed-up mouth. Her voice was thin and reedy. "It's been a terrible shock, Mrs. Harmon, as you can imagine," she said.

"Oh, I know," said Bunch. "It must have been. Do sit down. Can I offer you—well, perhaps it's a little early for tea—"

Mr. Eccles waved a podgy hand, "No, no, nothing for us," he said. "It's very kind of you, I'm sure. Just wanted to—well—what poor William said and all that, you know."

"He'd been abroad a long time," said Mrs. Eccles, "and I think he must have had some nasty experiences. Very quiet and depressed he's been, ever since he came home. Said the world wasn't fit to live in and there was nothing to look forward to. Poor Bill, he was always moody."

Bunch stared at them both for a moment without speaking.

"Pinched my husband's revolver, he did," went on Mrs. Eccles. "Without our knowing. Then it seems he come out here by bus. I suppose that was nice feeling on his part. He wouldn't have liked to do it in our house."

"Poor fellow," said Mr. Eccles, with a sigh. "It doesn't do to judge."

There was another short pause, and Mr. Eccles said, "Did he leave a message? Any last words, or anything like that?"

His bright, rather piglike eyes watched Bunch closely. Mrs. Eccles, too, leaned forward as though anxious for the reply.

"No," said Bunch quietly. "He came into the church when he was dying, for sanctuary."

Mrs. Eccles said in a puzzled voice, "Sanctuary? I don't quite . . ."

Mr. Eccles interrupted impatiently. "Holy place, my dear. That's what the vicar's wife means. It's a sin—suicide, you know. I expect he wanted to make amends."

"He tried to say something just before he died," said Bunch. "He began, 'Please,' but that's as far as he got."

Mrs. Eccles put her handkerchief to her eyes and sniffed. "Oh, dear," she said. "It's terribly upsetting, isn't it?"

"There, there, Pam," said her husband. "Don't take on. These things can't be helped. Poor Willie. Still, he's at peace now. Well, thank you very much, Mrs. Harmon. I hope we haven't interrupted you."

They shook hands with her. Then Eccles turned back suddenly to say, "Oh, yes, there's just one other thing. I think you've got his coat here, haven't you?"

"His coat?" Bunch frowned.

Mrs. Eccles said, "We'd like to have his things. Sentimental-like."

"He had a watch and a wallet and a railway ticket in the pockets," said Bunch. "I gave them to Sergeant Hayes."

"That's all right, then," said Mr. Eccles. "He'll hand them over to us, I expect. His private papers would be in the wallet."

"There was a pound note in the wallet," said Bunch. "Nothing else."

"No letters? Nothing like that?"

Bunch shook her head.

"Well, thank you again, Mrs. Harmon. The coat he was wearing—is that at the station? Perhaps the sergeant's got that, too, has he?"

Bunch frowned in an effort of remembrance. "No," she said. "I don't think . . . let me see. The doctor took his coat off to examine his wound." She looked round the room vaguely. "I must have taken it upstairs with the towels and basin."

"I wonder now, Mrs. Harmon, if you don't mind . . . We'd like his coat, you know, the last thing he wore. The wife feels rather sentimental about it."

"Of course," said Bunch. "Would you like me to have it cleaned first? I'm afraid it's rather—well—stained."

"Oh, no, that doesn't matter."

"I wonder where . . . Excuse me a moment."

Bunch went upstairs, and it was a few minutes before she returned. "I'm sorry," she said breathlessly, "my daily woman must have put it aside with other clothes that were going to the cleaners. It's taken me quite a long time to find it. Here it is. I'll do it up for you in brown paper."

Disclaiming their protests, she did so, then once more effusively bidding her farewell, they departed.

Bunch went slowly back across the hall and entered the study. The Reverend Julian Harmon looked up and his brow cleared. He was writing a sermon and was fearing that he'd been led astray by the interest of the political relations between Judæa and Persia, in the reign of Cyrus.

"Yes, dear?" he said hopefully.

"Julian," said Bunch, "what's sanctuary exactly?"

Julian Harmon gratefully put aside his sermon paper. "Well," he said, "sanctuary in Roman and Greek temples applied to the cella in which stood the statue of the god. The Latin word for altar, *ara*, also means protection. In A.D. 399 the right of sanctuary in Christian churches was finally and definitively recognized. Criminals and refugees have taken advantage of the right of sanctuary since very early times. In the

Bible, you may remember, Joab is mentioned as laying hold of the altar. The earliest mention of the right of sanctuary in England is in A.D. 600, in the code of laws issued by Ethelbert—"

He was, as often, disconcerted by his wife's reception of his erudite pronouncements. "Darling," she said. "You are sweet."

Bending over, she kissed him on the tip of his nose.

"The Eccleses have been here," said Bunch.

The vicar frowned. "The Eccleses? I don't seem to remember . . ."

"You couldn't remember," said Bunch. "They're the sister and brother-in-law of the man in the church."

"My dear, you ought to have called me."

"It wasn't necessary," said Bunch. "They were not in need of consolation. I wonder now." She frowned. "If I put a casserole in the oven tomorrow, can you manage, Julian? I think I shall have to go up to London. There's a special white sale at Burrows and Portman's. Besides," she added thoughtfully, "I think I ought to go and see Aunt Jane."

That sweet old lady, Miss Jane Marple, was enjoying the delights of the metropolis for a fortnight, comfortably installed in her nephew's studio flat.

"So kind of dear Raymond," she murmured. "He and Joan have gone to America, and they insisted I should come up here and enjoy myself. I so seldom get the chance of staying in London. And now, dear Bunch, do tell me what is worrying you."

Bunch was Miss Marple's favorite godchild, and the old lady looked at her with great affection as Bunch, thrusting her best felt hat farther on the back of her head, started on her story.

The recital was concise and clear. Miss Marple nodded her head. "I see," she said. "Yes, I see."

"That's why I felt I had to talk to you," said Bunch. "I don't really know what I ought to do. I can't ask Julian because—well, I mean, Julian's full of rectitude . . ."

This statement appeared to be perfectly understood by Miss Marple, who said, "I know what you mean, dear. We women—well, it's different." She went on, "You told me what happened, Bunch, but I'd like to know first what you think."

"It's all wrong," said Bunch. "The man who was there in the church, dying, knew all about sanctuary. He said it just the way Julian would have said it. I mean he was a well read, educated man. And if he'd shot himself, he wouldn't drag himself into a church afterwards and say 'sanctuary.' Sanctuary means that you're pursued, and when you get into a church you're safe. Your pursuers can't touch you. At one time even the law couldn't get at you." She looked questioningly at Miss Marple, who nodded.

Bunch went on, "Those people, the Eccleses, were quite different. Ignorant and coarse. And there's another thing. That watch—the dead man's watch. It had the initials W.S. on the back of it. But inside—I opened it—in very small lettering there was, *To Walter from his father,* and a date. Walter! The Eccleses kept talking of him as William or Bill."

Miss Marple seemed about to speak, but Bunch rushed on, "I know you're not always called the name you're baptized by. I mean, I can understand that you might be christened William and called Porky, or Carrots, or something. But your sister wouldn't call you William or Bill if your name was Walter."

"You mean that she wasn't his sister?"

"I'm quite sure she wasn't his sister. They were horrid—both of them. They came to the vicarage to get his things and to find out if he'd said anything before he died. When I said he hadn't, I saw it in their faces—relief. I think, myself," finished Bunch, "it was Eccles who shot him."

"Murder?" said Miss Marple.

"Yes," said Bunch. "Murder. That's why I came to you, darling."

Such a remark might have seemed incongruous to an ignorant listener, but in certain spheres Miss Marple had a reputation for dealing with murder.

"He said 'please' to me before he died," said Bunch. "He wanted me to do something for him. The awful thing is I've no idea what."

Miss Marple considered for a moment, then pounced on the point that had already occurred to Bunch. "But why was he there at all?" she asked.

"You mean," said Bunch, "if you wanted sanctuary you might pop into a church anywhere. There's no need to take a bus that only goes four times a day and come out to a lonely spot like ours."

"He must have come there for a purpose," Miss Marple said. "He must have come to see someone. Chipping Cleghorn's not a big place, Bunch. Surely you must have some idea of who it was he came to see?"

Bunch reviewed the inhabitants of the village in her mind before slowly shaking her head. "In a way," she said, "it could be anybody."

"He never mentioned a name?"

"He said Julian, or I thought he said Julian. It might have been Julia, I suppose. As far as I know, there isn't any Julia living in Chipping Cleghorn."

She screwed up her eyes as she thought back to the scene. The man lying there on the chancel steps, the light coming through the window with its jewels of red and blue . . .

"Jewels," said Bunch suddenly. "Perhaps that's what he said. The light coming through the east window looked like jewels."

"Jewels," said Miss Marple thoughtfully.

"I'm coming now," said Bunch, "to the most important thing of all. The reason really why I've come here today. You see, the Eccleses made a great fuss about having his coat. We took it off when the doctor was seeing to him. It was an old, shabby sort of coat—there was no reason they should have wanted it. I mean, they didn't look poor or as though a suit would mean anything much to them. They pretended it had sentimental value, but that was nonsense.

"Anyway, I went to find it, and as I was going up the stairs I remembered how he'd made a kind of picking gesture with his hand, as though he was fumbling with the coat.

"So when I got hold of the coat I looked at it very carefully and I saw that in one place the lining had been sewn up again with a different thread. Sewn up rather clumsily, as a man would sew it. I unpicked it and found a little piece of paper inside. I took it out and sewed it up again properly with thread that matched.

"I was careful, and I don't really think that the Eccleses would know I'd done it. I don't think so, but I can't be sure. Then I took the coat down to them and made some excuse for the delay."

"The piece of paper?" asked Miss Marple.

Bunch opened her handbag. "I didn't show it to Julian," she said, "because he would have said that I ought to have given it to the Eccleses. But I thought I'd rather bring it to you instead."

She handed the small docket across to Miss Marple.

"A cloakroom ticket," said Miss Marple, looking at it. "Paddington station."

"He had a return ticket to Paddington in his pocket," said Bunch.

"This calls for action," said Miss Marple. "But it would be advisable, I think, to be careful. Would you have noticed at all, Bunch dear, whether you were followed when you came to London today?"

"Followed!" exclaimed Bunch. "You don't think—?"

"Well, I think it's possible," said Miss Marple. "When anything is possible, I think we ought to take precautions." She rose with a brisk movement.

"You came up here ostensibly, my dear, to go to the sales. I think the right thing to do, therefore, would be for us to go to the sales. But before we set out, we might put one or two little arrangements in hand. I don't suppose," Miss Marple added obscurely, "that I shall need the old speckled tweed with the beaver collar just at present."

It was about an hour and a half later that the two ladies, rather the worse for wear and battered in appearance, their hair slightly disheveled, their hats askew, and both clasping parcels of hard-won household linen, sat down at a small and sequestered restaurant, called The Apple Bough, to restore their forces with steak and kidney pudding followed by apple tart and custard.

A smart young woman, with a lavish application of rouge and lipstick, entered The Apple Bough. After looking round vaguely for a moment or two, she hurried to their table. She laid down an envelope by Miss Marple's elbow.

"There you are, miss," she said.

"Oh, thank you, Gladys," said Miss Marple. "Thank you very much. So kind of you."

"Always pleased to oblige, I'm sure," said Gladys. "Ernie always says to me, 'Everything what's good you learnt from that Miss Marple of yours that you were in service with. Trained you proper,' he says, 'and don't you forget it,' and I'm sure I'm always glad to oblige you, miss."

"Such a dear, dear girl," said Miss Marple as

Gladys departed. "Always so willing and so kind. One wishes sometimes that they wouldn't wear so much lipstick—but I dare say it gives them self-confidence."

She looked inside the envelope and then passed it on to Bunch. "Now be very careful, dear," she said. "By the way, is there still that nice young Inspector Craddock at Melchester that I remember?"

"I don't know," said Bunch. "I expect so."

"Well, if not," said Miss Marple thoughtfully, "I can always ring up the chief constable. I think he would remember me."

"Of course he'd remember you," said Bunch. "Everybody would remember you. You're unique." She rose. "Well, I'd better hurry along or I shall miss the train."

Arrived at Paddington, Bunch went to the Left Luggage Office and produced the cloakroom ticket. A moment or two later a shabby suitcase was passed across to her, and carrying this she made her way to the platform where her train was already in.

The journey home was uneventful. Bunch got out of the train and made her way toward the exit, carrying the suitcase. She had nearly reached the doorway when a man, sprinting along the platform, suddenly seized the suitcase from her hand and rushed off with it.

"Stop!" Bunch yelled. "Stop him, stop him. He's taken my suitcase."

The ticket collector who, at this rural station, was a man of somewhat slow processes, had just begun to say, "Now, look here, you can't do that—" when a smart blow in the chest pushed him aside and the man with the suitcase rushed out from the station. He made his way to where a car was waiting.

Tossing the suitcase in, he was about to climb after it when out of the darkness a hand fell on his shoulder, and the voice of Police Constable Abel said, "Now then, what's all this?"

"Nonsense," said the man. "I don't know what this lady means. It's my suitcase. I just got out of the train with it."

"Now, let's get this clear," said Police Constable Abel. He looked at Bunch with a bovine and impartial stare. Nobody would have guessed that Abel and Mrs. Harmon spent long half hours in his off time discussing the respective merits of manure and bone meal for rosebushes. "You say, madam, that this is your suitcase?" said Police Constable Abel.

"Yes," said Bunch. "Definitely."

"And you, sir?"

"I say this suitcase is mine."

The man was tall, dark, and well dressed, with a drawling voice and a superior manner. A feminine voice from inside the car said, "Of course it's your suitcase, Edwin. I don't know what this woman means."

"We'll have to get this clear," said Police Constable Abel. "If it's your suitcase, madam, what do you say is inside it?"

"Clothes," said Bunch. "A long, speckled coat with a beaver collar, two wool jumpers, and a pair of shoes."

"Well, that's clear enough." He turned to the other.

"I am a theatrical costumier," said the dark man importantly. "This suitcase contains properties which I brought down here for an amateur theatrical performance."

"Right, sir," said Police Constable Abel. "Well, we'll just look inside, shall we, and see? We can go along to the police station, or if you're in a hurry we'll take the suitcase back to the railway station and open it there."

"It'll suit me," said the dark man. "My name is Moss, by the way. Edwin Moss."

Police Constable Abel, holding the suitcase, went back into the station. "Just taking this into the Parcels Office, George," he said to the ticket collector.

"Oh, ay," said the latter.

Police Constable Abel laid the suitcase on the counter of the Parcels Office and pushed back the clasp. The case was not locked.

Bunch and Mr. Edwin Moss stood on either side of him, glaring at each other.

"Ah!" said Abel, as he pushed up the lid.

Inside, neatly folded, was a long, rather shabby tweed coat with a beaver fur collar. There were also two woolen jumpers and a pair of country shoes.

"Exactly as you say, madam," said Police Constable Abel, turning to Bunch.

Nobody could have said that Mr. Edwin Moss underdid things. His dismay and compunction were magnificent.

"I do apologize," he said. "I really do apologize. I must somehow or other have left my own suitcase on the train. Please believe me, dear lady, when I tell you how very, very sorry I am. Unpardonable—quite unpardonable—my behavior has been." He looked at his watch. "I must rush now. Probably my suitcase has gone on in the train. What the company will say to me for having mislaid their properties! I shall have to see what can be done."

Raising his hat once more, he said meltingly to Bunch, "Do, do forgive me," and rushed hurriedly out of the Parcels Office.

"Are you going to let him get away?" asked Bunch in a conspiratorial whisper of Police Constable Abel.

The latter slowly closed a bovine eye in a wink. "He won't get far, ma'am," he said. "That's to say, he won't get far unobserved, if you take my meaning."

"Oh," said Bunch, relieved.

"That old lady's been on the phone," said Police Constable Abel, "the one as was down here a few years ago. Bright, she is, isn't she? Sharp as a needle. But there's been a lot cooking up all today. Shouldn't wonder if the inspector or sergeant was out to see you about it tomorrow morning."

It was the inspector who came, the Inspector Craddock whom Miss Marple remembered. He looked rather older and more careworn than when Bunch had seen him last, but he greeted her with a smile as an old friend.

"Crime in Chipping Cleghorn again," he said cheerfully. "You don't lack sensation here, do you, Mrs. Harmon?"

"I could do with rather less," said Bunch. "Have you come to ask me questions, or are you going to tell me things for a change?"

"I'll tell you some things first," said the inspector. "To begin with, Mr. and Mrs. Eccles have been having an eye kept on them for some time. There's reason to believe that they've been connected with several robberies in this part of the world. For another thing, although Mrs. Eccles has a brother named Sandbourn who has recently come back from abroad, the man whom you found dying on the chancel steps was definitely not Sandbourn."

"I knew he wasn't," said Bunch. "His name was Walter, to begin with, not William."

The inspector nodded. "Yes," he said, "they slipped up there."

"Who was he really?"

"His name was Walter Stevens, and he escaped some days ago from Charrington Prison."

"Of course," said Bunch softly to herself, "he was being hunted down by the law, and he took sanctuary." Then she asked, "What had he done?"

"I'll have to go back rather a long way. It's a complicated story. Several years ago there was a certain dancer doing turns in the music halls. I don't expect you'll have ever heard of her, but she specialized in an Arabian Nights turn. She wore bits of rhinestone and not much else and called the turn Aladdin in the Cave of Jewels. She wasn't much of a dancer, I believe, but she was—well—attractive. Anyway, a certain Asiatic royalty fell for her in a big way. Among other things, he gave her a magnificent emerald necklace."

"The historic jewels of a rajah?" murmured Bunch.

Inspector Craddock coughed. "Well, a rather more modern version, Mrs. Harmon. The necklace came from Cartier's. The affair didn't last very long—it broke up when our potentate's attention was captured by a certain film star whose demands were not quite so modest. She demanded marriage, a settlement, and considerable alimony. But none of that is our business.

"Zobeida, to give her stage name, hung on to the necklace, and in due course it was stolen. It disappeared from her dressing room at the theater and there was a lingering suspicion in the minds of the authorities that she herself might have engineered its disappearance. Such things have been known as a publicity stunt, or indeed from more dishonest motives. The necklace was never recovered, but during the course of the investigation the attention of the police was drawn to this man, Walter Stevens.

"He was a man of education and breeding who had come down in the world, and who was employed as a working jeweler with a rather obscure firm which was suspected of acting as a fence for jewel robberies. There was evidence that this necklace had passed through his hands, and indeed the actual setting of the jewels was found, so it looked as though he'd abstracted the emeralds and disposed of them.

"It was, however, in connection with the theft of some other jewelry that he was finally brought to trial, convicted, and sent to prison. He had earned remission for good conduct in prison and had not very much longer to serve, so his escape was rather a surprise."

"But why did he come here?" asked Bunch.

"We'd like to know that very much, Mrs. Harmon. Following up his trail, it seems that he went first to London. He didn't see any of his old associates, but he visited an elderly woman, a Mrs. Jackson, who had formerly been a theatrical dresser. She won't say a word of what he came for but, according to other lodgers in the house, he left carrying a suitcase."

"I see," said Bunch. "He left it in the cloakroom at Paddington and then he came down here."

"By that time," said Inspector Craddock, "Eccles and the man who calls himself Edwin Moss were on his trail. They wanted that suitcase. They saw him get on the bus. They must have driven out in a car ahead of him, and been waiting for him when he left the bus."

"And he was murdered?" said Bunch.

"Yes," said Craddock. "It was Eccles's revolver, but I rather fancy it was Moss who did the shooting. Now, Mrs. Harmon, what we want to know is, where is the suitcase that Walter Stevens actually deposited at Paddington station?"

Bunch grinned. "Aunt Jane's got it," she said. "Miss Marple, I mean. That was her plan. She sent a former maid of hers with a suitcase packed with her things to the cloakroom at Paddington. We exchanged tickets, and I collected her suitcase and brought it down by train. She seemed to expect that an attempt would be made to get it from me."

It was Inspector Craddock's turn to smile. "So she said when she rang up," he said. "I'm driving up to

London to see her. Do you want to come too, Mrs. Harmon?"

"We—ell," said Bunch, considering. "We—ell, as a matter of fact, it's very fortunate. I had toothache last night, so I really ought to go to London to see the dentist, oughtn't I?"

"Definitely," said Inspector Craddock.

Miss Marple looked from Inspector Craddock's face to the eager face of Bunch Harmon. The suitcase lay on the table.

"Of course I haven't opened it," the old lady said. "I wouldn't dream of doing such a thing till somebody official arrived. Besides," she added, with a mischievous Victorian smile, "it's locked."

"Like to make a guess at what's inside, Miss Marple?" asked the inspector.

"I should imagine," said Miss Marple, "that it would be Zobeida's theatrical costumes. Would you like a screwdriver, inspector?"

The screwdriver soon did its work. Both women gave a slight gasp as the lid flew up. The sunlight coming through the window lit up what seemed like a treasure of sparkling jewels, red, blue, green, orange.

"Aladdin's Cave," said Miss Marple. "The flashing jewels the girl wore in her dance."

"Ah," said Inspector Craddock. "Now, what's so precious about it, do you think, that a man was murdered to get hold of it?"

"She was a shrewd girl, I expect," said Miss Marple thoughtfully. "She's dead, isn't she inspector?"

"Yes, died three years ago."

"She had this valuable emerald necklace," said Miss Marple musingly. "Had the stones taken out of their setting and fastened here and there on her theatrical costume, where everyone would take them merely for colored rhinestones. Then she had a replica made of the Cartier necklace, and that of course was what was stolen. No wonder it never came on the market. The thief soon discovered the stones were false."

"Here is an envelope," said Bunch.

Inspector Craddock took it from her and extracted two official-looking papers. He read aloud: "*Marriage certificate between Walter Edmund St. John Stevens and Mary Moss*. That was Zobeida's real name."

"So they were married," said Miss Marple. "I see."

"What's the other?" asked Bunch.

"A birth certificate of a daughter, Jewel."

"Jewel?" cried Bunch. "Why, of course. Jewel! Jill! That's it. I see now why he came to Chipping Cleghorn. That's what he was trying to say to me. Jewel. Mrs. Mundy, you know. Laburnum Cottage. She looks after a little girl for someone. She's devoted to her. She's been like her own granddaughter. Yes, I remember now, her name was Jewel, only of course they never call her anything but Jill."

"Mrs. Mundy had a stroke about a week ago. I've been trying hard to find a good home for Jill. I didn't want her taken away to an institution. Her father must have heard about it in prison and managed to break away and get hold of this suitcase from the old dresser he or his wife left it with. I suppose if the jewels really belonged to her mother, they can be used for the child now."

"I should imagine so, Mrs. Harmon. *If* they're here."

"Oh, they'll be here all right," said Miss Marple cheerfully.

"Thank goodness you're back dear," said the Reverend Harmon, greeting his wife with affection and a sigh of content. "Mrs. Burt really gave me some very peculiar fishcakes for lunch. I didn't want to hurt her feelings, so I gave them to Tiglath Pileser, but even he wouldn't eat them. I'm afraid I had to throw them out of the window."

"Tiglath Pileser," said Bunch, stroking the cat, "is very peculiar about what fish he eats. I often tell him he's got a proud stomach."

"And your tooth, dear?" asked her husband. "Did you have it seen to?"

"Yes," said Bunch. "It didn't hurt much, and I went to see Aunt Jane, too."

"Dear old thing," said Julian Harmon, "I hope she's not failing at all."

"Not in the least," said Bunch with a slight grin.

The following morning Bunch took a fresh supply of chrysanthemums to the church. The sun was once more pouring through the east window and Bunch stood in the jewelled light on the chancel steps. She said very softly under her breath, "Your little girl will be all right. I'll see that she is, I promise."

Then she tidied up the church, slipped into a pew, and knelt for a few moments to say her prayers before returning to the vicarage to attack the accumulated dust of two neglected days.